STORM SURGE

THE SHADOW GUARDIANS BOOK 2

CB SAMET

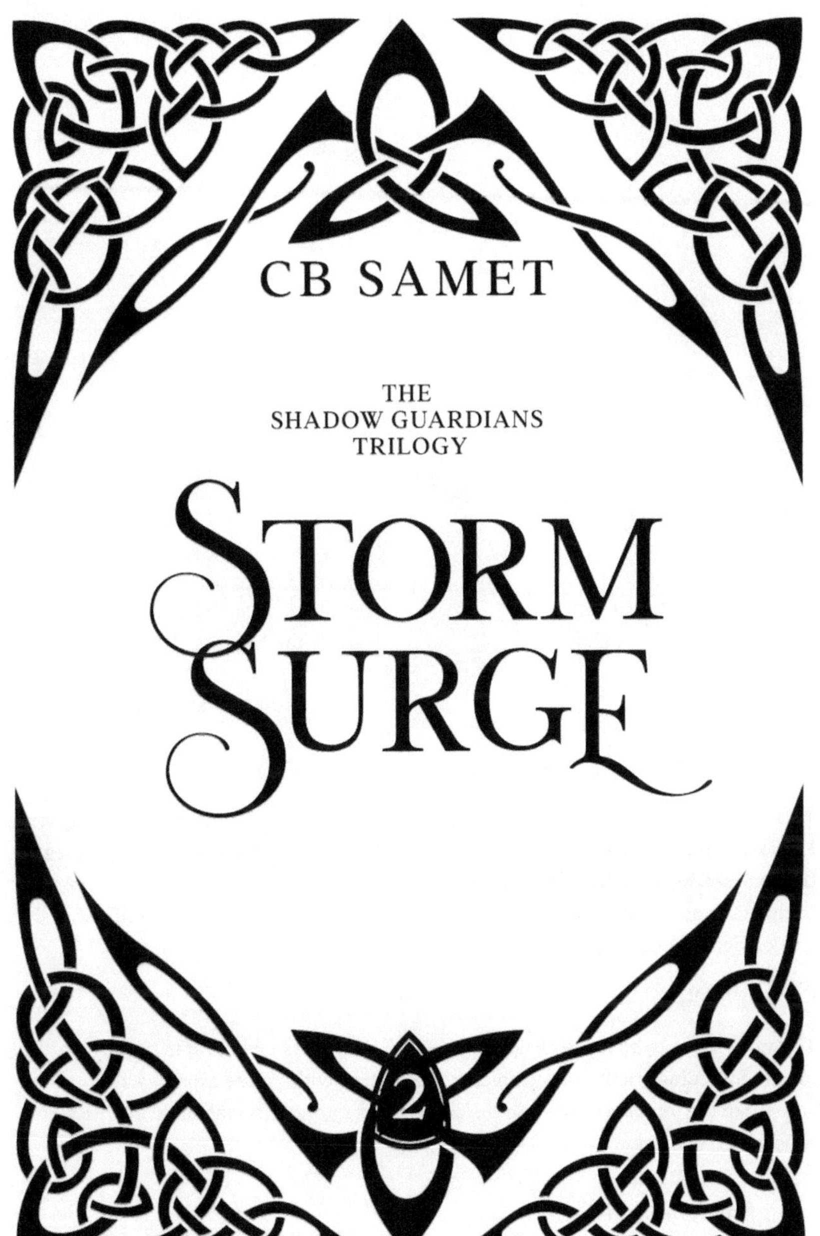

CB SAMET

THE
SHADOW GUARDIANS
TRILOGY

Storm Surge

CHAPTER
ONE

Storm exhaled through gritted teeth as she shifted her weight off her left leg—the one with the bullet wound. As she watched from across the street, the last of the patients exited the free clinic, a standalone, single-story, faded, brick building. With the establishment finally closing, she could receive treatment in private.

As she emerged from the alley where the ride share had dropped her off, three men approached the clinic. The Caucasian and two Latinos sported bold tattoos on bare arms and bulges at their lower backs. She suspected they were gang members by their appearance and the shifty way their eyes darted around the dim and empty parking lot. In any case, their behavior betrayed their dubious intentions.

Using a paint can, the tallest of them sprayed the security camera above the door. After jimmying the lock and opening the door, they shuffled inside the clinic, drawing their weapons.

I don't have time for this.

Swearing, Storm crossed the street as the men entered the building. They were interfering with her plan to get medical care. She'd already spent two hours with a bullet in her shin. She wanted no more delays.

Besides, Dr. Bryce Chambers—owner and operator of this fine, dilapidated health clinic—was her mark. He had the right mix of debt and desperation to patch her up, take cash, and not ask questions about how she ended up with a bullet in her leg. She couldn't simply pick another clinic to invade after hours.

Cautiously limping toward the clinic, she noticed through the window that the waiting room lights were off. Silently, she opened the door with its newly broken bolt. As she crept through the entry door, men's voices reverberated from across the dim room. The gang members were demanding money.

"I've given you everything from petty cash. We don't have any more than that, and we don't stock any narcotics at the clinic." The deep voice with a hint of Texan twang must have belonged to the physician. His tone was firm, laced with more irritation than fear. "This is an indigent care clinic. People pay what they can, which is usually nothing. No, don't take supplies. You're stealing from patients in this community. *Your* community."

Storm crept around the short entry wall to see the receptionist's desk. One gang member pointed a gun at Dr. Chambers. The physician was younger than she'd expected, perhaps mid-thirties. His dark brown hair was cut short and blended with a week's growth of beard. Another man rummaged through drawers and cabinets. Judging by the clamor down the hallway, the third gang member was ransacking one of the treatment rooms.

Storm slunk against the wall in the shadows. She slid beneath the window as she made her way to the clinic rooms. Her leg throbbed. Fortunately, the delinquents were making enough racket she didn't have to be incredibly stealthy—unlike most of her other assignments.

She peeked into the room where a young Latino man rapidly opened and closed cabinets as if searching for the Holy Grail. She needed to pick off the lone thief before taking on the others. After making a quick mental map of the room, she braced herself for action. This was going to hurt, and her leg was likely to bleed again.

In three quick strides, she was in the room and vaulting over the exam table. She kicked at the man with her uninjured leg, her calf-length, rubber-soled boots solidly contacting with the side of his head.

He grunted and dropped to the hard linoleum floor.

She pounced. While he was still dazed, she drew out a pair of flex cuff ties from her jacket and secured his hands together behind him, followed by tying his feet. She snatched a roll of gauze off the ransacked countertop and stuffed it in his mouth as a gag before he gained his senses and called for help.

"Julio?" a voice sounded from down the hall.

Storm lifted the gun from Julio's pants. A .38 snub nose revolver. The small bullets couldn't do much more than slow attackers, unless one had good aim under pressure to land an accurate, injurious shot.

She possessed such marksmanship, but she didn't feel like killing anyone tonight, especially when they didn't fit the profile and she wasn't getting paid to take them out.

She positioned herself against the wall to the right of the open door to the exam room and waited for Julio's friend.

The scrawny, pale-skinned man carelessly rushed his entry.

Storm cracked the butt of the gun against his forehead, and he stumbled backward in stunned surprise. Chopping her right hand into his neck over the larynx, she incapacitated his ability to speak or scream.

As he made a gaping, fish-mouthed expression, he attempted to raise the gun in his right hand. Storm slipped behind him and unleashed a punch to his lower back. Kidney shots were quite painful. With any luck, he'd think twice about robbing anyone again.

He fell to his knees, the grip on his gun faltering. In one smooth motion, she stepped on the weapon and slid it away from him. She tied off his hands and feet, this time using the porous self-adhesive bandage roll from off the exam room counter. She left him gasping and writhing on the floor with a swollen larynx, a goose egg on his forehead, and a contused kidney.

Slinking her way down the hall, she quieted her labored breathing. She was more winded than she liked from the vigorous effort of disarming two men, making her wonder if she'd lost more blood than she'd initially thought.

"Julio? Mickey?" the third man called from the reception area.

Storm could feel the warmth of fresh blood oozing into her bandage.

Son of a beiskaldi, she swore internally with a wave of annoyance. She was supposed to be getting this bullet out right now, not dealing with these punks.

When the last gun-toting criminal stepped into the hallway, Storm put the barrel of the .38 to the man's temple as she grabbed the wrist of his gun wielding hand. He jerked away from her, but she pushed the muzzle more firmly against him.

"No, no," she chided softly. "It's time to accept defeat."

He stiffened and glared at her sideways, releasing the grip on his gun.

The physician lashed out a cowboy boot, striking the assailant squarely in the back. The man flew forward, crashing into the opposite wall.

Storm ejected the magazine and handed the pieces of the gun to Dr. Chambers, who accepted them with stunned surprise. Turning, she knelt and tied the gang member's hands and feet with another two flex ties. The man hurled expletives in Spanish at her.

She turned and appraised the physician. He wore jeans and scuffed, brown, cowboy boots. His collared shirt was rolled at the sleeves, and a stethoscope hung in a loop from a belt hook.

"Dr. Bryce Chambers?" she asked.

"I'm a little concerned about saying yes after you disarmed three men so effortlessly."

"You want me to untie them?"

"No." He set the gun down on the counter and extended a hand. "Bryce Chambers."

He had a handsome face with warm, hazel eyes that held a hint of mischievousness. Around him, a faint aura glistened—a white hue that brightened his entire body. She stifled her surprise and shook his hand firmly, ignoring the heat radiating from his touch. Long fingers wrapped around her hand. His palm was heavy with callouses, like a man who worked with his hands, not in a medical office.

"Are you some type of vigilante?" he asked.

She snorted. "No." She had been called many things, but never a vigilante. "But I am in need of your services."

"Okay." Placing his hands on his hips, he looked back down at the gang member glaring at the pair of them. "I should probably call the police."

She shrugged. "That's up to you. My opinion, if you want to make sure they don't bother you again, you need to put a bullet in each of their heads."

She'd said the words more to intimidate the criminals listening to their conversation, but she must have sounded convincing because the physician gaped at her.

The man on the ground, eyes wide in alarm, vigorously shook his head.

Her gaze angled around the lobby at the peeling paint and worn furniture. "I could do it for you, but you couldn't afford me."

Dr. Chambers shook his head. "I don't want to kill anyone, and I don't want you to kill anyone."

Half-amused, she smirked. "Your risk, doc."

"I guess it is. And don't call me doc."

CHAPTER
TWO

Bryce followed the woman in her black burglar outfit as she limped down the hallway of his clinic. Moments ago, men had held him at gunpoint while robbing and vandalizing his workplace. This mysterious woman had saved his clinic. Probably saved him. The least he could do was address whatever medical ailment she'd come to have treated. Yet, uneasiness had him wanting to be rid of someone who would talk about killing so cavalierly. Although he couldn't tell how much was sincere and how much she'd said for the shock factor, such a notion went against what he was and the oath he'd taken to preserve life.

She turned into an empty exam room. With a smooth twist of her neck, she flicked long strands of dark, snarled hair over her shoulder. "You coming?"

He walked past the first room, glimpsing the bound Latino man on the floor who didn't appear to have any serious injuries, and reluctantly followed the stranger into the vacant exam room.

She closed the door behind him and hoisted herself with easy agility onto the exam table.

"I will treat you, but I need to get the cops headed here for these men," he said.

"No cops while I'm here."

He felt his jaw muscle tick. She obviously wanted after-hours, off-books medical care, which meant she was avoiding authorities.

"Okay. Let's play out your scenario." Even as he spoke, he smoothed antiseptic gel on his hands and slipped on a pair of gloves. "I don't phone the cops, and they question me about why I didn't call for so long. I'm forced to give a description of you, and after I treat you, there's likely to be lots of your DNA and fingerprints lying around."

He didn't mention the external cameras watching the front and back doors. She might have been caught on video also, but he didn't want her stealing his footage that also had the robbers.

With a grimace, she tugged off her left boot and rolled up her pantleg.

He pulled scissors out of a drawer and pulled up a rolling stool. After sitting, he began cutting away the sloppy, blood-soaked bandage she'd obviously placed in a hurry.

When her pale skin was exposed, he used a moist, clean gauze to wipe away the blood. "You've been shot." He looked up into her face, noticing for the first time a pair of unusual violet irises. She was beautiful, with high cheekbones, long lashes, and light, creamy skin.

She blinked. "Yes, I already know that."

His mouth quirked. "This is why you came to my office after-hours and why you don't want cops."

"He's good looking and clever," she announced to the room.

Bryce felt his cheeks grow hot at her compliment though her tone had been mocking rather than sultry or flirtatious. He scowled. Bullet wounds were reportable violence. Now he really did need to call the police.

"Want to share with me how you got shot and why you want to keep it a secret?" He also wanted to know how she remained calm with a bullet wound. He'd seen grown men twice her size reduced to blithering tearfulness from injuries like hers.

"No."

"Are you in danger?"

"Not anymore," she said on a sigh, the exhaustion in her exhaled air practically palpable.

He dabbed at the wound with clean gauze. "Are you trying to be mysterious?"

"Right now, I'm just trying to get medical help. How much do you charge for a bullet removal? You can charge more for not asking questions."

Bryce grunted. "It's not exactly on the easy treatment checklist I created for this clinic. I'm more of a bronchitis, diabetes, and hypertension physician these days." He prepared a syringe of lidocaine and then opened a sterile pack of medical forceps. "I wouldn't charge you after saving my clinic from those gang members anyway."

"I can pay."

"Judging by your leather boots, leather jacket, and the diamond ring on your necklace, I bet you can." He looked up into those purple eyes again. In a word—spellbinding. "Besides," he continued, "you won't feel like paying me by the time we're done."

"Why is that?"

"I don't keep narcotics here, and this is going to hurt as much as getting shot did." He wiped antiseptic around the wound.

Fortunately, the bullet hadn't lodged in or near any major blood vessel, so it wasn't a threat to life or limb. It would, however, leave a nasty scar and throb with pain for weeks.

"I see you're packing under that jacket. Why didn't you use that on the men trying to rob this place?"

"I pull my gun when I need to. I didn't need to."

He squinted as he inspected the area closer. "It looks like you've started healing around it. How long has the bullet been in your leg?"

"Too long."

Does the woman ever answer a question directly?

"You'll need a tetanus shot after this."

"Skip it."

When he wriggled the end of the bullet, testing how embedded it was, she sucked in a breath. It was the first sign of anything resembling fear or concern he'd seen since meeting her. Mysterious though she was, and obviously no stranger to pain, he wondered if this was her first bullet wound.

"Last chance to go to a real hospital and have this removed properly," he told her.

Shaking her head, she leaned back on the exam bed with her legs dangling off the end. She gripped the sides of the narrow table.

After adjusting his position on the rolling stool, he injected the skin around the bullet wound with lidocaine.

"It burns."

"That's just the local anesthetic, and it will only make a dent in the pain when I pull the bullet out."

"I'm ready."

He doubted that, but he dug in with the forceps anyway, working the tip into the surrounding skin. The bullet had embedded in the tibia. Since the tissue seemed to be already healing, he wondered again how long she'd been afflicted with the projectile. She threw an arm over her face, sobbed, and bit down on the cuff of her jacket.

He worked quickly, because tender and slow would only prolong the pain. When his instrument grasped the bullet securely in its serrated edges, Bryce gripped the tool firmly and pulled as hard and as fast as he could.

Her scream was muffled by the jacket, but he cringed at the sound of her suffering. He'd never made a patient cry out from pain, and the feeling was beyond lousy. So much for 'first, do no harm.'

She fell silent and limp. He suspected he would faint too if someone yanked a bullet out of one of his bones.

After cleansing the area again, he applied a pressure dressing and taped it down. Gingerly, he pulled her pant leg down over the bandage. She needed a hospital and x-rays, not a quick care clinic.

As he checked her pulse at the wrist, he stared at the sleeping beauty. He was tempted to move strands of hair that had fallen across her face, but without permission, it felt like a violation of her space. Why did he want to touch her?

He definitely didn't want the sort of trouble a woman who could restrain three men without making a sound would bring. He needed simplicity in his life right now.

He needed to think about Olivia.

STORM OPENED her eyes to a dimly lit room. She was lying on a well-worn couch. As she looked at her surroundings, she recognized the waiting room of Dr. Chamber's clinic. Her throat felt parched, and she needed water and sleep after her long day.

Then she remembered the bullet. Reaching down, she felt the area where the pant leg was now rolled down. Fresh bandage. At last, she'd be able to quickly heal the injury with the projectile now removed.

Listening to the surrounding sounds, she heard no police sirens and no sweaty gang bangers swearing on the floor. Clinking and scuffling emitted from one of the clinic rooms.

She slipped her boot up over her foot and calf. As she stood, her leg throbbed, and she bit back the pain and headed for the front door. In two uneven steps, she paused, feeling an unusual urge to see Dr. Chambers again.

Ridiculous.

Perhaps she would take one look, just to see if she could determine the source of that soft aura she'd noticed earlier. She turned and walked toward the exam room. Inside, he was tidying the space. His keen eyes focused on his task and his square jaw set in concentration. He'd rolled up his sleeves even further, revealing defined forearms and a glimpse of firm biceps. Those must have been how he'd been able to move her from the exam room to the couch.

"Thank you."

He turned to look at her. "Back on your feet already," he observed.

"Thank you, Dr. Chambers," she repeated.

"Call me Bryce. And you are?"

"Storm."

"Storm—?"

"Just Storm."

"Storm. You certainly know how to make an entrance." Bryce gave her a grin.

As he did, she admired his glow again—faint, white tendrils dancing along his skin. This close she saw those hazel eyes again. No, not hazel. Golden eyes, matching the sun-kissed highlights in his otherwise brown hair.

She cleared her throat. "Have you got any water?"

He pulled a clean sheet of paper over the exam table and nodded. "Follow me." Leading her to an employee kitchen, he fixed her a glass from the water cooler. As he passed it to her, she thanked him, drank it, and fixed herself a second glass.

"What happened to your attackers?" she asked, taking another long gulp.

He leaned on the counter, amusement in the quirk of his lips. "You're referring to the ones who had their butts kicked by a woman half their size with a bullet stuck in her leg? I opted to let them off with a warning. Well, you provided the warning."

"I might not be here next time they come back."

He arched an eyebrow in an expression that made her heart kick faster. "I'd be surprised if you were."

"What do I owe you?"

His brow furrowed. He pushed off the counter and walked down the hall toward the front of the clinic. "Nothing. You paid in full when you stopped the robbery."

Her gaze flickered around the room as she followed him. "You might work in a nicer place if you accepted payment from patients."

Bryce stopped and turned to look at her, his expression darkening. "The clinic functions just fine."

She cocked her head to one side, wondering why he chose to take offense at her observation. However, she'd been told—mostly by her sisters—that she could be 'abrasive,' so perhaps Bryce felt she was being rude.

"Are you going home soon?" she asked.

He gave her a skeptical glance as he walked around, turning off the lights in all the exam rooms.

As she followed toward the front of the clinic, Storm admired Bryce's fluid movements while he deposited his stethoscope on the receptionist desk and grabbed his brown sport coat. She exited the building after him and waited as he pulled the broken front door shut.

Outside, the fall air was cool—perfect weather this time of year in Texas. The streets were wet from a light rain while she'd been in the clinic.

He sighed. "Do you need a ride somewhere?" His lack of eye contact suggested he was ready to be rid of her.

She arched an eyebrow at him. Since she'd saved him, he might express more gratitude to the woman who rescued him. Well, the bullet removal had been free.

"I'd like to make sure you arrive home safely." Feeling drawn to him despite his sudden cool demeanor, she followed him to his truck and walked around to the passenger side.

Bryce opened the driver's side door but didn't climb inside the gray F150. He leaned over the hood and spoke firmly. "I appreciate what you did back there, and I repaid the favor, but you're not coming home with me. I've been taking care of myself just fine for thirty-four years without a bodyguard."

Four years older than me, she noted.

Storm found his irritation amusing, but she was also exhausted and not in the mood for an argument. She'd suffered a bullet wound —her first after eight years in the business—followed by a tedious background check to find the right local physician who would be the least likely to report injuries. After all that, she'd had to save him and disarm three thugs.

She couldn't explain why seeing Bryce home felt important, but it did. And she never ignored her intuition. Although she didn't possess her younger sister's power of premonition and telepathy, Storm trusted her gut feelings.

She climbed into the passenger side. "I could tail you, but that's a lot more work than I feel up to doing right now. So, let's get you to your house safely. Then, I promise to leave you unguarded."

He sat in the driver's seat but didn't start the engine. "Why are you doing this?"

"I don't know. I don't leave a job half done. Leaving you at the clinic feels incomplete. Unsafe."

After starting the engine, he backed out of the parking lot and turned onto the main road. "I'm a job now?" He gripped the steering wheel firmly.

"That wasn't meant to offend you," she said.

Am I abrasive or is he just irritable?

Perhaps today had been long for him also.

"What sort of jobs do you do?" he asked. "They seem to entail getting shot and knowing how to sneak around disarming people."

She shrugged, feeling no need to sugar coat her answer. "I'm an assassin."

THREE

Bryce's truck swerved slightly as he let out a nervous chuckle. He gripped the wheel tighter with now sweaty palms. He couldn't possibly have just allowed an assassin into his vehicle.

"Relax. You're not my target," she said.

"I don't find that statement as reassuring as you may intend it to be. Who is your target?"

"I'm currently between targets. I finished my assignment this morning, and I'm not planning on taking another one until after my leg heals." She brushed a strand of hair off her shoulder.

"How generous of you."

"You're judging me?" Storm gave a humorless chuckle. "The surgeon drowning in debt who leaves private practice under dubious circumstances to run a general medicine indigent care clinic has problems with my line of work?"

Bryce felt his blood boil. "You don't know a damn thing about me."

"Nor do you know much about me. I'm not here to piss you off, so let's call a truce. I won't judge you about your life choices, and you won't judge mine."

Storm's voice was infuriatingly calm. He glanced at her as she regarded him with those big, beautiful eyes. Her attractive features —smooth cheekbones, full lips—annoyed him. What kind of name was Storm?

He turned to stare out the windshield as bright headlights passed him at high speed on the interstate.

After a few minutes of tranquil quiet, he felt calm again. "So, you're an assassin? I take it you're not interested in traditional employment."

"I have a unique skill set."

"I can't argue with that. How did you acquire said skills? Don't answer that if you have to kill me according to some assassin code."

She gave a sweet, silky laugh that unnervingly aroused him. "I had a calling early in life. I veered from traditional education and studied martial arts and weapons training."

"Killing doesn't bother your conscience?" he asked hesitantly.

"Choir boys don't end up on my list."

"Passing judgment doesn't bother you?"

"I don't have to judge anyone. Their fate was determined by their actions leading up to the point when I entered their lives." She reached down and rubbed at the wound under the bandage on her leg.

"But you end someone's life. You aren't troubled by that?"

"No. Maybe I'm missing some neural synapse which prevents most people from doing what I do. I'm not claiming my reaction to my occupation is normal or appropriate, but I don't lose sleep over it."

"You don't lose sleep over killing people?" Perhaps for his own health, he should stop questioning her, but her candid answers fascinated and frightened him.

"I don't enjoy it. I don't make people suffer. I don't drone on a long monologue about why they're a target. I don't demand atonement or confession. I simply send smudged souls back to the Maker. He or she can sort them out from there."

He or she? Bryce decided against a religious discussion with a cold-blooded killer.

He maneuvered the turns home mechanically as they rode in silence. Was she a cold-blooded killer? Nothing about her was cold—dismissive and a little cavalier, yes, but not cold. Yet she'd said she was an assassin. He couldn't reconcile what she claimed to be against the woman who sat beside him.

When the crunch of gravel sounded under his tires, he brought his mind back to the present. From the motion of his truck down the driveway, the floodlight on his porch burst on, illuminating the side of the house and gravel drive.

He turned off the truck and sat quietly. Beside him was a beautiful and deadly woman whom he had driven to his home. If she knew about his clinic and had this "unique skill set" as she claimed, he had no doubt she would have been able to find his home anyway. The best he could do was not upset her and end up on her naughty list.

Now, how do I get rid of her?

She sat looking at his house with a perplexed expression, as though also trying to decide what was next. He wanted to remind her she'd said she would leave after she saw him safely home. Perhaps she hadn't considered his home might be remote and leaving wasn't as simple as hailing a cab. He certainly hadn't.

"There. You've seen me home safely. Do you have a phone? You can summon a rideshare. Where do you live? Are you staying in town?"

"If you would feel more comfortable, I can sleep in the truck," she offered, apparently with no intention of leaving.

He scowled. "No, I would not feel comfortable with you sleeping in the damn truck." He got out of the Ford, slammed his door, and walked around to her side. Feeling on edge, he was all too aware he was being rude to someone who had saved his clinic and possibly his life. He yanked her door open.

She blinked at him.

"You're not sleeping in the damn truck," he growled as much as said.

She arched an eyebrow at him with a look that made him simultaneously want to kiss her and slam the door shut in her face.

He cleared his throat and clamped down on his temper, which seldom manifested on the surface like this. After a deep breath, he said, "Please come inside. I have a guest room."

After sliding out of the truck, she stood close to him. The sudden urge to gather a handful of those dark knots and tangled hair irked him. He stepped back, closed the door, and stuffed his hands in his back pockets.

She took an uneven step forward.

"Wait." He pulled his hands back out and put them up in a halting gesture. "Just wait a minute. You shouldn't put your full weight on that leg." He ran an arm around her waist and helped support her into his house. With every step, he silently chastised himself for having succeeded in getting his hands on her. Now he had to remove them from her somehow.

Bryce turned on the kitchen light without leaving her side and dropped his keys on the counter. "Let's get you to the sofa."

This entire time, she hadn't so much as squeaked about the pain. Turning her in his arms, he eased her onto the couch but hesitated. She was fully in his embrace now, on the sofa with him leaning over her. She looked up at him with mesmerizing eyes.

Oh, hell.

Rational thought escaped him. He leaned into her and when she didn't pull away, kissed her. She returned the kiss, opening her mouth to him and pulling herself up to press her body into him. Hunger and desire swirled in him like gasoline and sparks, igniting a fire down to his core. When she wrapped her arms around him, he scooped her into his arms and carried her to the bedroom, intermittently kissing those succulent lips.

She sank fingers into his hair, her touch sending the heat between them into dancing flames. As he set her down on the bed, he positioned himself above her. She grasped his shirt collar and pulled him closer. He savored her lips again, wanting to devour every inch of this woman he hardly knew.

She took off her leather jacket to reveal a holster and weapon. The look was sexy as hell, despite knowing she'd called herself an assassin. Even sliding out of it was sexy. When she set the gun aside, his hands were back on her.

As they tugged clothing off each other, he kept attentive to every motion, expression, and sound. Any second, she would tell him to stop. Any second, she would make him come to his senses before they were both naked.

"Are you sure?" he asked, kissing her neck and stroking hands around her breast to make sure she understood he was asking for her consent and not making a show of any reluctance on his part.

"Yes." Her voice was husky, needy.

When their bare skin touched, flames soared into a raging fire. He remained in control long enough to pull a condom from his nightstand and slip it onto himself. He kissed her neck, intending to work his way lower for more foreplay.

Instead, she pulled him closer with tender, soft hands caressing him. Angling her hips, she slid onto him. He gave her a moment to adjust before moving in long strokes. Her skin and warmth felt divine wrapped around him.

Her hunger for him showed in every touch and every moan. And she didn't even know him. The entire situation was surreal. He careened out of control, but his body refused to stop something so sublime.

Her breathing became ragged as she moved her hips faster, calling out his name.

His moment of ecstasy followed hers, punching through him and ripping him apart like an earthquake. They rocked in unison, bodies moving like one. When his mind reconnected, he eased himself off Storm and held her tenderly in his arms.

In a few moments, she was deep asleep.

BRYCE WOKE and stretched an arm across his bed. Empty. He opened his eyes to the morning sun streaming in through his window. He was alone.

"Storm?" He felt the sheets where she'd been.

Cold.

She must have left before dawn.

After he threw off the blankets, he pulled on a pair of jeans and walked through his house. "Storm?"

Silence.

He started a pot of coffee, tugged on his boots, and walked outside to feed the horses.

She'd left without a trace.

But last night hadn't been a dream. The pleasure was real. He could still smell and taste the intensity of her. He scrubbed a hand through his hair. She must hate him. The things he did to her. To her? With her. Multiple times, since she'd awakened after her nap and wanted more.

She'd been enjoying the fervent passion, hadn't she? She had been with him every step, right? Had he been too rough? Too much?

He'd never lost himself in the throes of passion and indulged all night like that—and certainly wouldn't have considered doing the things he did with a stranger.

An assassin.

His mind retraced the events, arousing him all over again. He shook his head, doubts and insecurities transforming into frustration. How dare she just leave? He looked around at the flat, rural land spanning in every direction.

"And where the hell did you go?"

His ranch was a hundred acres. She didn't have a car, and she hadn't stolen his. She would have a hefty hike—in the dim light of dawn with a leg wound—to make it to a major road where she could catch a rideshare or hitchhike. Since he hadn't heard the crunch of tires on his gravel drive, he doubted she'd taken a rideshare directly.

Hitchhike with a stranger? Someone else she might spend a night with? The thought sickened him, but his reaction was also disturbing. He had no claim to her.

He hadn't even had the decency to keep his hands off her and just let her sleep. Had she left angry? Perhaps she was on foot somewhere and he could track her down and demand to know why she had left. Simultaneously, he felt some measure of relief that she was gone before Olivia would return home from her grandmother's house.

Dolly and Faith waited by the fence for him, greeting him with soft neighs.

"Yeah, yeah. I'm coming." He stalked to the barn and put a scoop of feed in each of the two buckets. After carrying them to the fence, he hoisted them over and onto their respective hooks.

The horses stuck their heads into the buckets and commenced chomping.

"What the—" Bryce stared at Faith, who was wearing a bit. "Come here, girl." Reaching up, he tugged off the bridle.

The horse, undisturbed, resumed eating.

Bryce stepped on the first rung of the fence, swung a leg over, and landed on the other side. He inspected his horse. Small triangles of sweat foamed under her forelegs and between her thighs. Someone had run his horse while riding bareback.

Storm.

If the woman had ridden north to the boundary of his land, she would be a tenth of a mile from Highway 80. Easy for an attractive woman to flag down a ride from there.

So, she was gone.

He wasn't big on most cry-in-your-beer country songs, but suddenly he felt like one. She rode him, then rode his horse, and then rode right out of town.

FOUR

Storm crept across the bow of the yacht as it streamlined slowly through a glassy gray ocean. The sun hadn't yet breached the horizon, but she had enough light to navigate stealthy steps along the boat. She wore all black along with a slender bullet-resistant vest and black gloves. Her hair was braided back to keep strands out of her vision.

She kept her Sig Sauer in front of her, the suppressor firmly in place, hoping the muffled noise wouldn't be distinguishable over the hum of the engine to those inside the boat and steady thrumming breeze to those on deck.

Her phone rang—a gentle beeping through her single Bluetooth earpiece. She tapped the earpiece twice to accept the call, only audible to her. "Hello?"

"Storm, I'm returning your call, but only to say you have to stop calling me."

"Denny, thanks for calling back."

"Why are you whispering? Are you on a *job*? Why are you taking calls on a job?" His voice sounded horrified.

A man twenty feet away port side was leaning over the railing, perhaps on the lookout or perhaps just enjoying the ocean breeze. She took aim and fired, the spitting sound of the gun breaking the tranquil silence. He fell overboard, taking his Smith and Wesson with him. The splash was contained, so she hoped his coworkers hadn't been alerted.

"Your call is important to me. You're important to me," Storm said.

"I shouldn't be. I don't want to be."

"I need your advice."

"I'm not your psychologist," Denny replied.

"You are *a* psychologist."

"But I can't be yours. We dated, which makes counseling you unethical."

"We had *one* date. A sole dinner a year ago. Now we're not dating, so we're good."

"It's still unethical," he protested.

"So don't bill me."

Denny sighed. "I also know what you do for a living, which puts me under duress. It makes me feel like I have to talk to you or the consequences will be far graver than a bad patient review."

She smirked. "So bill me." She slid along the bow to the starboard side. She'd never once threatened Denny, so his duress was entirely self-inflicted—as a psychologist, he ought to have recognized that.

She took aim and shot another gunman. Since the crew was heavily armed and well-funded, she wondered how much they had demanded for ransom.

Listening for a moment, she heard no shouts or commotion to suggest the men aboard the yacht knew they were under attack.

Denny remained silent.

"I met someone, and I haven't been the same since." Firing another shot, she killed a man on the stern. She kicked the body down the back steps, and it rolled into the water before it could stain anything. "I've turned down jobs—"

"Sounds encouraging."

"—and I've taken a few unusual jobs."

"Unusual?"

"The jobs aren't the point. For the last four weeks since our night together, I can't stop thinking about him. We had sexual chemistry. What if we're also a good relationship fit? Shouldn't I find out?" Quietly, she stepped with stealth up the stairs to the captain's lair.

A man with his back to her gripped wheel. His Smith and Wesson rested in a holster. Unlike everyone else so far on the boat, he had no black aura.

"You're dwelling on a single date?" Denny asked.

Storm replaced her gun quietly into its holster. She pulled out her wire. Gripping it in her gloved hands, she brought it around the man's neck and cinched it.

He clutched at the wire frantically.

She kicked at one knee, bringing him to the floor where strangling him into unconsciousness would be more manageable.

"Yeah. Is that normal?" she asked, the strain in her voice apparent.

Denny grunted, and she sensed this was his way of communicating that nothing about her was normal.

She continued, "I want to see him again, but I left abruptly, so I don't know if he even likes me." She shuffled her feet to stay behind the man, then dug in her heels to keep him steady. The man clawed frantically at the wire as he sputtered, but Storm held fast.

Bryce's caresses and kisses had suggested he liked her, but his mood leading up to sex had suggested he didn't. Because she hadn't dated in many years, she was in uncharted territory.

Denny said, "You should consider the danger your lifestyle might bring to someone. If you really care, staying away might be safer."

The boat's pilot crumpled to the ground as his face transformed from red to a deep shade of bluish purple. She released him when he passed out.

This one got to live. She secured his hands and feet with flex ties before stretching his shirt over his head to blindfold him. He hadn't seen what she looked like and never would.

"I can discuss those concerns with him. He knew my vocation when we slept together." She cut off the engine and readjusted her gloves.

"Most men, given the opportunity to sleep with a beautiful woman, aren't considering the long-term ramifications."

Storm stepped carefully down the stairs and waited at the entrance to the berth. "So, we can take it slow—you know, aside from having rushed into bed together. Maybe I could invite him to my family's Christmas dinner." She was even considering going home for Christmas, as she hadn't been home in years. The last time she'd seen her family was at her older sister, Raine's, wedding a year ago.

A voice called from below deck. "TJ? What's going on?"

Thunderous footsteps of a man coming up the stairs echoed. Two-fifty maybe.

Aren't there any small *villains on this boat?*

She pressed her body flat against one wall, out of view from below deck.

Through the earpiece, Denny said, "I thought you hated your family Christmas get-togethers."

The man led with his gun as he came up the steps. Storm grabbed the gun with one hand and the man's wrist with her other. She brought the entire weight of her body down and flipped him forward using his own momentum.

"I don't hate Christmas." She certainly didn't hate her family, either. She loved them dearly, which was part of the reason she had become the killer she was.

The big man stumbled on the last step and landed on his right shoulder with a crunch. He released a roar that shattered her remaining element of surprise.

Well, it wasn't going to last forever.

She sighed. "I hate my mom nagging me about being alone. I

hate the looks of pity from my family about... well, you know. Anyway, if Bryce comes with me, I can enjoy Christmas more." She wrenched the Desert Eagle from the man's hand. The .50 caliber bullets were good for putting down a gorilla and good for close range if one's accuracy sucked. However, it was too messy to use on the deck of a seven-million-dollar yacht.

She tossed the gun overboard and spun on her rump. Kicking out a leg, she struck him in the face as he tried to push himself up, and he crumpled back to the deck.

"Do you have a good story for your family about how you met Bryce, or will that be an awkward recounting?" Denny asked.

More footsteps clamored up the stairs.

"Good point," she said, grabbing the donut-shaped buoy from the side of the ship and hurling it at the next man. "You're probably going to suggest I don't ask him to lie for me." She wouldn't have done that anyway. Although she eliminated smudged souls, she lied to no one and wouldn't ask anyone to lie for her. Avoidance, however, was something she was guilty of.

"You're right," Denny said.

Christian Delaney, the ringleader of the boat thieves and kidnappers, half-ducked and half-blocked the flying life saver ring as he fired a wild shot in Storm's direction.

"Was that a gunshot?" Denny asked, his voice an octave higher.

Spinning across the floor, she kicked Christian's ankle, thrusting him off balance. Leaping up, she struck him in the jaw with her fist before wrestling the gun out of his hand, digging her fingertips into his median nerve. When he released the weapon with a cry, she struck him in the temple with the butt.

He fell to his knees, dazed.

"Storm?" Denny's voice emitted as a terrified whisper into her earpiece.

She picked up the foam donut and squeezed it over Christian's torso. Fortunately, he was smaller than the other gunmen.

"Relax. I'm alive," she told Denny. She was certain she heard the psychologist sigh through the phone as if he'd been holding his breath on behalf of her safety.

She began to tie off the life saver rope to the railing, when the big man on the deck recovered faster than she expected. When he stood and took a step toward her, drawing a knife, she fired Christian's gun. Single shot to the chest. The man with the knife crumpled to the floor.

So much for not making a mess of the boat.

Christian used the opportunity to stand and charge, ramming his restraining donut into her. She grunted from the impact but side-stepped as he continued his momentum forward and tripped over the body on deck. Unable to catch himself with his arms, he fell face forward and unleashed a string of curse words.

Denny audibly swallowed. "Do you want to call me back at a better time? Or never?"

"No," she said to Denny. "Let's summarize, and then I'll let you get back to your other patients."

"You're not my patient," Denny repeated.

"If I'm going to ask Bryce to my family Christmas dinner, I need to first see if he is comfortable with my occupation—"

"No one is comfortable with your occupation."

"—and I need to be prepared to be truthful with my family about him. Anything else?"

"You could use your talents to save lives instead of taking them, as I suggested a year ago after our one date."

"I take lives to save lives, remember?" she said plainly. "Thanks, Denny." Reaching across with her left hand, she disconnected the call on her headset.

Discussing her issues with Denny always made her feel better. She recognized her social skills were often lacking, and therapy brought a certain clarity.

She set the gun down and rolled Christian toward the latched door at the stern. After propping him up, she pointed the gun back at him as he sat regarding her with cold, dark eyes. Blood dripped down the side of his face—dark and thick.

"Christian Delaney," she greeted the man restrained with the buoy ring who stared at the barrel of her Sig.

"Do I know you?" His long hair was pulled back into a low ponytail. A pocked-marked face hardened around a pair of gray eyes while his dusky aura whisked around him like a toxic smoky haze.

"You've hired me, but people who hire me don't know me."

"J-7." His already pale complexion blanched. "You never miss a mark."

"Is she still alive?" Storm asked.

"She is. I swear." He squirmed against the restraining ring.

"Good condition?" She set the gun down on the ledge of the bulwark.

He smiled a mouth full of crooked yellow teeth and metal fillings. "Mint condition. What's your price?"

"To let you live?"

He nodded.

She smirked. He was a gunrunner, kidnapper, rapist, and overall sleaze bag. A smudged soul. She had taken his money for a job once but only to eliminate an equally smudged soul.

You don't get to live.

"I don't leave a job unfinished," she said.

"Tell me, J-7, what does the codename mean?"

He was stalling, but she could indulge him for a few minutes. "J-7 was the last call my fiancé made before he sank my battleship." And that was the last night they'd spent together before he died.

Game night.

Christian's brow furrowed in confusion.

"You've never played Battleship?"

"No."

Using his own gun, she pulled the trigger and shot him between the eyes. His head snapped back, and she reached over and undid the latch, opening the door and letting his limp body fall overboard and into the ocean. She watched him bob in the water as his form rapidly decomposed, transforming into a large, inky-black oil stain rippling on the surface.

Another smudged soul.

It floated near the stains of the other men she'd sent overboard. She turned and looked at the one she'd shot who was now decomposing on the deck. The dark stains might never come out of the wood.

Storm holstered her gun and started down the stairs. "Sophia?"

No reply.

After descending eight steps of polished mahogany wood, she entered a large room with wide rectangular windows revealing an expanse of ocean views. A kitchenette was at the far end, with the living room nearest her and a dining table with cushioned chairs secured to the floor between the two. White leather couches took up one wall, curving around the corner. She crept across the linoleum floor to another set of stairs, making a tight curve down to a narrow hallway with light-gray carpeted flooring.

"Sophia, your mom sent me. She's worried about you. She wants me to bring you home. All the bad men are gone."

Whimpering came from one room.

Storm tried the door. Locked.

"Sophia, are you able to open the door and let me in?"

Her mother's instructions to Storm had been explicit. Retrieve her daughter from the kidnappers and try to minimize emotional trauma to the girl.

"Emotional trauma?" Storm had asked the mother when they'd spoken on the phone several days ago. The girl had been kidnapped. What could Storm possibly do that was worse?

"You need to kill those bastards, but I don't want her seeing violence and blood and dead bodies."

Oh, yeah, that emotional trauma.

"Got it," Storm had said.

"And don't scare her."

"Scare her?"

"Use a sweet voice. Not like what you're doing now. She's a child."

"Kid gloves."

"Exactly."

Storm heard the click of Sophia's door unlocking. She opened the door to see the eight-year-old staring at her with enormous blue eyes framed by curly red hair.

Storm knelt down at her level. "Hi, cutie. My name is J-7."

The girl looked from Storm's boots, up her black leggings, to her bullet-resistant vest, black gloves, and finally to her face. "That's a weird name."

"It is a weird name. I'm kind of a weird person." She gave her a lopsided grin.

Sophia smiled, lighting up her freckled face.

"Are you hungry?" Storm asked.

Sophia nodded.

"Me, too. Let's find some food."

Sophia took the hand Storm offered, and they walked to the galley of the yacht, where they washed their hands and made peanut butter and jelly sandwiches.

Storm had never done a hybrid mission involving a child—part assassination part rescue. Sophia had been kidnapped, and on her parents' boat no less. Her mother feared if the police or coast guard went after the kidnappers, Sophia would be killed. Instead of alerting authorities, she'd hired Storm to take a motorized boat to the yacht. Fortunately, Sophia's mom had taken precautions in low-jacking the boat with an additional tracking mechanism beyond the manufacturer's standard anti-theft device. Storm had paid a captain to pilot her close but not within sight. Guided by GPS, she'd driven her small motor-powered raft and cut the engine to row the last mile in silence to the yacht in the dark of night.

Sophia and Storm sat down and ate the sandwiches, washing them down with a glass of milk.

"Are you ready to go home?" Storm asked.

Sophia nodded.

"You know how to drive a yacht?"

The girl shook her head, curls swinging.

"Me neither. Maybe we can find a manual."

"Or a YouTube video," Sophia suggested.

"Yeah, or that."

CHAPTER
FIVE

Bryce nursed his beer as he listened to country music. Across the table, Landon cracked open peanuts and dropped the shells on the floor before eating the nut. Beside Landon, his wife Wendy sipped wine as she tapped the toe of her shoe to the beat of the music.

"C'mon, buddy, it's been three years. When are you coming back?" Landon prodded. He was a burly man in his mid-thirties with black hair.

Bryce shrugged. "When I'm ready. And I'm *not* ready."

Wendy adjusted a strap on her purple dress. "Don't you miss it? Miss the rush? Miss saving lives?"

The three of them had completed surgical residency together. Inseparable, they had all moved to Dallas to practice. Bryce and Landon had been general surgeons while Wendy did reconstructive and cosmetic surgery.

I do miss it, Bryce thought.

There was nothing quite like having his hands on someone's vital organs. But with the responsibility came the risk. Malpractice insurance was astronomical, which meant he had to work extra hours to make those payments, in addition to the mortgage, student loans, and raising a child. After Olivia's mother, Erin, died, giving up eighty-hour work weeks to raise his daughter wasn't a hard choice.

Bryce chose the free clinic with flexibility where no one faulted him for keeping banker's hours to drop off and pick up Olivia from daycare. The grant funding to run the clinic was minuscule, but it paid the bills. With Olivia having recently started kindergarten, going back to being a practicing surgeon was something to consider, but only if he could find the right fit. He would need to find a position that didn't involve twelve-hour work days and frequent weekend calls. And it needed to be within a reasonable commute from his ranch.

Bryce realized Wendy was still waiting for an answer.

"Sometimes I miss it." Performing surgeries, the impact to patients' lives had been more immediate and dramatic compared to clinic. But the long-term rapport with many of his patients at the clinic was rewarding.

He thought about Storm and how he wouldn't have met her if he'd been working in his private practice surgery position instead of the free clinic. Taking out her bullet had reminded him of his former glory, and he'd spent days researching job openings that looked utterly unappealing. Too many hours. Too far from home.

Wendy gave him a sad smile with a full set of red lips. Large eyes and high cheekbones were framed by a brown bob cut. She was an attractive woman, and he often wondered why she partook in plastic surgery herself. He wasn't sure if it made her more beautiful or more like a wax figurine.

Regardless, she and Landon had been amazing friends after Erin's death. They'd helped Bryce through the grieving process. Although Bryce and Erin had been divorced over six months and had been out of love longer than that, her death had been sudden and tragic. Olivia had lost a mother she now barely remembered.

When Bryce saw a woman in black with long dark hair enter the bar, he snapped to attention. No, she wasn't Storm. The stranger walked to the bar and ordered a drink. Of course, Storm wouldn't randomly walk into the same bar he happened to be frequenting at the time.

As he took another swig of beer, he thought about the mysterious woman he had no way of contacting and shouldn't even be wishing he could hold again. His mind drifted to her smooth skin against his lips, fingernails digging into his skin, and hot, wet thighs.

"Bryce?"

He looked up at Landon.

"Were you actually checking out a woman?"

"I—"

"Because that's the first time in a long time, and it gives me hope."

Wendy leaned forward, all intrigue. "Are you thinking about dating again?"

"I guess so."

Her eyes widened even though it didn't crinkle the smooth glossiness of her skin. "Are you seeing someone?"

"Not exactly."

His friends stared at him with a mixture of awe and amusement.

Bryce scrubbed a hand across his face. "I met a woman about a month ago."

"That's great," she cooed.

Bryce shook his head. "I thought things went well." Skin on skin and succulent, scathing kisses. "But I haven't heard from her since." He'd hoped to hear from her, but he also worried about their compatibility. He would never know if they fit well outside the bedroom if she didn't return.

Except, if she truly was an assassin, they were definitely not compatible. Then why did he want to see her again? He reminded himself, for the hundredth time, how he should be relieved she'd left for good.

Landon gave a lopsided grin and punched Bryce in the arm. "Shake it off, buddy. Nobody bats a thousand when they first take the field after an injury—in your case, a leave of absence."

"Can you call her?" Wendy asked.

"She didn't leave a number."

Wendy's expression turned pitying.

Bryce stood and dropped money on the table. "I'm going to make it an early night. I'm taking Olivia to the zoo tomorrow."

"Okay. Keep trying. We're proud of you!" Landon called after him.

Storm woke to the smell of coffee. The automatic machine she'd programmed yesterday had kicked on, filling her rented condo with the delectable aroma. She usually slept heavily, sometimes forgetting where she was because she traveled so frequently. Coffee—medium roast—was the smell of home, even if she didn't have a single location which anchored her geographically.

Had she slept twelve hours?

The boat ride to Galveston had been hours of hoping she didn't crash the yacht. Then she'd had to sneak off the boat as Sophia's mom walked onto it. Storm had completed forty-two missions. Not a single person who'd hired her knew what she looked like. Or her real name.

"Will I see you again?" Sophia had asked when Storm said goodbye.

"No. People rarely meet me once, and seldom a second time."

"Like the Tooth Fairy?"

Storm had cocked her head to one side. "Definitely not like the Tooth Fairy."

More like a dark fairy slaying even more monstrous creatures, Storm thought.

Kid gloves, she'd reminded herself. "Maybe a little like the Tooth

Fairy if she came out to fight the bad guys instead of paying for lost teeth."

"What if I need help again?" Sophia asked sadly.

"Your mom knows how to reach me." With that, Storm left the boat. She hid nearby and waited until Sophia was in her mother's custody before summoning a rideshare.

Surrounded by boats rocking gently under the dock light, she'd heard Sophia's mother emit shouts of joy. The mother's sound of delight and the knowledge she had reunited mother and daughter sent an uncomfortable shiver of warmth down Storm's spine. She had a loving mother—one she hadn't taken the time to visit except every few years. She hadn't seen her mother since her oldest sister's wedding.

Exhausted after the rescue, she'd gone to the condo and to bed.

Now, she padded on bare feet to the kitchen and poured a cup of steaming coffee, adding a splash of vanilla spice creamer.

She thought about her strange behavior over the last few months. Killer for hire was losing its appeal even if she was eliminating evil. Why had she changed? Because of one night with a man?

No.

She'd been thinking about her family more since Raine's wedding. Her night with Bryce was a reminder—a taste—that she didn't have to be alone. Should she end her self-imposed isolation and reconnect with friends and family again? Could she?

Oh, that night—fingers caressing her flesh, heated panting, and rough urgency. After Bryce lay spent beside her, the animalistic hunger had been replaced by a gentle embrace. She'd thought that was the conclusion of their evening, but Bryce had invited her into the shower.

He'd wrapped the dressing of her bullet wound in plastic wrap, and under steaming streams of water, he had explored every inch of her body with his fingers and lips. He'd vacillated between tender and firm, experimenting and tuned-in to what she enjoyed and what tipped her over the edge into ecstasy. All the while his glowing aura surrounded him—breathtaking and beautiful.

Out of the shower, the lovemaking had continued. She'd never had a lover so attentive... or tireless.

The next morning, she'd woken in a panic and left while he slept. She didn't want to steal his truck and didn't want to summon a rideshare to his ranch and risk creating an electronic trail back to his place. Instead, she'd borrowed his horse. Growing up in Texas with neighbors who owned horses, she'd taken her share of trail rides in her youth. Because the saddles were locked in the barn, she'd grabbed a bridle off a hook and set out north, bareback on one of Bryce's mares.

Since that night, time had slipped by as she dueled with her emotions. Time and distance, however, hadn't alleviated her desire to see him again. Instead, she was taking on reckless jobs, like a kidnapping. Kidnappings put her at risk of identity exposure whereas assassinations were clean in and out jobs.

She needed to see Bryce again. If he wasn't still attracted to her or his fear of her work trumped his desire for her, as Denny suggested, then she could get back to her normal business.

BOLVERKR STEPPED into the chilly night air wearing black pants and a dark windbreaker. He loved the cold and made an effort to take assignments north of the Mason-Dixon Line. He never traveled near the equator, and he preferred to work during the winter. His current task in Alaska was sublime. Fall temperatures peaked at fifty degrees and plummeted into the teens at night.

Bolverkr's skills ranged from sniper killing to remote bombing to hands-on murder. He didn't have a particular pattern, unless flawless success counted as a mode of operation.

Since the act of hiring a hitman—the highest form of premeditated murder—was an attempt by people to distance themselves from the act, he preferred to keep his clients engaged by having them choose the method by which their victim died. The deep-rooted hate of a person, enough to want to end their life with advanced planning, could be nothing but personal.

If his employers tried to dismiss the method by which the victim would die, Bolverkr would insist they choose or he wouldn't take the job. He was acting on their will, acting as the catalyst to create their darkest wishes. They needed to own the death, take responsibility for their darker side.

By selecting the method of death along with their commitment to have someone assassinated, his clients kept his conscience clear. Bolverkr wasn't the monster. The people who paid to have someone killed—their way—were the real monsters.

His current client had chosen an ax. He literally wanted the woman who'd cheated on him to be axed to death. The money was good, so she would get the ax. He'd have to burn his clothes after to eliminate the evidence, so he'd packed pants and shirt in the bag he carried.

He stood outside the woman's home in the shadows of her porch. Mozart emitted from the dining room where light shone through sheer curtains and spilled onto the snow-covered ground outside the house.

As he breathed the crisp, revitalizing air, he knew his conscience was clear. Well, almost. The only kill he could claim for himself—unpaid and unsolicited—was a Valkyrie. The demon who'd killed his mother had met a gruesome fate at Bolverkr's hands. Gruesome and well-deserved. The Valkyrie had been easy to spot with her holier-than-thou disposition and shimmering golden aura—repulsively warm and luminous. She hadn't been so haughty when her blood and life seeped out of her.

He'd never encountered one since her and wondered if she'd been the last. But that couldn't be true, since he'd heard the powerful woman and Helheim descendent in Europe had put a bounty on the heads of all existing Valkyrie.

As his mind focused back on the present, Bolverkr gripped the ax in his hand. His breath condensed in the frigid night air. Time to earn his payday.

Storm fought the fluttering in her chest as she pulled into Bryce's driveway. Before reaching the end, she did a quick three-point turn and backed the rest of the way down. She parked her black Audi R8 facing the road out of habit of always having a quick escape route. Taking a few steadying breaths and aware she was never this nervous before an assignment, she summoned her courage. Since this was nothing more than a social visit, she shouldn't have these absurd butterflies.

As she exited the sports car, she smoothed her jeans and walked toward the sound of a deep, encouraging voice by the corral. Her boots crunched on the gravel until she reached dirt. The estate was even more beautiful at sunset.

She wasn't dressed in all black this time and wasn't sporting a fresh bullet wound. Hometown girl look. She wouldn't apologize for her occupation, but she could dress casually and not remind him she was an assassin. She left her gun in the glove compartment.

Bryce leaned against the fence with his back to her. The setting sun in front of him accentuated his broad shoulders. He was watching someone on horseback ride in a circle around the edge of the fence. As Storm approached, she could tell the helmeted rider was a girl, perhaps six. She looked tiny on the back of the horse and yet entirely in control.

When horse and rider reached one end of the corral, the girl kicked the animal into high gear. They raced around three barrels with speed and agility.

"Well done, Olivia!" Bryce called.

Storm stood beside Bryce and leaned on the fence.

He jolted. "Storm, I didn't hear you."

He also didn't look happy to see her. Not a trace of delight.

This might be a brief visit.

"Sorry. Habit." Swell. And now she had reminded him of her day job.

He looked at the rider, who was cantering along the edge now, and back to Storm. "What are you doing here?"

"I came to see you." She kept her voice even, although she was beginning to think she'd made a mistake by coming back to his home.

"This is a social visit?" His jaw tensed.

"Yes." Her voice hardened as his unspoken rejection of her stung. "If I were on the job, you'd never know I was here."

He turned his gaze toward the sunset.

She lowered her voice. "I would never hurt you." It pained her to think he'd even considered the possibility.

"You can't just show up unannounced."

"I failed to get your number before I left." She could have easily discovered his phone number, but she'd wanted to make a personal visit.

He gripped the fence. "Without so much as a goodbye."

"I—" she hesitated.

He was angry at her for leaving, which meant he had wanted her to stay. Was she to conclude that he'd missed her?

If so, why is he unhappy I'm back?

"I'm here now," she said.

"You can't just show up unannounced."

"Yes. You mentioned that. Rule number one. Got it. Other rules I need to know?"

"What? No. We don't need to establish rules because you're leaving."

His tone hurt. She tried to read his expression, but he wasn't making eye contact with her. Had he forgotten their amazing night together?

He turned toward her, towering over her. "You need to leave, Storm."

She took a step closer, her cheeks flush with anger and humiliation. Did he think he could intimidate her? Did it mean nothing to him that she came out to his home to see him? She had taken a kidnapping case because of him. Everything was changing.

He reached for her, and she wasn't sure if he planned to kiss her or shake her.

"Okay, Daddy, I'm done riding."

Bryce stepped back from Storm before touching her.

She turned and looked at the little girl. Two brown braids protruded from her helmet. Faint freckles dotted her cheeks and nose.

Daddy.

Bryce was a father.

Why didn't Storm know that? Because she hadn't treated him like a mark. She hadn't delved deep into his background like she did for someone with a price on his head.

She thought of Denny's words of caution. Her type of employment could put someone she dated in danger. And his child.

Olivia, he had called her.

Bryce glowered at Storm before jumping the fence and giving his full attention to Olivia. He talked about how well she rode and praised her posture as he walked beside the horse and back to the barn.

Was she supposed to back off knowing he had a child? Storm was no amateur. No one who hired her saw her face or knew her real name. She had a good cover. A real cover.

Bryce watched Olivia slide off the saddle and unstrap her helmet. His daughter being within a hundred feet of an assassin frayed his nerves.

"Who's your lady friend?" Olivia asked.

He tied Faith to a rope and unbuckled her girth belt. "Just someone I met at the clinic."

Someone who'd left him before dawn. Six weeks without a word, which was fine because he didn't need her kind of trouble—although he'd nearly just kissed her again.

Anger. Arousal. The sight of her made him irrational. As a father and a physician, he was never irrational. He had Olivia to consider. He took off the bridle and saddle and hauled them to the tack room where he shelved them.

Oh, and the look on Storm's face when she realized he had a daughter—shock with a side of dismay. She would leave for certain now. Clean break. The one-night stand would remain forever that, which would be for the best.

He lifted Olivia up so she could brush Faith. "We need to finish up so you can practice your letters. Grilled cheese sound good for supper?"

"Yeah. Is your friend staying for supper?"

"No."

When they were done grooming, Olivia skipped on her way to the house, and Bryce fed the horses oats before putting them out to pasture.

As he walked back toward the house, he was surprised to see Storm leaning on the fence. He didn't like the zing of excitement he felt at seeing her persist.

"You're still here."

She smiled.

He noticed for the first time she had perfectly placed dimples. Were assassins allowed to have dimples? It seemed like those alone broke some type of code. He kept walking past her, afraid that if he stopped, he would grab her and indulge his fantasy about kissing her again.

She stuffed her hands in her pockets and fell into step beside him.

He noted she walked without a limp.

"Your leg is healed."

"Thanks to you."

He grunted.

"How's your clinic doing?"

"No more robberies. Thanks to you." He paused. "That's your car?"

"You like it?" She grinned.

Did he like her high-end luxury sports car that was probably worth more than half his house? "Yeah, I like it."

"I have a boat, too."

He cocked his head to one side, wondering what type of boat she had if this was her car. Deciding he didn't want to know, he resumed walking.

When they reached the porch, he swung the door open and stopped, turning to look at her. The last remnants of the setting sun gave Storm a glowing, angelic outline. She regarded him with those big, beautiful eyes.

"I have a daughter. You're an assassin. This won't work."

She arched an eyebrow as one corner of her mouth turned up. "I don't see how the two are mutually exclusive."

"Why are you grinning?" he asked.

"If you didn't like me, you wouldn't be thinking about the long-term ramifications of dating someone in my line of work."

He shifted his weight and ground his teeth. "Not a word from you in six weeks and you just drop by?"

"I dropped by to ask if you would be interested in going to my family's Christmas dinner. If Olivia isn't busy, she can come too."

He gaped at her before taking a step inside the house.

"Daddy, are you making supper?" Olivia asked from the kitchen table.

He motioned for Storm to come inside the house. "Are you serious about Christmas?" He infused his voice with as much incredulity as he could, keeping his voice low so Olivia didn't hear his incensed tone.

"I took courses in cultural studies, not relationships. I haven't been on a date in... in a while." She touched her fingers to the necklace with the diamond ring he'd noticed at the clinic the night they'd slept together. Behind the ring was a trifold Celtic knot pendant.

"Most relationships have a period of dating before meet-the-parents," he said.

When she smiled, he realized he hadn't given her an outright 'No.' Why didn't he just say no?

"You're right," she said. "But I thought meeting my family might make you feel less threatened by my occupational choice."

He paused in the foyer and lowered his voice. "They know you're an assassin?"

"No. They know I'm a travel blogger."

He arched an eyebrow. "Travel blogger?"

"I post about food, sightseeing, and culture."

"That's your cover?"

She stepped close to him. Too close. The creaminess of her skin reminded him of how she'd felt naked in his arms. His gaze trailed from her full lips to her enticing purple eyes.

"More than a cover, it's a career. I'm an influencer. I have over three hundred thousand followers on my social media platforms. *Asgardian Adventurer.*"

He blinked at her.

"So you lie to your family about your more lucrative job?"

"An omission to protect the people I love." Her gaze turned distant, giving him the sense she genuinely cared about her family.

"But you told me the truth?"

"You asked me what I did for a living in a situation where I'd been shot. You would have thought I was lying if I'd answered 'social media influencer' or 'travel blogger.'"

He couldn't argue with her infuriating logic. She hadn't lied to him. But what else was she omitting about her life, and why did he care?

"So, can we date?" she asked.

She smelled like lilacs. His ears rang and his head grew fuzzy. He couldn't think straight with this woman so close to him.

"I... I need to make dinner." He walked through his living room and into the kitchen.

STORM FOLLOWED Bryce into the kitchen. Everything about his house interior looked cozy, from the brown sofa covered in soft throw blankets to the pictures of him and Olivia on the walls to the worn, dark, oak furniture. She tried to remember what she'd seen her first night here, having obviously missed evidence of him having a daughter. The house had been dark, and she'd been too hot and bothered kissing Bryce to notice Legos in one corner of the room.

The physician wasn't happy to see her, but he wasn't turning her away either—mostly. Mixed messages to stay and leave were woven in his words and body language. She hoped his interest in her would win over the fear he had of her occupation.

"I'm sorry for leaving and taking so long to come back." She lowered her voice.

She'd had occasional one-night stands when the loneliness of her life seemed all-consuming, but she'd never tracked the man down later to try to establish a real relationship. They had been nothing more than a quick release. A distraction from the violence and death she dealt with day in and day out. This was what she'd told herself for years, but now with this need to spend time with Bryce, perhaps those encounters had been a balm to ease the ache of loneliness.

He glanced at her as he pulled out a loaf of bread and placed a pan on the stove.

"What are you sorry for?" Olivia asked her.

Kid gloves, Storm remembered. She leaned on the counter and looked at the young girl. She had Bryce's amber eyes.

"When your dad and I met, we became friends. But I left without saying goodbye, and I just now came back to say hi."

Olivia frowned.

"I know," Storm continued, "it isn't nice to treat friends that way."

The girl's face brightened. "But you said you're sorry. So it's okay now. Daddy, is it okay now?"

He buttered the bread, staring at it intently as though he was painting a Monet masterpiece with every stroke. "Did you finish your letters, sweetie?"

Olivia resumed her tracing.

"Maybe we can get to know each other?" Storm asked Bryce.

He turned and placed the bread in a pan on the stove, adding cheese between the slices. "This is me. I live here. I have a daughter and a few horses, and I work at the clinic you've already visited. Born and raised in Texas. I went to medical school at Baylor. I completed residency at Emory."

"And you like grilled cheese," she added.

And you have an amazing aura, she thought, wondering if he knew the significance. What supernatural powers did he possess? She opted not to ask him in front of his daughter. Olivia had a very faint white aura but was so young she might not be manifesting any abilities yet.

"Olivia likes grilled cheese," he corrected. He pulled out pre-cut carrots from the fridge.

"What do you like?"

He flipped the sandwich in the pan and started spreading butter on another one. "Simplicity. Safety. And Thai food."

"Thai. There's a cozy little restaurant in Bangkok—The Sixth. Great food, though a little different from Americanized Thai food."

He blinked at her.

"What's a Bang-kok?" Olivia asked, grinning as she sounded out the word.

"It's a city in a country called Thailand. Wonderful food. And you can ride elephants in Thailand."

Olivia's eyes went wide. "I want to ride an elephant!"

Bryce chuckled and finally cracked the first smile since Storm's arrival. "Do you, now?"

Storm pictured Olivia on top of the large animal. She would be so small up there. She imagined an elephant wouldn't go fast enough for a little girl accustomed to barrel racing, yet the novelty of riding an elephant might be enough to entertain her.

"We're going to the fair next weekend. Wanna come?" Olivia asked Storm.

Bryce's mouth gaped open as he dropped carrots onto Olivia's plate.

"I'd love to!" Storm replied, sensing she needed to snatch the invitation before the girl's father retracted it.

"Daddy, that's too many carrots. That's seven, not six."

"Yeah, well, you got two runts in there, so it's about six normal sized baby carrots."

She crinkled her nose.

He flipped the second grilled cheese, finished cooking it, and slid it on a plate to Storm.

She smiled. "Thanks!"

"It's just a sandwich."

She felt like it was more than a sandwich. She felt like maybe it was acceptance. Maybe it was a start.

After he made one for himself, they all sat at the table together.

"Daddy, can I please have ranch dressing for my carrots?"

"I'll grab it." Storm hopped up and fetched the bottle from the fridge. She'd just intruded on their father-daughter dinner and secured an invitation to the fair; the least she could do was grab ranch dressing for Olivia.

She poured a dollop onto Olivia's plate before returning to her seat.

"Thanks."

"She's very polite," Storm said to Bryce.

"I'd like to claim that's always the case, but I think she may be trying to impress you."

"It's working." Storm winked at Olivia, who giggled.

Dinner proceeded with Olivia explaining to Storm the intricacies of her classmates in kindergarten. There were nice ones, ones who misbehaved sometimes, and others who were downright mean—hateful, she called them.

Not so different from the adult world, Storm thought.

"What do you want to be when you grow up?" Storm asked.

"An astronaut."

"Way cool."

Bryce smiled. "We're trying to focus on robust careers. In Texas, school activities are too often divided into football players and cheerleaders. I don't want her falling into stereotypes."

"What about a doctor?"

Olivia shrugged with a mouthful of grilled cheese. "I don't know. What Daddy does is kind of gross."

Storm's gaze slid to Bryce, thinking of the bullet removal he'd performed. "He helps people."

"If I terraform other planets, I'll be helping people, too."

"Wow. I don't think I knew what terraforming meant when I was your age."

When dinner was over, Storm insisted on doing the meager amount of dishes because Bryce had cooked. While she cleaned the kitchen, he got Olivia through her bath.

She finished, drying her hands on the kitchen towel and sensing she needed to wrap up her stay. Bryce walked her to the door.

As they reached his porch, she turned around. "I am sorry, Bryce, for dropping in unannounced. Thank you for dinner and the company." She was still basking in the wonderful normalcy of the family dinner she'd enjoyed. Between her travel blog and her other occupation, she rarely socialized. Until she met Bryce, she hadn't wanted to. He reminded her of the human connection she'd been avoiding all these years.

His expression looked fraught with turmoil. "This probably isn't a good idea, Storm."

Even as he said the words, he stepped close enough she could feel the heat radiating from his body. His eyes roamed her face, settling on her lips.

Despite her heart beating fast and loud, she could practically hear the war waging inside his head. Part of him clearly wanted to kiss her again, and part of him was vying for control and seemed disgusted by his own lust.

She only needed to lean forward an inch to help him with his decision, but self-respect held her in place. If some part of him didn't want her, then he wouldn't get to have her. She understood he was in turmoil, but he would have to sort out those emotions before they could be intimate again. Seducing him wouldn't set his mind at ease over his daughter either.

She debated telling him how she was sure she'd found him for a reason, and something drove her back to him, gnawing at her as if he needed her, or maybe she needed him, but that sentiment made no sense. She didn't need anyone. Did she? When she tried to define her feelings—not simple lust—she couldn't pinpoint what it was. All of this jumbled contemplation seemed like too much too soon.

"Goodnight. I'll see you next week for the fair." She slipped away and walked to her car.

CHAPTER
SEVEN

Bryce had spent a busy day on his feet seeing patients. Medicine wasn't as simple as prescribing something and saying 'see you in a few months.' At the indigent care clinic, he had a finite set of resources, as did his patients. People ran out of insulin test strips or didn't have money for an antibiotic prescription to treat their infections or arrived hypertensive because they couldn't afford their blood pressure medication. He did the best he could with what he had to offer them.

He had compassion, and that was free. He had advice on lifestyle changes, most of which cost nothing. Sometimes the best medicine was an empathetic ear and reassurance.

Today, a patient had come in with chest pain. Bryce gave him an aspirin to chew, a nitroglycerin tablet under the tongue, an EKG, and a trip via ambulance to the emergency room. The man needed a cath lab, not a clinic visit.

At times, Bryce missed his surgery practice—the feel of warm organs and his power to cure in a single procedure. Yet, with declining health care reimbursements, he'd lost all personal touch with his patients when he'd been a surgeon. Since surgery paid better than seeing follow-up patients, he'd been relegated primarily to the operating room, and a nurse practitioner saw all of his inpatient and outpatient return visits. He'd felt like half of him was missing when he didn't get to see his patients after a procedure he'd performed. The decline of the physician-patient relationship to make room for efficiency and covering profit margins had left him incomplete.

At least in his clinic, he saw patients time and again through follow-up visits. He didn't have the dramatic effect of a surgical cure, but he had a rapport with his patients and his bedside manner was intact.

His phone rang. After checking caller ID, he answered. "Hi, Landon."

"Bryce, buddy. We're going to a Gabby Barrett concert on Saturday. You want to come?"

Bryce thought of the fair with Olivia. "No, I've got plans."

"Oh, hot date?"

Landon's question reminded him that Storm was accompanying them to the fair. Bryce's emotions rolled with a mix of excitement and worry. He wanted to see her again, although that made no rational sense.

I can't be with an assassin, he thought.

At Bryce's long pause, Landon asked. "Are you seeing someone?"

"Yes," Bryce drew out the word.

Was he seeing someone? How was a question like that so complicated? He regretted his answer, as it would inevitably lead to more questions.

"We are talking about a woman and not just your daughter?" Landon teased.

Just his daughter would be fine by Bryce. He would have a wonderful time with Olivia alone. In fact, he wondered why he'd allowed Storm to intrude on his outing with Olivia at all.

"We're going to the fair. Olivia and a date." Crap. Not a date. Storm was not a date. Olivia had invited her, not him.

He didn't want the complexity of a relationship right now, especially one with an assassin. Storm was dangerous, even if she didn't act like a threat to him. Her relaxed behavior clearly resulted in him making poor decisions, like allowing her near his daughter. Oddly, he didn't feel threatened by her specifically, even though she'd admitted to being capable of murder. He feared how the danger surrounding someone in her line of work could affect him and his daughter.

"Nice." Landon's word had an 'attaboy' feel to it.

"Is he coming to the concert?" Wendy's voice sounded in the background.

"He's taking a date to the fair," Landon replied.

Bryce gripped his phone in frustration. Not a date. Storm was a complication.

"Oh! Exciting!" Wendy gasped.

"Have a great time," Landon said.

"Thanks, man." Bryce hung up the phone and deflated into his office chair.

When Storm arrived at Bryce's house dressed in jeans, boots, and a t-shirt, Olivia and Bryce emerged. The little girl waved enthusiastically, pink boots thudding down the porch stairs. Bryce looked delicious in his worn blue jeans, despite the lack of a smile on his face. Storm was determined to show him she was a good person, mostly, even though he'd already passed judgment.

She'd worn a purple shirt with a peace sign—a gift her mother had given her years ago. She left her Sig in the glove compartment and slipped her phone into her back pocket as she exited her car.

Olivia beamed at her. "Storm! The fair is going to be great. By the end of the day, you won't want to leave."

Storm smiled as she followed them toward Bryce's truck but didn't know what to say to the girl's strange declaration. In Storm's experience, such a statement might be considered prophetic. Her father possessed something supernatural, evidenced by his aura. Did Olivia have special insight, or was this a normal child's enthusiasm?

Storm looked to Bryce for guidance, but he didn't make eye contact with her. He opened the backseat door of his extended cab truck and helped Olivia into her booster seat. Without a trace of warmth, he opened the passenger side door for Storm.

She looked at him, waiting for some type of warmer greeting. Even a slight smile would suffice.

Nothing.

Olivia in the backseat gave her a bright smile. Walking around to the other side of the truck, Storm climbed into the back of the extended cab to sit next to Olivia. Since the girl had invited Storm and was thus far the only person excited to see her, she decided to sit with her.

Olivia's eyes glowed with delight.

Bryce slammed the door shut before climbing into the driver's seat.

"Have you been to the fair before?" Storm asked.

Olivia's mouth quirked. "Of course. Have you?"

"It's been a long time. What's your favorite thing to do?"

"Eat cotton candy."

"What's your second favorite thing to do?"

"Watch Daddy try to win a prize for me by shooting the metal ducks."

"That sounds fun."

"What do you like to do?" Olivia asked.

"I like the Funhouse with all the mirrors that make you look weird."

Olivia giggled. She picked up the Stetson in the back seat and set the too-big cowboy hat obviously belonging to her father on her head. "My head is fifty-five centimeters around."

"Oh?"

"We measured our heads in school. Did you know the sperm

whale has the largest brain? And the pentaceratops has the biggest skull?"

"I did not know any of that," Storm confessed, amused and impressed.

Olivia continued to rattle off animal facts, and Storm was delighted to listen during their drive to the fair.

BY THE TIME THEY ARRIVED, Olivia and Storm had the day planned. Bryce's mood seemed gloomily unchanged as they parked and entered the fairgrounds.

Olivia took Bryce's hand in one of hers and Storm's in the other as she led them to the rides, bobbing in her cowgirl boots with each step. Her tiny hand was warm and soft, reminding Storm of Sophia's and all the trust the little girl and her mother had put in her to get her home safe.

Seeing the bustling fair and swirling rides brought Storm back to her own childhood, which seemed a lifetime ago. Country music blared as the smell of funnel cake wafted through the air. Nostalgia had her seeing glimpses of her and her sisters in their youth, dashing between rides and games, while Raine, the oldest, tried to herd Storm and Sky. Sky was easy to spot with her red hair streaked with gold highlights and brightly colored dress.

Did her little sister still skip happily through life? Storm wondered.

Sky had seemed happy at Raine's wedding and before that at a tropical vacation the sisters had taken. Deep down, was she happy though? Storm hadn't taken the time to ask.

Olivia rode all the rides she was tall enough for while Bryce snapped photos on his phone. At last, he seemed to relax and enjoy Olivia's enthusiasm. After cotton candy, they walked to the animal barn where the 4H Club had their prize animals on display.

"Do you have any other animals or just the horses?" Storm asked Olivia.

"We have a barn cat. Her name is Summer. She keeps rats out of Dolly and Faith's horse feed." Smiling, she pet one of the pigs.

"I saw you riding," Storm said. "You've got talent."

"Daddy says I have a knack."

Bryce smiled, landing a pair of adoring eyes on his daughter.

"I agree with that," Storm said.

They left the large barn and joined the throng of people walking between the ride lines.

"Look, Storm! The house of mirrors." The girl grabbed her hand and dragged her into the funhouse.

Inside, they made faces and wriggled their bodies while laughing at the contorted images.

After the mirrors, they reached a game where Bryce shot the ducks to win a prize. Of the five shots, he knocked down three metal ducks and won a small teddy bear.

Olivia was ecstatic as she clutched the small furry animal. Bryce smiled down at her.

"Nice shooting, cowboy." Storm winked at him.

"Thanks."

"Now, it's Storm's turn," Olivia said.

"No, I'm good, thanks." She looked dismally at the toy gun with its slightly bent, rusty barrel.

"Come on," Olivia pleaded.

Storm glanced at Bryce for support.

With the twinkle in his eye, he paid the attendant. "By all means, Storm, show us your skills."

After narrowing her eyes at him, she picked up the rifle. In smooth motions, she cocked, fired, re-cocked, and fired successively five times. All five ducks fell.

"Wow! That was awesome!" Olivia jumped up and down.

Bryce blinked.

After Storm picked her prize, they left the fairgrounds. When they reached Bryce's truck, he fastened Olivia and the stuffed animals in the backseat—Bryce's prize a fraction of the size of the one Storm had won. The little girl had grown quiet, with a pair of eyelids hanging as heavy as the late afternoon sun.

"She's worn out," Storm commented.

Bryce closed her door and walked with Storm to the passenger side. He reached for the door but stopped and pinned Storm between him and the truck.

He spoke in a low voice. "What are you doing, Storm?"

She looked into his eyes, surprised to see resignation in them. "What do you mean?"

"You can't befriend Olivia to get to me."

His words cut her like a knife.

Zero trust.

Storm's mouth went dry as her heart withered. "I know you don't know me, but I'm not like that. I don't manipulate people. That was not my intention today. From the minute I arrived at your house this morning, you were rude. I chose to spend time with the only person who wanted me at the fair." And to think, Storm had been congratulating herself on getting along with a child, something she'd rarely ever attempted.

Bryce's expression softened, but he didn't go so far as to apologize. As his posture relaxed, his body moved closer to hers. Rock solid, she knew, beneath those clothes. Knowing what he felt like, she wanted to slide her hands along his chest and down his back.

But he didn't trust her, and seducing him now wouldn't bridge that gap.

"I'm sorry for my behavior," he said in a low, rumbling voice.

She reached up and straightened part of his shirt collar. "Give me a chance."

He shook his head. "I'm a single father. I can't afford to take chances. But I am glad you came. Olivia had a great time with you there."

Storm wanted to lean into him, close the distance, and kiss away the worried look on his face. But she didn't want to push. He apparently already felt like she'd spent the day pushing her way into his life.

"Let me show you who I am before you throw me away. Then, if you still want me gone, say the word and you'll never see me again."

Closing his eyes, he touched his forehead to hers. For a moment, they breathed together, the same air in the same space. She wanted to tell him he needed her but didn't know how to say that without sounding crazier than he already thought she was. After all, she couldn't explain why she felt this way.

He reached up and ran a thumb over her lips. She closed her eyes, soaking in the gentle sensation and forcing herself not to move to kiss him.

When he opened the door, she took her cue and climbed inside the truck.

They didn't speak on the drive back. Bryce's wariness toward her was a barrier, but she wouldn't fault a father for thinking of his daughter's safety. Feeling acutely aware of her lack of relationship experience, Storm knew she was ill-equipped to pursue someone who planned to resist her every step of the way.

Why was she bothering? She'd never subjected herself to the ill behavior of others. But Bryce was different. He made her feel different. He drew out emotions—far deeper than the initial sexual attraction—that she'd buried long ago.

She also couldn't ignore the nagging sensation of danger encroaching. The feelings weren't the acute rush of abdominal discomfort she felt when threats were imminent, but a faint clawing as if something advanced over the horizon, distant and ill defined.

He needs me, but I don't know why.

CHAPTER

EIGHT

Bryce drove his truck, listening to the hum of the engine while Olivia slept in the back seat and Storm stared out the passenger truck window. He'd hurt her feelings and needed to quit being a jerk to her simply because he couldn't process his own emotions.

She'd shown up wearing snug jeans hugging her curves and a purple t-shirt matching her eyes stretched over a perfect pair of breasts. He would know—he'd had his hands on them in an intimate moment. Nothing about the outfit was risqué or provocative, but his hormones regressed to that of a teenager.

"Let me show you who I am," she'd said.

What had she meant?

The entire time at the fair, she had focused her attention on Olivia, and his daughter had a wonderful time because of it. Storm didn't flirt with him, try to hold his hand, or try to force eye contact. He realized she was doing more to gain his trust by ignoring him and showing affection to Olivia. Then he'd stupidly accused Storm of orchestrating the entire event.

He'd ruined a perfectly pleasant day at the fair.

59

Storm pressed a hand into her stomach.

"Are you okay?" he asked.

"Stomachache." She squeezed her eyes shut.

"Something you ate at the fair?"

"No. I only get them when something is about to happen. Don't go onto the interstate." Her voice was pleading.

"Why not? We're right here."

"No. Go straight and then take the road on the left," she said followed by a gasp.

He obeyed her instructions. "Do you need a hospital?"

"No. It'll pass."

He turned down the country road, which began as asphalt and changed to gravel.

Storm straightened in her seat. "Can you stop for a minute and let the pain pass?"

"No problem." Bryce let his foot off the gas. Gently, he applied pressure to the brake pedal. Nothing happened. He pumped the pedal, but the brakes didn't engage.

What the—

Thankfully, no cars were ahead of him. He looked in the rearview mirror. No cars were behind him, either.

The truck was slowed by the natural friction of the gravel road. He helped it slow by pulling up on the emergency brake.

Turning toward Storm, he asked again, "Are you okay?"

She had a hand to her temple. "It's passing."

He hopped out of the truck as he released the hood. After popping it open, he inspected the engine. Next, he grabbed a flashlight from his truck bed toolbox and looked under the vehicle. On the driver side firewall in the engine compartment along the underside of his vehicle, he found the culprit.

Storm emerged beside him, holding a bleary-eyed Olivia on one hip. "She wanted to see what was going on."

"Brake line's been cut." Bryce stood and dusted the dirt from his jeans.

Storm's expression turned concerned, but she didn't seem surprised.

"How did you know?" he asked.

"I didn't." She set his daughter down beside her.

Olivia walked away from the truck and toward a fence on the side of the road.

Bryce crossed his arms. "But you knew not to take the interstate. We could've been going seventy miles per hour when the last of the brake fluid ran out." He didn't want to find out how dangerous pulling the emergency brake at high speeds surrounded by eighteen-wheelers would have been.

She shot him a look, and he suspected it was because his tone was more accusatory than grateful. "I get stomach aches sometimes and feelings, but nothing I can explain logically."

Bryce ran a hand through his hair as he looked at their surroundings. Pastureland spread out in all directions. He would have to call a tow truck to pick them up.

"Do you know anyone who would want to hurt you?" Storm asked.

Bryce let out a short, sharp laugh. "I was going to ask you the same thing."

He slammed the hood of the truck shut.

Anger flashed in Storm's eyes with a hard look he'd never seen from her before. She pointed a finger at his chest and spoke in a clear, cold voice, low enough his daughter wouldn't hear. "Listen to me very carefully, Dr. Chambers. No one who knows what I do knows my face. If I'm ever targeted by an assassin, it will be a clean kill—sniper shot. Only amateurs pull stunts like cutting brake lines."

Cheeks flushed with rage and indignation, she turned away from him. She walked off the road toward Olivia.

Well, once again, he'd been a jerk to her. He ran a hand through his hair. She made him crazy. In her proximity, he couldn't think straight. He vacillated between wanting to strangle her and kiss her.

As Bryce reached into his pocket for his phone to call roadside assistance, Olivia screamed.

Storm scooped up his daughter in her arms with lightning-fast speed and carried her to the truck.

"What happened?" he demanded.

"Snake. She's okay."

Bryce grabbed the shotgun out of the storage bin in the back of his truck. In three quick strides, he was by the fence. He located the snake and raised the gun to pull the trigger, except the snake was already still, save a slight rattling of its tail. On closer inspection, he could see that the reptile's neck was broken.

Storm and Olivia climbed into the bed of his truck.

He put the shotgun back and hopped into the truck bed with them. "Everyone's okay?"

Tears streamed down Olivia's face. "It bit Storm. It came after me, but she blocked it."

Blocked it and broke its neck somehow, he thought.

Bryce seized Storm's hand and inspected the purplish swelling. He sucked in a deep breath as his blood turned to ice. "Okay. Stay calm. Keep the wound below the level of your waist and let it bleed."

She did as he instructed. He checked his watch—he needed to get her to a hospital within thirty minutes. The nearest one was twenty minutes by car, but he didn't have a functioning vehicle.

"Bryce," Storm's soft voice called to him.

He looked into her eyes, knowing she would soon have light-headedness, sweating, and salivating. As he observed her breathing to see if she was struggling, he was amazed to see she was calm and her chest rose and fell serenely. Laying fingers over her wrist and feeling for a pulse, he noted it wasn't racing. In fact, his pulse was faster than hers.

"Bryce, I'll survive this. Tell me how to buy time."

"If you can keep calm and keep your heart slow, it will slow the spread of the poison into your body."

"I can do that."

He pulled out his phone and dialed 911. While he gave them details, Storm spoke in a soothing tone to Olivia as she stroked her hair. After giving the dispatcher his location and details about the snakebite, he dialed his mom's number.

"Hey, Mom, a friend of mine was bitten by a rattler. I'm waiting for an ambulance, but can you come get Olivia for the night?" His daughter didn't need to see this emergency from start to finish.

Storm sat in his truck bed and leaned back against the cab with her eyes closed. If Bryce didn't know better, he'd think she was taking a nap. Olivia lay with her head in Storm's lap.

"Sure. I'll be there right quick. Is your friend okay?"

"I don't know, Mom."

Storm was breathing, but that could change at any moment. She could have an anaphylactic reaction, and her throat would swell shut. Or she could develop systemic coagulopathy, damaging the circulatory system and her organs.

"I'll text you my location," Bryce told his mother.

"I'm already out the door."

"Thanks."

He hung up the phone and walked back over to look at the dead rattlesnake. He snapped a picture of the reptilian corpse with his mobile phone in case he needed to show it to anyone when they arrived at the ER. Turning back to the truck, he hopped into the bed.

Olivia sat up. Her tears had dried, and she appeared calm. "Shhh. Storm is resting. She said she's going into a trance. When she wakes up, she'll be okay. She doesn't need a hospital."

Bryce scowled at the absurdity of that notion. "She's going to the hospital." He felt Storm's slow and steady pulse. How was she doing that?

Olivia smiled. "She said you'd say that."

Bryce had to time her pulse against his watch to be sure his mind wasn't playing tricks on him. Thirty-two. Thirty-two?

"Storm?"

Was she actually meditating?

Sure, who doesn't put themselves in a trance after suffering a snake bite?

The minutes seemed to tick by as he waited for the ambulance. He wished he had a blood pressure cuff, but even without one, he could tell her pulse was strong. Storm was not in shock. In fact, of the three of them, only the physician on scene seemed to be the one in shock.

When the ambulance arrived, Bryce slid the sleeping beauty to the end of his truck bed before scooping her into his arms. The heavy vehicle crunched loudly on the gravel after cutting off its siren. Two men hopped out of the front and came around to open the back doors. The paramedics helped Bryce situate Storm on the stretcher as he explained what had happened.

"I'm Dr. Bryce Chambers. This is Storm. A rattlesnake bit her on her hand." He gave them the exact time of the bite.

Moving out of their way, he stood outside the back doors as the medics took vital signs and started an IV. He paced the road.

A heavyset one with a nametag that read 'Staley' cleaned the bite wound with antiseptic. "Uh, Doc?"

Bryce stepped closer.

"No disrespect, but if that's a rattlesnake bite, then I'm a ballerina."

Bryce climbed into the ambulance and re-inspected Storm's wound. The puncture wounds, which ten minutes ago looked swollen and purple, were now flesh colored and slightly red.

Bryce blinked in disbelief. "I'll show you the snake."

He climbed out of the ambulance with Staley following. They walked off the road toward the fence while the other medic stayed with Storm.

The paramedic scratched his head and leaned closer to look at the dead snake. "Huh. Well, don't that beat all, Doc? Guess we'll take her in for observation?"

They walked back to the ambulance, where Bryce climbed in the back to see Storm.

"Did she faint?" the other paramedics asked. "She's not rousing to my questions."

Bryce took her uninjured hand and stroked a strand of hair out of her face. "Storm, sweetheart, can you open your eyes?"

She squeezed his hand as her eyes fluttered open. Those beautiful purple irises, brimming with life, gazed up at him. Maybe she was an assassin. Maybe there was more here than he comprehended. But she had saved his daughter, and that spoke more to her character than an occupational title.

"How'd I do?" Storm asked, licking her lips as she blinked sleepily.

"You did good." He smiled, leaned forward, and kissed her forehead.

Storm's gaze focused on the inside of the ambulance. Small, compact cabinets with clear windows stored breathing masks, tubing, IV fluids, bandages, and tape. She sat on a hard stretcher elevated to a forty-five-degree angle. Intravenous fluids trickled into her.

Looking down at the hand where the snake had bitten, she saw it was almost healed. She felt tired and groggy, as she always did when her body was taxed with healing itself, but the cool fluids running through her veins revitalized her.

"They're going to take you to Longview Regional Medical Center. I'll come when I can get a ride."

"I don't need a hospital."

The paramedics stopped their tinkering in the back of the truck and listened to their conversation.

Bryce scowled. "This is nonnegotiable."

She calmly sat up on the stretcher, not intimidated by his doctor tone. "I appreciate your concern, but I'm okay."

"A rattlesnake bit you. This is serious and could be life-threatening."

"Bryce, look at my leg."

"Your leg?"

She held one leg two inches off the stretcher and waited for him to follow the instructions.

He rolled up her jeans and removed her boot. With a tender finger, he stroked over where her bullet wound had been. He stared at her perfectly unmarked skin in amazement.

"I can explain, but when we're alone," she said.

The bigger paramedic blinked at Bryce. "What's the plan, Doc?"

The paramedic's partner began taking a repeat blood-pressure measurement.

Outside the ambulance, the crunch of gravel signaled the arrival of another vehicle.

Bryce leaned back and scratched his chin. "I guess we're going home."

The paramedic shifted his weight on the bench. "Normally I'd have her sign an AMA waiver, but other than looking slightly pale, she seems fine. Vital signs are all good, which is damn strange, because she should be really sick right now after a rattler bite. Will someone watch over her for the next twenty-four hours?"

"Yes," Bryce said without hesitation.

Storm arched an eyebrow at Bryce, who'd been ready to be rid of her an hour ago. He shot her a look back that seemed to implore her not to fight him on this one.

A petite woman appeared, walking toward Bryce's truck. "Hey, Olivia, sweetie. How are you?"

"Granny!"

"Our ride's here," Bryce told her.

The paramedic removed Storm's IV. As they began stowing their supplies, Bryce helped her out of the ambulance. His hands holding her arms was the first lingering physical contact they'd had since their night together. The warmth of his touch seared her mind with memories of his body over hers.

"Mom, thanks for coming," Bryce said.

The small woman had a great bushel of blonde curls hiding

brown and gray roots. With a sweet, albeit overly lipstick-laden smile, the woman beamed. "Of course, hon."

"This is my friend, Storm. She doesn't need a hospital after all. Can you take Olivia and her home instead?"

"Of course. What happened to your truck?" Her voice was a sticky, sweet Texan twang.

The sound of it reminded Storm of her high school friends. She and her family had moved to Texas when the sisters were young, and the accents had taken adjusting to. Of the three of them, Sky, the youngest, had been the only one to acquire a slight Texan accent of her own.

Bryce's face darkened as he answered his mother's question. "A malfunction."

He escorted Storm into his mother's minivan. She focused on each step, still feeling lightheaded from healing.

"Are you okay?" he asked.

She nodded.

Bryce pulled out his phone again. "I need to call the police about the brakes and have my truck towed."

"I'll be fine," she assured him.

Olivia climbed into the child's car seat beside Storm.

His mother hopped in the driver's seat. "My name is Maddison. Folks just call me Maddie."

"Thank you for the lift, Maddie," Storm said.

Bryce turned to make his call but just as quickly turned back to Storm. He cupped her chin in one hand as he leaned closer. "Thank you for what you did for Olivia." His rich, golden-brown eyes overflowed with gratitude and affection. As he leaned in closer, he gently pressed his lips to hers.

Heat filled her from her abdomen and up into her chest. Too soon, he stepped back and closed the door.

NINE

While Maddie saw to Olivia's bath, Storm wandered around the kitchen and living room of Bryce's mother's home. She lived in a single-story ranch-style house with spacious rooms and an attached garage.

Storm had cooked spaghetti carbonara for dinner using a recipe she'd learned during a trip to Rome, while Olivia talked nonstop about the fair to her Granny. The adorable little girl had been brimming with energy. She reminded Storm of family and what life had been like growing up as a little girl without thinking of creatures lurking in shadows.

Now, all was quiet.

Maddie seemed to have an interest in ravens. Glass figurines, wood carvings, and paintings with ravens decorated her house.

One painting, a bird with shimmering obsidian wings and dark eyes looking right at her, seemed almost alive. Storm touched a finely carved and painted piece of wood. The bird's feathers were delicately sculpted. She admired the black creatures—in life and in art.

In Greek mythology, they were seen as bad luck, and in other folklore, their presence was a bad omen. Swedish stories depicted them as ghosts of the slain without a Christian burial. The Germans believed ravens represented damned souls.

In Christianity, the raven was more complex—at times saving saints or as examples of God's provisions in Psalms, and at times, a symbol of vice.

"Do you like ravens?"

Storm turned to see Maddie had entered the room. She must have finished tucking Olivia into bed.

Bryce's mother continued, "I think they're beautiful. Majestic."

"They are," Storm agreed. "You have an amazing collection."

"Thank you. They get a bad rap sometimes."

"So they do. In Norse mythology, Odin had two ravens—Huggin and Muninn, Thought and Memory—who flew around the world for him."

Maddie smiled. "Odin was also known as the Raven God. I'm a Christian, but I do like to read about ancient religions."

Storm thought about Bryce's aura, wondering what it meant and if Maddie, with an affinity for Norse mythology yet no aura of her own, knew of her son's ability.

"They are entertaining," Storm said instead of asking anything supernatural that might sound bizarre to Bryce's mother.

"Well, Olivia has requested her special guest tuck her in."

Storm placed the figurine back in its spot. "Oh? What do I do?"

"Tell a story or read a book. Since Christmas is getting closer, she'll probably want *The Grinch*."

Storm walked toward the girl's bedroom. "I can do that." When she arrived, Olivia had the book ready. Her room was decorated in all things pink and horses. Storm wondered if Olivia's bedroom at Bryce's house had a similar décor. She sat on the edge of the girl's bed and picked up *The Grinch*.

"Today was fun," Olivia said.

"Sure was."

"Will you be here tomorrow?"

"I don't know." She reached up and stroked a hand over Olivia's head. Then, she opened up the book and read.

Before she finished the story, the girl had fallen asleep. As she tucked the covers around Olivia, Storm recalled the kidnapped girl she'd spent a brief time with. Her interactions with these girls suggested she was capable of compassionate behavior.

Was she the Grinch whose walls of isolation were crumbling?

She hadn't explored this side of human compassion in years. She hadn't allowed herself to feel so much. After walling off her pain and isolating herself for so long, she didn't know if she could return to having relationships with people she cared about—other than her sisters. For the first time in a long time though, she felt like trying.

When Storm returned to the kitchen, Maddie had two glasses of red wine waiting for them. "I had Merlot or Merlot."

Storm smiled. "Merlot it is." Wine seemed a perfect end to this crazy day.

"You're okay after the snake scare?"

"I'm okay. I hate that I worried everyone."

"I'm relieved you're not injured." Maddie leaned on the countertop and added, "Bryce has never brought a woman to meet Olivia, much less spend a day with her."

Storm grinned. "Actually, Olivia is the one who invited me to the fair, not Bryce."

"Oh." Maddie's brow furrowed. "How did you meet Bryce, then?"

"He patched up my bullet wound." Storm might kill smudged souls, but she didn't lie. She certainly wouldn't create a web of lies around the mother of the man she wanted to date.

"You were shot?" Maddie's mouth formed a surprised 'O.'

"Just careless." Storm waved off her concern.

The woman relaxed slightly.

In Texas, a careless gunshot wound would imply a hunting mishap or cleaning misfire, so this was likely Maddie's assumption. In actuality, Storm's mark had pulled a Colt out of his boot she hadn't known he was carrying. "Anyway. Bryce helped me, and Olivia asked me to the fair."

Maddie smiled. "Well, she might've been the one who invited you, but Bryce was the one who kissed you."

Storm tucked a stand of hair behind her ear. "Ah. You saw that."

"I know chemistry when I see it. I also know people, and I've got a good feeling about you, Storm."

Storm tipped her wineglass back and drank.

You'd be the first, she thought.

STORM ROUSED at the sound of footsteps in the room.

"Sorry to wake you." Bryce stood, still dressed in the jeans and shirt from the fair.

"It's okay." She glanced at the clock. Eleven pm. She patted the empty spot beside her. "You look like you need sleep."

Maddie had told Storm to make herself comfortable until Bryce returned. Neither had expected him so late, so Maddie had gone to bed and Storm had dozed on the bed in Maddie's guestroom. She'd considered leaving several times but had wanted to see Bryce.

He crawled into bed beside her. As he eased himself quietly closer, she accepted him into her arms. He laid his head on her shoulder, and she relished the feel of him close, emitting warmth.

"Are you okay?" Storm asked.

"I am now." His eyes were closed, his breathing slow and steady. "How are you? How's the snake bite?"

She had felt the last of the poison seeping from her body by the time she read Olivia her bedtime story. "All healed."

He opened his eyes but didn't move away. "How is that even possible? I've been a physician for a long time. I've never seen anything like that. And the bullet wound is gone, too. Completely healed with no scar tissue."

"I'll tell you everything. It might take a while and be better received when you're not exhausted." She ran a hand gently through his hair and massaged his scalp.

Storm could tell he was tired. He might be more receptive to what she had to say if he was well-rested. On second thought, he might be most receptive if he wasn't entirely sober. Yes, the truth over drinks one evening. Once she opened up to him, she would ask him about the supernatural in his life, because something lurked in that glowing aura of his, whether he knew it or not.

When he didn't answer right away, she asked. "What did they say about your truck?"

"Someone cut the brake line. I gave a statement to the police. I can pick it up from the shop on Wednesday." He stroked a hand lazily up and down her arm.

"Who would do such a thing?" She'd had stomachaches or nausea when untoward events might happen most of her life. Her inklings were nothing like true prophecies some Vanir conjured. Storm could never pinpoint what the event would be, only that a threat was eminent.

"I don't know," Bryce said. "I have no enemies I know of, and certainly no one psychotic enough to risk the life of a child."

Storm continued to feel his soft hair and warm scalp. She had told Denny that Bryce needed her, and she'd been right. She wasn't just drawn to him for the lust of his kiss and the comfort of his embrace.

He needs my protection.

"We'll figure it out," she promised.

He drew his hand along her stomach, making the skin quiver. Her breath hitched as he ran a finger under the waistband of her jeans. Turning her head toward him, she met his heady gaze. His aura glowed luminescent and white, highlighting the gold flecks in his eyes. He stretched up to kiss her with those full, succulent lips as his hand slid beneath her jeans.

He kept the intensity of the kiss as he brought his hand back up and undid the top of her pants before sliding his hand back down.

She kissed him deeper and angled to maximize the pleasure of his touch. Writhing in ecstasy, he took her to the brink of passion and beyond with only the stroke of his fingers.

When he finished and she lay in boneless contentment on the bed, he pulled the throw blanket from the end of the bed over both of them. "Sleep," he whispered. "We'll talk more tomorrow."

"Daddy!"

The warning came seconds before Olivia pounced on Bryce, who was still lying in his mother's guest bed. He let out a grunt as she landed on top of him. Wrapping his arms around her, he pulled her close as she giggled.

"Daddy, you're still wearing clothes."

"I got home late."

"Granny's cooking waffles."

He lifted his head and blinked against the bright sunlight streaming through the room. The clock read eight AM. He had caressed Storm until he passed out from exhaustion. The bed still smelled like her.

"Daddy, where's Storm?"

"I don't know. Did Granny say?"

"Nope. She said she left like a ghost. Bypassed the alarm system."

Bryce's heart battled with a mixture of relief at Olivia not finding them in bed together and withering disappointment Storm was gone again. For three days or three months? This woman was such a rollercoaster ride. She confused him when she was near him and drove him crazy when she left. The only time he wasn't doubting and questioning everything about her was when she was in his arms or him in hers. He ran a hand through his hair as he stood.

After he'd left Storm with his mother, he had questioned his decision. He'd just thrown the three women in his life together without him present. It could be a recipe for disaster. Not because of

Storm—based on her protective instincts with Olivia she wasn't a threat to his family, though her occupation might be if it brought other danger—but three women possibly conspiring against him was enough to make any man sweat.

"You want waffles?" his daughter asked.

Bryce kissed Olivia's cheek. "Yeah, I want waffles. Granny's already cooking, huh?"

She rubbed his cheek. "You're scratchy."

He chuckled and ran his fingers over his stubble. He hadn't shaved in two days. "I suppose I am."

Olivia hopped off the bed and dashed out of the room.

Bryce pushed to his feet and walked to the bathroom. After freshening up, he entered the kitchen with its cheery yellow decor and broad windows over the sink.

He gave his mom a quick hug. "Thanks, Mom, for picking them up and taking care of Olivia."

His daughter took a seat in front of a cut up waffle, strip of bacon, and a glass of orange juice.

"Of course, dear. Your friend did most of the work. She insisted on cooking us all dinner—spaghetti. A bit different though. Not tomato based but an egg and bacon sauce. It was quite delicious. After that, she tucked Olivia in, bedtime story and all."

Bryce snagged a crispy piece of bacon from a serving platter and took a bite. Chewing, he tried to picture this domestic recap his mother gave.

"She said you met at your clinic?" His mom intently watched the waffle cooking as if it required the precision of surgery. Obviously, she was burning with curiosity for more of the story.

He thought about the ruffians Storm had disarmed at the clinic. "She helped me at the clinic a while back. Then we went to the fair."

"I invited her," Olivia touted.

"She did." He walked to the refrigerator and poured himself a glass of juice, busying himself to hide his worming discomfort at discussing a woman with his mother and daughter.

His mom took the waffle off the griddle and placed it on Bryce's plate. "Oh, Storm left this for you. I found it on the counter." She pulled a folded note out of her apron pocket.

Bryce stared at it. Good news or bad? They weren't actually dating, so she couldn't very well break up with him via a note. After taking the piece of paper, his waffle, and juice, he sat across the table from Olivia. He could feel all female eyes on him as he read it.

Bryce,

I had a wonderful time at the fair. I knew you wouldn't want mixed messages for Olivia. Since we don't know what we are yet, I didn't want to confuse her by staying in bed with you. I'd like to see you again. Friday. I'll find you so we can talk about what I am.
—Storm

Friday. His stomach did a giddy flip at the thought of seeing her again. Why was he so excited? This wasn't passing notes in high school. He folded it and tucked it into his blue jeans pocket.

When he looked up to eat his waffle, his mother and daughter were staring at him. Maddie's mouth twitched in a poor attempt to hold in a delighted smile.

"She had things to do. She'll be back." He cut into his waffle.

"Today?" Olivia asked.

"Not today, sweetie. Besides, you and I already have riding plans."

Olivia smiled.

Bryce took a bite of his waffle, hoping the horseback riding wouldn't involve snakes.

TEN

Storm picked the lock to Denny's office after hours. She needed to talk to him after having seen Bryce again.

Watching the doorway to his office, she noted the psychologist was oblivious to her presence. He was a sturdy black man in his thirties. Broad shoulders were a testament to his college football days he'd once told her about with a wistful nostalgia.

He relaxed into his office chair and poured a glass of bourbon from his desk drawer. After taking a bite of his sandwich—turkey and Swiss on rye by the looks of it—he washed it down with the liquor.

"Good evening."

Denny bolted upright and choked on his alcohol. "Storm." He gasped and coughed as his eyes watered.

"Sorry. I didn't mean to scare you."

"You pick my lock and slink in here like a wraith. What did you expect?" He blotted his eyes.

She cringed, not having intended to cause him obvious pain and discomfort from accidentally snorting the bourbon. "Point taken." She began walking toward the couch.

"No, no, no. You are *not* my patient." Denny came around the desk.

Storm stretched out on his couch and propped her head up with a pillow.

He crossed his arms in obvious irritation. "You didn't mention you're wanted by the FBI."

She arched an eyebrow. "Beg your pardon?"

"An agent came to my office asking about you," he said.

"Tall and lanky with a splash of arrogance?"

"Yes. Brown hair, navy suit. Very official looking."

"Special Agent Decker," Storm mused. "What did you tell the FBI agent?"

"The truth—you're not my patient and I don't know where to find you. He told me to tell you to call him if I saw you."

"Okay. Message delivered."

"Storm, this is serious. I can't aid and abet a criminal."

"Tell me what happened." She closed her eyes to focus on the scene.

"He dropped in—no forewarning or call. He showed me his credentials. I almost had a heart attack thinking I'd done something. My mind raced—no unpaid parking tickets, no overdue taxes. I thought maybe one of my patients accused me of something. Then I thought one of my patients had done something." Denny paced the room, wiping his palms on his pants as he did when he was nervous.

Storm was tempted to offer him the couch but wasn't sure if he'd find that offensive. "All that flashed through your mind with one glance at his FBI badge?"

Denny shot her an irritated look. "I let him in. He sat at the chair." He gestured to the one across from his desk chair. "He told me he was looking for a woman. I jokingly said, 'aren't we all,' mostly out of relief to know he wasn't after me for something. I don't think he has a sense of humor. Anyway, I asked him if this was a missing person's case. That's when he showed me your picture."

Denny walked around to his desk, pulled out a bottle of antacids, and took two. "He knew right away I'd recognized you. Hard not to. He said he wanted to find you."

"What did you tell him?"

"That I don't know where you are. I don't even know your last name. I pulled the client-doctor privilege bit, but—as I've told you before—that doesn't apply if you intend on hurting yourself or someone else."

"I'm not intent on hurting anyone."

Denny continued without missing a beat. "He seemed surprised you'd be talking to a psychologist. I explained how you aren't technically a client. You saved my life, we talked, now you won't stop talking to me."

Storm chuckled. She remembered the incident. She'd yanked Denny back from stepping into traffic. He'd gone white as a ghost before fumbling through an invitation to dinner. They'd had that date but no chemistry. Now, she consulted him for emotional therapy.

"Then Agent Decker left you alone?" she asked.

"No. He asked more questions, during which time I avoided telling him anything about your claimed crimes, smudged souls, or what we talk about. He knew I was holding back. He pointed out that if I don't take payment, don't keep a file on you, and just listen, our relationship is more of a friendship. All well and good, but I told him I still don't know where you are. When he finally left, he asked me to tell you to call him."

"Did he tell *you* to call him or just deliver a message?"

He rubbed his palm over his chest. "Just the message."

"Then you've fulfilled your obligation, and you're not doing anything wrong."

Denny pinched the bridge of his nose. "Gossip about Feds investigating me or my practice or my clients could be detrimental."

She felt a pang of regret at the stress the situation was causing him. "I'm sorry, Denny. Will Decker is my brother-in-law. I'm not wanted by the FBI."

He deflated into the chair nearest the sofa. "Why didn't he just say that?"

"He was probably protecting me and my sister. They work for a secret organization. He doesn't know you, doesn't know if he can trust you. He's not going to share connections but guard them."

"He knows what you do for a living?"

"The world is more than what you perceive it to be, Denny."

Stretching her arms then relaxing her hands on her abdomen, she said, "You'll be happy to know I'm making progress. I feel like I'm finally healing."

His brow furrowed. "You're referring to the incident with your fiancé?"

"Yes."

Denny leaned forward. "I could tell something changed."

"Why do you say that?"

"You always wear black. The queen of macabre is suddenly wearing pink today."

Storm recalled selecting the pink cardigan to wear today when she'd recalled the fun at the fair with Olivia.

"Why do you think you feel differently?" Denny asked.

Storm closed her eyes. "I know what you're asking. Is it because of Bryce? I think it's because of what he represents. He's like a tall drink of hope. When I'm with him, I don't even think about smudged souls." She thought about friendships and family —concepts she'd avoided and thought her heart had been closed to.

With a smile, she continued, "His little girl is a delight, too. She's a ball of energy and childhood bliss."

"How do you feel about exposing Bryce and his daughter to what you do?"

Releasing a hefty sigh, she wriggled deeper into his couch. "I know you think I'm a monster, and maybe Bryce does, too, but I protect people—good people. The more time I spend with Bryce and his daughter, the more I feel like they need me. I can't explain it."

He reached over to his glass and took another swig of bourbon. "Could you be confusing your feelings with *you* needing them?"

"Yes. That's possible. But not the only reason. I wouldn't subject myself to Bryce's mood swings toward me if this were just about me. I wouldn't tolerate it from anyone else."

"Mood swings?"

"He's as cold as a Frost Giant one minute and hot as the burning crown of Sutr the next. I can't tell if he wants to kiss me or hurl me into the next oncoming stampede."

"Why do you think he behaves that way?" Denny's voice held a fascination she hadn't heard before.

Perhaps this attachment to someone was a bold, new development any psychologist would find enthralling.

She puffed her cheeks and blew out a breath. "Damned if I know. He needs to make up his mind."

"And what if he chooses the stampede?"

She scowled. "I still need to figure out why he needs me."

Denny rubbed his temples and eyed the unfinished glass of bourbon on his desk. "Most people don't force themselves into a relationship."

"I'm not most people."

Denny snorted.

She narrowed her eyes at him before deciding to let it go. "Besides, I'm persistent, not forceful."

"So says the woman who picked the lock to my office."

"Precisely my point. There was no *forced* entry."

Denny scrubbed his hands along his face in evident exasperation, but she thought she spied a smile hidden under there. It faded quickly.

"Boundaries. I need to establish boundaries. How did I allow you onto my couch and into a counseling session?" Standing, he walked across the room and opened the door. "Storm, I need you to sort out your relationship with Bryce on someone else's couch."

Sitting up, she blinked at Denny. "You're the only one I trust."

His expression morphed into a strange mixture of pride and terror at her compliment.

As she stood, she pursed her lips. "Is this because of the FBI thing?"

"Although I don't want any involvement with someone wanted by the FBI—or her FBI brother-in-law flashing his badge around—my inability to be your psychologist predated my awareness of that and began the moment you told me you're an assassin."

She walked toward the door. "Only of—"

"—smudged souls. Yes, I remember. Whatever that means."

She responded to his irritation with a look of pity. "Do you want me to explain it to you? It might take a while."

"No." He ushered her out the door. "No explanation needed."

She shrugged.

"What am I supposed to tell Special Agent Decker if he comes back?" Denny asked.

As Storm walked away, she tossed the words over her shoulder, "The truth. I'll call him when I'm ready."

ELEVEN

Back in her apartment, Storm called her sister. "Hey, Sunshine."

"Oh my goodness, Storm. It's so good to hear your voice. It's been too long. I was drying out herbs yesterday, and I smelled funnel cake. Was I sensing you? I felt like it was related to you some-how." Sky's voice sounded light and airy.

"I was at a fair. I was thinking of the three of us. Remembering you with pigtails and a sundress."

"Sometimes that's still me," Sky said. "You went to a fair?"

Storm ignored the disbelief in her sister's voice. "I went with a friend and his daughter. I had a great time."

She'd even snapped a few photos along the way of the bustling fair and thought perhaps she would make it a topic of her travel blog at some future date. She never uploaded to her blog in chronological order or of the location she was currently at. If anyone was trying to track her down, she wouldn't make it easy for them by creating a trail through her travel blog. Still, Special Agent Will Decker had tracked her to Denny, and his discovery felt like a chink in her armor. She would have to ask the FBI agent how he'd made that connection.

"A friend," Sky said, sounding like her interest had been piqued.

Storm suspected her tone of voice hadn't suggested a more intimate relationship between her and Bryce, but Sky was invoking her ability to see into people, into Storm in this case. She'd known calling Sky would expose her to her sister's powers and all the uncomfortable emotions swirling in Storm.

"I hope more than a friend," Storm confessed. "Sometimes it's hard to tell."

"I like the sound of this. How did you meet?"

Storm gave a dry chuckle. "I forced him to patch up an injury, scared him to death by telling him what I do for a living, and elbowed my way into his life." She walked to her bedroom and pulled out exercise clothes. She needed to get in an hour of training today.

Sky giggled. "Subtle was never your style."

"I'm worried about him, though. I sense danger. He has some type of supernatural powers based on his aura, but we haven't talked about what that is yet. He only recently learned about my healing ability. I haven't wanted to ask him what he knows about the shadow world in front of his daughter. In any case, I sense danger, and I'm wondering if you could shed light on any of this."

"Maybe if I met him, but not from a distance. You and Raine are the only ones I'm emotionally attached to and able to sense the good and bad from a distance, even then I usually have to be focused on you to feel your emotions. Everybody else I have to be in proximity to, and even then I don't always have your foreboding. Mine is more of an inner thoughts rather than premonitions."

Storm knew this from when they'd grown up but hadn't inquired in a while if any new developments had occurred with Sky's abilities. "Yeah, okay. I just thought it was worth asking. I really need to stay close to him and get to the bottom of it."

"Let us know if we can help in any way." Sky's voice turned tentative as she added, "Are you coming home for the holidays?"

"Maybe, if I can understand Bryce's situation and resolve the issue." If she could do that and tell him what she was with an explanation of why she was an assassin, maybe she and Bryce had a chance at a relationship.

At Sky's long silence, Storm added, "I'll try. It's hard to come home. It's hard to face those memories." There were places she'd spent with her fiancé which she'd never returned to. Her family had known him, embraced him.

"We have lots of wonderful memories to return to as well. Besides, you don't have to face memories alone. You never have to face anything alone."

A lump formed in Storm's throat. "Love you, Sunshine." She disconnected the call.

Alone.

She had done everything alone for so long, she didn't know how not to. Bryce and Olivia were proof that maybe she was ready to accept people she cared about back into her life. She hadn't realized how much she'd missed the comfort of family. The father-daughter duo stirred long quiescent feelings in her.

Storm spent the next week treating Bryce like a mark, investigating every aspect of his life. She needed to find the threat. He'd married during medical school and a few years later, during surgical training, had Olivia. Sixteen months later he'd divorced, a mutual, faultless dissolution by all appearances. Storm couldn't dig up any smearing of each other on social media. Six months after that, his ex-wife died in a car accident. Her blood alcohol level had been well beyond the legal limit. Bryce had been in a surgery at the time. Where had Olivia been? Probably with Maddie, Storm guessed.

An accident? Storm felt skeptical now, knowing Bryce's truck brakes had been severed. If his wife's car had been mangled and investigators ruled it a drunk driving accident, had anyone even bothered to inspect the break line? Storm didn't believe in coincidences and knew to trust her gut.

So, who was after Bryce, and if his ex-wife's accident wasn't an accident, who would want them both dead? And why?

And why the gap of years between events?

After Bryce's ex-wife's death, he quit surgery and ran a free clinic funded through local donations, philanthropic foundations, and government grants. When Storm had first investigated him before approaching him to fix her wound, she'd thought perhaps there had been malpractice reasons behind the sudden change in career path. What surgeon with medical school debt leaves a lucrative practice to work at a free clinic?

Now she understood.

A loving single father had put his career on hold so his daughter had the support she needed.

From various social media apps of his friends and family, she pieced together Bryce's routine. On weekdays, he went to the clinic after dropping Olivia at school. He left the clinic to pick up Olivia Monday through Wednesday. On Thursday afternoons, her maternal grandparents picked her up, and she stayed for dinner and overnight. On Friday afternoons, Bryce's mother picked her up, and they had dinner and a sleepover together—which explained why Olivia hadn't been home the night Storm had spent with Bryce.

He spent Friday nights at the Roadhouse Saloon with Wendy and Landon Cabot. The Cabots had been married twelve years. They were debt-free with no children and currently investing in a start-up project of eco-friendly houses run off solar panels.

Storm sat in her car, watching the free clinic while Bryce worked inside, oblivious to her presence. She wanted to see if he had someone else watching him and where the vulnerabilities were in his routine.

While she observed, she phoned a friend. "Hi, Denny."

"I need to change my number," he grumbled.

"That isn't an effective barrier against me calling you."

"What is?"

She couldn't think of a suitable answer, so she proceeded to the point of her call. "I read your book."

"You and my mother. That makes two." He was trying for sarcasm, but Storm detected a trace of pleasant surprise in his voice.

"I thought it was very good. I can use those techniques with Bryce."

"They're meant to be used in any relationship—friendly, romantic, professional." Changing the subject, Denny asked, "Did you call your brother-in-law?"

"It's on my to do list."

"Great." Denny sighed.

"So, the technique you described in your book requires first a statement of empathy?"

"Yes."

"Then what I need or want?"

"Yes." His weary tone carried through the phone.

"Then a suggestion or a solution?"

"Yes."

"Can we try it? You know, role play?"

"Storm—"

"I won't take much of your time." She knew he didn't answer the phone during client sessions, so she wasn't interrupting his work.

He didn't reply.

"Okay. So, I know Bryce isn't happy about what I do."

Denny let out a small *pfft* sound.

"My empathy statement could be, 'I know my job of assassinating people makes you uncomfortable.'"

"Consider rephrasing that."

"My waste management job?"

"Is that what it is?"

"Maybe."

"First, you need to figure out what it is you think you do."

"Okay. I'll work on that, but then I say, 'let me explain why I do it, so you can understand.'"

"Is there a good explanation?" he asked.

"Well, I think so."

The line went quiet, and Storm could envision Denny looking bleary-eyed and haggard as he rubbed his temples.

"Denny."

"Yes, Storm."

"I know that my forcing our friendship causes you worry and stress."

He didn't reply as she tried the tactic on him.

She continued, "But I value your expertise, and I appreciate being able to talk with you." Her words were genuine.

A resigned sigh sounded through the phone. "Okay."

"So, can I call you from time to time? As a friend and counselor?"

"Yeah, you can call me," he said.

"Next time, you can tell me your worries."

"Sure."

She added earnestly, "You're not in any danger from me, Denny."

"How is work going?" Even as Bryce asked his friend, he watched the front door of the saloon.

"Fancy Like" by Walker Hayes played through the speaker as people danced and waitstaff moved through crowded tables. The scent of bar-b-que and beer filled the bar.

Landon looked at his wife and then back at Bryce. "Going well. How's the clinic?"

"Good." The week had passed with the usual runny noses, minor injuries, and chronic conditions. Now it was Friday—the day Storm had promised to return. She'd said she would find him, so he'd stuck to his routine.

Wendy crossed her arms. "What's going on?"

Bryce turned toward her as she arched a sculpted eyebrow at him. "Nothing." He sipped his water. He didn't know what time Storm would show up, and he didn't want to be three beers deep when she strode through the door.

"Nothing?" Landon munched on a handful of peanuts. "You're watching the door, drinking water, and excited."

Busted.

"I met a woman. The woman I went to the fair with might meet up with me tonight." As he said the words, he felt a ridiculous grin spread across his lips.

Landon's eyes widened. "That's great. Isn't that great, hon?"

Wendy appeared less excited, unless that was a plastic surgery side effect, but added, "It is great. What does she do?"

"She has a travel blog. She rates and reviews vacation spots, hotels, restaurants, and transportation services. She's an influencer on social media."

Bryce had investigated Storm's website during the week. *Asgardian Adventurer.* It had appeared wholly legitimate, as she'd claimed, with a blog and links to all major social media platforms flourishing with posts and followers. Her reviews were thoughtful, thorough, and indicative of an extensive travel history. In fact, he found himself intimidated by her robust globetrotting.

Not one of her social media sites had pictures of herself. There were photos of food, wine, restaurants (inside and out), beautiful balcony scenery, hotel rooms and their views, but no Storm. Thinking of the fair and giant stuffed animal prize, he couldn't help but draw a parallel on how her skills shooting camera pictures and rifles were both excellent. Too bad she hadn't—couldn't—throw a few selfies into the mix.

"An influencer?" Wendy sipped her wine.

"And she may have saved Olivia's and my life."

"What? How so?" Landon asked.

"While we were at the fair Saturday, someone cut my truck

brakes. Storm had some type of premonition and kept me from getting on the interstate."

Wendy sat back, mouth open in amazement. "Wow. I've got goosebumps just hearing that story."

"Storm." Bryce watched her walk through the door wearing jeans and a floral print top. Her long, dark hair hung in silky ringlets, and thick locks swept across her brow.

He stood and walked toward her. They met halfway on the dance floor as "I Cross My Heart" by George Strait played through a jukebox.

Bryce took one of her hands in his and placed the other on her hip. "Dance with me. Just for a moment. My friends are eager to meet you because I haven't brought a woman here since my divorce. Once I take you over there, they might not give you back. Not easily, anyway."

As Storm smiled, she placed her hands behind his neck.

His heart thrummed with excitement. "I'm glad you came."

"I promised the truth. Do you still want it?"

He stared into her captivating violet eyes as they swayed. Her throat bobbed in a swallow. She was nervous. The woman, a world traveler who'd fought armed men in his clinic, conquered rattlesnake venom, and gave him the most amazingly sensual night of his life, was afraid of secrets she wanted to share.

Yes, he would tell her his too.

"I'm listening." He gave her a reassuring squeeze where his hand rested on the small of her back. He was ready to take this plunge with her.

TWELVE

Storm felt the warmth of Bryce's body close to hers and struggled to focus on the topic of conversation. He smelled of sage and leather.

"You've seen that I have fighting skills and healing skills." She needed to tell him what she had told no man—ever. Only her sisters and her brother-in-law knew what Storm was. Her truth. Her ancestry. "My abilities come from my bloodline, my ancestors."

As they danced, she glimpsed Bryce's friends, Landon and Wendy Cabot. She knew them from their background checks—both surgeons. She watched Wendy for a moment as she talked to her husband. Tuning in her senses, Storm detected Wendy's aura and the dull greenish color it oozed. Was she ill?

"Bloodline?" Bryce prompted.

Storm's gaze shifted to a man hunched over his beer at the bar. His aura was a smeared tarry black, one of the thickest she'd ever seen. She tensed and clenched her teeth as a roaring crescendoed in her ears and her blood pressure rose.

"Storm?"

She focused back on Bryce. Right, bloodlines. "I'm descended from Asgard. I can see people's auras as it relates to their bloodlines—Dark Elves, Giants, Asgardians—and their souls, good versus evil." She glanced again at the man at the bar. "Dark Elves and evil have distinct gray-black auras. The potency of their darker side is manifest in thicker auras. Meaning, the more they manifest evil in doing evil deeds, the more pronounced their aura is."

"Asgardian? You're talking about Norse mythology?"

"Yes—Odin, Frigg, Thor, Loki—all that."

"And you have supernatural powers from these mythological gods?" The skepticism in his voice turned palpable as the heat he'd been emitting in her direction cooled.

"Remote descendent. My skills are minor compared to the once true Asgardians and Vanir."

"Who live in other realms?"

"No."

"No?"

"Lived not live. Past tense. The old gods are gone—not that they were actually gods—just supernatural beings that early man deified. In any case, Ragnarök happened, gods are gone, and magic is diluted."

"But *you* have magic? Like your ability to heal?" His tone was soft, and she thought she detected a hint of acceptance.

"Minor gifts," she clarified. "Me and probably a few thousand people across the world have some inherited genes from Asgardians." And more from other destroyed realms, but she would delve into that later.

Bryce frowned. "This sounds—"

"—far-fetched? Unbelievable? Crazy? It took me a long-time to process it. I don't expect you to understand, at least not right away."

Odin and Frigg! she swore silently.

She was doing a poor job of delivering the message she had carefully rehearsed as she continued to be distracted by the smudged soul at the bar. She'd been nervous to begin with, and the Dark Elf's presence was making her explanation rushed and irritable sounding.

Before the night was through, she needed to discover the man's evil deeds.

She'd made a mistake. She should be having this conversation with Bryce somewhere quiet and private. Just like the first night they'd met, she was botching this part.

"Storm." Bryce took her chin and turned her face to him. "I saw you heal a rattlesnake bite with my own eyes. I'm trying to be open-minded. How do you know what you say is true about the link to Norse mythology?"

"A lot of research and dreams over the years." Dreams that were memories belonging to others. Memories of her descendants.

"So you see auras, and you have accelerated healing abilities?"

"Yes. You have a beautiful, glowing aura, Bryce. It's one of the things I first noticed about you."

He looked wary and uncomfortable at her statement. "How does that translate into you being an assassin?"

The answer to this question had many layers of complexity. She'd planned to meet him and spend the next several hours baring her soul but hadn't considered she might run into a Dark Elf at the bar—really dark, judging by his aura.

She wanted to confide in Bryce how her fiancé had been murdered before her eyes by a Dark Elf. She'd done nothing to stop it. That day, her future had changed forever. But she was fumbling her way through this discussion and the discomfort rattled her.

She tried for a briefer version. "A smudged soul has succumbed to evil. There is no hope of redemption. They've done dark deeds and will continue to do so."

He swallowed. "So, you kill them?"

She met his eyes with a hard stare. "I keep them from hurting others. To do that, they must be killed."

As the song ended, they lingered a moment.

"I can do better. I can explain better. I'm sorry."

"Let's take a breather, and we'll resume the conversation in a minute. I'd like you to meet my friends." He gave her a reassuring squeeze on her hand and escorted her to the table with his friends. "Landon and Wendy, this is Storm."

Landon stood, smiled, and shook hands. "I'm so glad Bryce finally decided to share you with us." His grip was firm and his smile genuine.

Wendy smiled and waved. "We're glad to meet you."

"Thank you." Storm took her seat, angling her chair to monitor the man at the bar.

Bryce sat beside her, but his body language had stiffened. He didn't lean closer, touch his leg to hers, or take her hand. In her distracted state, she'd failed to express herself clearly. Or maybe she had. Maybe this was the inevitable conclusion to any relationship with her.

There would be no fixing it tonight, because she needed to deal with the Dark Elf at the bar.

"Bryce tells us you travel and have a blog?"

Storm turned a friendly expression to Wendy. "I critique tourist sites, from the pool to the food to the size of the bathroom."

What was the strange color around Wendy. It was Grinch green and smokey. Was she sick? Something terminal? She otherwise looked healthy. Her lipstick was a shade bright, but her smile seemed pleasant, even if it didn't reach her eyes.

"Landon and I want to travel to St. Maarten. Have you been there?"

"I've been to most of the Caribbean islands."

Wendy clapped her hands together in delight. "Oh, wonderful. We'll have to search your blog for dos and don'ts."

Landon's lips curved in an attempted smile that didn't convey enthusiasm. Was he not looking forward to an island vacation with his wife?

He changed the subject. "Bryce was telling us about his brake malfunction. He said you had some type of premonition?"

Storm rolled her shoulder. "Feelings I get sometimes."

Like knowing your wife is sick.

She wondered if Landon knew. Perhaps he did, and that was the lack of anticipation at the upcoming vacation. One last trip before— what? Storm wasn't going to ask.

Time for a topic change.

She said, "You're both surgeons? That must translate into many long hours."

They glanced at Bryce, probably assuming he'd told her about them, and Bryce managed to hide his surprise at how much Storm knew. Unless he suspected she had investigated his friends the way she'd investigated him before hobbling into his clinic the first night they met.

Landon nodded. "We get Friday nights together, but not much else."

"Then St. Maarten may be just the getaway you need," Storm said.

He took Wendy's hand in his, though it looked more reflexive and habitual than affectionate.

Wendy smiled. "The two of you should come with us."

Bryce coughed. "We just met. I'm sure we're not ready to fly to a tropical island for a week."

Storm was ready. In an uninterrupted week, she could explain everything to Bryce. With understanding would come acceptance. Maybe. Or maybe she was delusional to think Bryce could ever accept who she was.

It didn't matter, since she would have to follow the biker when he left the bar. When she left unexpectedly in the next few minutes after the fumbling half-explanation she'd given Bryce on the dance floor, he'd be done with her.

She realized Wendy was staring at her. "No trips," Storm confirmed. "My schedule's full, and Bryce has Olivia to consider. Taking a vacation with a woman he only recently began seeing wouldn't send the right message to his daughter." She made the statement matter-of-fact, as if the topic were something they had discussed.

She didn't need to discuss it with him to be certain Bryce would agree. He always considered the implications of his actions on his daughter. He was a good father that way.

Bryce blinked at her.

"Olivia is such a sweet girl," Wendy began.

The man at the bar stood and dropped cash on the counter. He adjusted his blue jeans and walked toward the restroom. Storm debated her next course of action. She could follow the Dark Elf and deal with him before he had a chance to commit his next evil deed, or she could not sabotage her attempt to grow a relationship with Bryce and stay. The latter felt wrong and selfish. She would have to hope Bryce would give her a second chance to explain. Next time, she wouldn't pick a bar to have this conversation.

How to deal with the Dark Elf? She could confront him in the restroom, but that could risk witnesses. She would have to get him in his vehicle and away from public eyes.

"Can you excuse me? I need some fresh air."

I'm unbelievably lame.

She would have to work on fixing her sudden disappearance later. She couldn't tell Bryce in front of his friends that she needed to excuse herself to go kill a Dark Elf.

She stood and walked toward the front door—a predator planning to wait for her prey.

Bryce watched Storm exit the bar. One minute they were discussing vacations and Olivia and the next she needed fresh air. Who needs fresh air in a non-smoking bar? The woman who waltzed into his clinic sporting a bullet wound wouldn't suddenly get claustrophobic talking to his friends, unless she was an introvert out of her comfort zone.

Had he upset her? Surely, she would understand his hesitance to accept her claim to be a descendant of Asgardian bloodlines. Not that he had a better explanation.

Oddly enough though, her words rang true, and he had his own secrets he wanted to share with her. Secrets he'd told only his mother.

Bryce narrowed his eyes as the door closed behind her. Rising from his seat, he tossed money on the table to cover their beers. "I'll be back."

Landon saluted with his beer as Wendy gave a perplexed expression.

Bryce caught up with Storm outside. Her face looked troubled, but she wasn't looking at him. She was watching some pudgy biker walk toward his motorcycle.

"Storm?"

She looked at him, her eyes clouded with worry. "I'm sorry. He's a Dark Elf. I can't let him get away."

"Wait. Let me tell you about me. I think we have a connection."

If she would stay, he had his own supernatural story to tell. Maybe she could shed light on the things he didn't understand.

Obviously distracted, she walked away from him.

"Storm!"

As she climbed onto the stranger's motorcycle, she tossed her long hair over her shoulder and whispered something in his ear. The man smirked at Bryce and nodded before revving his engine.

Bryce stood and watched them drive away. He felt utterly bewildered. He might have been jealous, but no way was she leaving for a romantic interlude with that man. One minute she was explaining her mythological heritage and the next she was riding on a motorcycle with an urgency like she was on some type of mission. A Dark Elf? Was she on a mission?

Has the assassin come out to play?

He rubbed his neck and walked back into the bar.

"Where's Storm?" Landon asked.

Bryce slumped into the chair and took another gulp of his beer. "I honestly don't know."

"And then she was gone," Landon said wistfully.

"Are you okay?" Wendy asked.

"I'm fine."

Landon punched his arm lightly. "Don't sweat it, buddy. I saw the way she looked at you on the dance floor. Whatever came up, she'll be back."

"Yes, she will." He didn't know when or for how long, but Storm would be back.

Would she bring the answers she promised? Or would she speak in riddles and leave again?

How do you catch an Asgardian and pin her down?

THIRTEEN

"This guy won't leave me alone," Storm told the biker as she tossed her hair over her shoulder. "Can I grab a ride?"

Before the man could answer, she was already climbing on the motorcycle behind him. The words Bone Crusher was spray painted in cursive on his Harley. The biker nodded as he revved the engine.

Storm glanced back at Bryce, who stared at her with a perplexed expression. Her heart sank. This was not how she envisioned this night progressing, and she should have picked a better setting to talk to him. She wanted to be in his arms, not holding the waist of a biker who reeked of body odor, regurgitated beer, and death. But she had to put her romantic desires aside and eliminate this danger—this Dark Elf descendant—from society.

In a half hour and dizzying number of turns on remote roads, Bone Crusher pulled into the driveway of a small, run-down house in the middle of nowhere, Texas. No other vehicles were parked in the lot.

She got off the bike and straightened her dress. "Talk about your fixer upper." She surveyed the trees and lack of neighbors. In such a place, no one would hear him scream.

If a Dark Elf dies in a forest and no one is there to hear it, does it make a sound?

"You're purdy." Bone Crusher reached toward the saddlebag on his bike.

Storm reared a foot back and slammed it into his knee. He howled in pain as he crumpled to the gravel driveway. She reached into the sack from where he'd been attempting to retrieve something and withdrew a revolver. She aimed his own gun at his head.

He threw his hands up in the air. "I'll give you whatever you want."

"I want you to be a better man, but that's not something you're capable of being." She pulled the trigger. The shot rang through the night air. A conspiracy of startled ravens flew out of a nearby tree, black wings on a gray sky.

As the Dark Elf slumped to the ground, his body morphed into a black ooze that bubbled and sizzled as it settled into a puddle on the gravel before soaking deeper. She gained no satisfaction from the act. Her gift—curse?—of seeing auras and understanding the relationship of their potency to the crimes of who she killed had led her down this path to becoming judge, jury, and executioner.

What made her any better than them?

Some days she wasn't sure.

She cocked her head to one side to listen to the surrounding stillness. She glanced at the house. In the split second before she'd shot Bone Crusher, his eyes had darted to the house. The shack wasn't anything to behold, not something to be missed when he died. Why look there in the last precious moments before death?

Storm walked toward the house, gun still in hand. She eased the unlocked door open, all senses on high alert. The shack was bathed in blackness, and she opted to leave it that way. A dim glow of the moon cast just enough light for her to see the outline of furniture and walls. She walked in measured steps, listening to the sounds of her boots creaking the floorboards.

She paused by a wooden door with a padlock. Was he hiding a gun cabinet or something else? Was he trying to keep others out or keep something in?

She crouched with an ear to the door. No growling, so at least she knew a rabid dog wasn't salivating on the other side. She wrapped her knuckles on the door twice, making a distinct sound that wouldn't be mistaken for any normal creaks and moans of an old house.

A faint whimper sounded from the other side.

Storm walked back outside to Bone Crusher and took the keys off the ground near where his corpse had dissolved and left only tainted clothing. Back in the house, she sifted through the set until she found the one fitting the padlock. After unlocking and removing it, she swung the door open on a creaking set of hinges. Stairs led down to a dim basement.

She descended them, but with the angled ceiling, couldn't see into the room. "I'm coming. If you need help, I'll help. If you ambush me, I'll shoot you down."

"Help," a woman's voice croaked.

When Storm reached the bottom, a woman in chains was curled into a ball on the concrete floor. Her stomach churned at the sight of a tortured human being.

"Ah, *helvete*," Storm swore. "I'll call for help," she told her.

She pulled out her phone and pressed a number as she went back upstairs. As the phone rang, she rummaged through Bone Crusher's kitchen and fixed a glass of water.

"Hello?" a woman's voice answered.

"Raine, I've got a victim for you. She's in this guy's basement—a Dark Elf I just dealt with. I'll text you the address."

"Okay. Storm, wait."

She hung up the phone.

Walking back down the steps, she led with the glass of water. "Help's on the way."

The woman on the floor stared at her through stringy, matted hair.

Storm set the glass of water down near her. She wanted to help and unchain her, but she wasn't sure that was the safest thing for this woman. Based on her condition and the way the restraints had formed callouses around her wrists and ankles, she'd spent more than a few days down here. The psychological trauma alone might make her a danger to herself or others.

The woman drank the water, watching Storm with wary, wide eyes.

"I won't hurt you, and that man who chained you can't hurt you ever again. What's your name?" Storm asked.

"Tonya."

Storm considered the chains again. To unchain her would involve touching the woman, and she may not want to be touched.

Storm placed another phone call. "Denny."

"Storm, I'm in the middle of—"

"I've got a kidnapping victim here, and I need your advice." Denny fell silent, but by his nasal breathing, he was still on the line and listening.

"Authorities are on their way, but I'm not sure what to do until they arrive." She wanted to help the woman, but she also needed to be gone before anyone arrived and began asking questions. She could stay until sirens were audible and offer what comfort she could.

"Okay." His voice was sad and solemn. "I'll try to help."

She looked at Tonya. She thought perhaps whatever needed to be said would be better coming from a woman rather than a man. "I'm going to stay with you until police arrive. Okay? My friend on the phone is going to talk to me, and I'll talk to you."

BRYCE WOKE THE NEXT MORNING, prepared coffee, and started on a breakfast of eggs and bacon for him and Olivia.

As he stirred the eggs on the pan over the stove, he thought about Storm's words last night. Norse mythology. Asgardians.

With that in mind, he'd done a little internet investigation last night about Norse mythology and the unique powers of the different species of the Nine Realms. He found groups claiming to be descendants of Norse gods or from other realms, some with members-only sections requiring an account.

He swiped a hand through the air over the stove, and a semi-transparent rainbow appeared. Smiling wistfully, he recalled how he'd created lights and imagery for Olivia when she was young. The illusions entertained her, but he'd stopped when he thought she was at the age of reason where she would wonder how he'd done it.

He'd had the ability since turning eighteen, having discovered it by accident when he was studying calculus and could project the formulas and move them around in the air with his mind. During college, he'd made money on the side doing magic shows. He'd used his ability throughout college to help him study. Medical school anatomy was easier when he could create three-dimensional images of the human body in the air to rotate and study. As a surgeon, he could visualize an entire operation before he performed it.

He had asked his mom in a roundabout way about "magic" in the family, but she'd seemed oblivious. Finally, he had showed his abilities to her. She'd been shocked and amazed but cautioned him not to let others see his gift out of fear of their reactions. He knew better than to advertise his abilities, but he'd never found a satisfactory reason for where they'd come from.

Now, with Storm talking about the Nine Realms bloodlines and having witnessed her healing abilities, he wondered if his illusion abilities originated from—what?—Vanir. Those who'd lived on Vanaheim were said to have magic.

"Morning, Daddy. Ooh, a rainbow!"

Oops. He'd forgotten he'd left that hanging in the air. Too late to cover it up now. He sent the colors soaring to the ceiling and erupting in fireworks, complete with popping noises.

Olivia laughed and clapped. "I forgot about your pretty pictures. Do it again!"

He smiled. "Maybe another time. Breakfast is ready." He moved the cooked eggs onto the plate and added the bacon.

What if Storm could shed light on his abilities? What if he didn't have to hide them from Olivia anymore?

They sat at the table and ate together, talking and making plans for the day.

Olivia stood abruptly, her fork slipping from her grip and clattering to the floor. Her eyes glazed over as her voice took on a commanding, ethereal tone.

> *"Death comes this night*
> *She hunts hungry*
> *Seeks your plight*
> *Bloodshed before morning light."*

Bryce's stomach rolled, threatening to expel his morning coffee. "Olivia, sweetie, are you okay?" He placed reassuring hands on her arms as he tried to keep calm against the ball of ice forming in his stomach. If she snapped out of this trance to find her father in shambles, he would scare her.

She hadn't had a vision in two years. At that time, she'd predicted the death of her daycare teacher from an accidental shooting. Although the news called it accidental, Olivia's vision had made it sound intentional.

"Daddy?" Olivia blinked as her eyes focused.

He smoothed a hand over her hair. "Hey, sweetie. Are you feeling okay?" If these were going to become recurrent events, he would have to rethink public school. Fortunately, so far, her visions had only happened in front of him.

"What happened?" she asked.

He fought his racing heart to keep a calm exterior for her. "Maybe you stood up too fast. Do you feel lightheaded?"

"A little."

He searched her face. Like last time, she showed no evidence of having heard her own words.

She placed a small hand on his cheek. "Can we ride today?"

He laid his hand over hers and smiled. "I'd love to ride with you today."

"First, I need to draw," she said.

He nodded with a swallow. Last time, after a vision, she'd drawn a stick figure of a man with a gun. As much as he disliked his little girl creating frightening pictures, he would allow her to her draw since he thought perhaps she needed it as a way to expel the information she'd channeled.

"Okay. I'll get dressed while you draw." He fetched paper and crayons and placed them on the table in front of her.

As he walked to the bedroom, he wondered if Storm would know anything about Olivia's premonitions. The eeriness seemed to fit Storm's world. He could ask her.

But what if she's this hungry hunter bringing death?

BOLVERKR EXITED the terminal and scowled at the sky. The late autumn temperature was sixty-five degrees in Dallas. Much too warm. He'd only agreed to this job because the person hiring him was paying well—a hundred grand for a contract kill would do nicely.

Checking his messages on his phone, he was startled to see one email in particular with a callback number. After finding a quiet corner away from the bustling travelers, he dialed the number.

"This is Helen. Is this the assassin known as Bolverkr?"

"Yes." He drew out the word, his mouth going dry.

How did one address the descendent of the goddess of darkness?

Mistress? Ma'am? Queen? Your Highness? He wasn't her servant, but one didn't piss off Hel.

"I understand you have taken a job to assassinate a physician named Bryce Chambers?" Her voice had a German accent with a seductive edge.

"Yes."

"Would you consider adding two additional tasks to this job?"

He swallowed. When Helen asked… she wasn't actually asking. She was a powerful woman, and rumor in the shadow world was that she would one day rule Midgard—Earth. He wasn't sure if that was true, but a Jotun could hope. He hated walking among so many lesser humans, hiding his true self.

"Of course."

"Excellent," she purred. "Listen carefully…"

As he obeyed, he walked to the garage and located his rental car. The smell of gasoline and smog assaulted his nostrils, while the humidity, however faint this time of year, irked him. He preferred cold and dry. But he wouldn't remove his blazer; he was a professional and always traveled as such.

"Do you understand?" Helen asked when she'd finished.

"Perfectly."

His dull kill just became interesting.

FOURTEEN

Bryce reheated Olivia's eggs and bacon before sliding the plate in front of her with a clean fork. She moved her drawing aside and drank her orange juice. He tried not to stare at the big blue Frankenstein's monster on her page, especially because he had no idea what the vision and subsequent drawing meant.

"Salt and pepper," she said.

"Please," he corrected her.

"Please."

"Coming right up," he said.

A knock came at the door.

"I'll do it myself," Olivia said, reaching for the salt and pepper containers.

"Easy on the salt," he called back to her as he walked toward the door. "I don't want to have to revoke salt-sprinkling privileges again."

He hoped Storm was at the door. She had some explaining to do. First her Asgardian descendant claim, followed by leaving the bar early, followed by hopping on the back of a Harley with an expression suggesting she'd rather be anywhere but with the biker. A Dark

Elf, she'd said, in a tone suggesting she needed to deal with him. After she cleared the air about last night, he could show her his abilities and see what she thought about his magic. The future held exciting possibilities.

Bryce swung open the door. "Storm—"

On the other side of the screen door, a tall lanky man in a navy suit stood on Bryce's porch. He gave an easy smile with a knowing look in his eyes as he raised a credentialing pack. Bryce glimpsed the letters FBI.

"Daddy?" Olivia called from the kitchen.

"I'll be just a minute, sweetie. There's a salesman here." He opened the screen door and stepped over his threshold, pulling the front door shut behind him.

"I'm Special Agent Will Decker of the FBI." He handed Bryce a business card as if he needed to emphasize he wasn't a salesman.

Bryce inspected the card, probably longer than he should have. He wasn't sure he wanted to ask the nature of the agent's business.

Bryce extended a hand. "Bryce Chambers." No sense in not being polite.

"Dr. Chambers, correct?" There was that smile again, as though Decker wanted Bryce to feel relaxed in his presence.

Bryce judged the man's age—late-thirties, perhaps a few years older than himself. He had a firm shake.

"That's right."

"Would you prefer to stay on the porch or talk somewhere else?" Decker asked.

Bryce opened his arms. "Here in Texas, some of the best conversations happen on the porch."

"That they do." The FBI agent walked the length of the porch and looked at the barn. "Fine piece of property you have here."

"It's home."

Decker nodded, turning around and leaning against the railing. He gave a closed mouth quirk of his lips, as though recognizing Bryce had yet to ask why the FBI was knocking on his door. "I'm looking for a woman. Her name is Storm Thoren." He pulled out his phone and flashed a picture of her.

Storm Thoren.

Bryce's heart sank like a stone in quicksand as he stared at her beautiful face in the photo. She looked younger as she gazed into the distance on what appeared to be the shores of a tropical beach.

Oh, Storm. What kind of trouble are you in?

"So, you've seen her?"

"I have."

"When?"

"Last night."

Decker's eyebrows shot to his forehead. He stood straighter. "What's your relationship with Ms. Thoren?"

"Hell if I know." Bryce sat heavily in one of his rocking chairs. "She stopped a gang from robbing my clinic back in September. Then she showed up at my place six weeks later. We took my daughter, Olivia, to the fair last Saturday. Last night we had drinks at the Roadhouse Saloon."

"Storm went to a fair?" Decker's perplexed expression accentuated his thin nose.

Bryce supposed the FBI agent was unaccustomed to the people he hunted having days of leisure.

Decker's eyes flickered to the house. "Is she here now?"

"No. We went home separately last night."

"Do you know where she is right now?"

Chasing a Dark Elf?

Bryce exhaled, genuinely relieved Storm had never told him where she lived so he didn't have to betray her. Why did he want to protect her? She needed to face whatever laws she'd broken.

Like murder.

"No. She's never told me where she lives." If she had, he may have tracked her down last night and demanded answers. Bryce rubbed the back of his neck. "Can you tell me what this is about, Special Agent Decker?"

"No, but if you would ask her to contact me when you see her again, I'd be grateful." He glanced at the card still in Bryce's hand as he retreated down the steps toward his car.

Bryce stood, took a step forward, and asked the question he didn't want to know the answer to. "Is Storm in some kind of trouble?"

Decker shrugged but with a strange sadness in his expression. "When is Storm not in some kind of trouble?"

Bryce watched the FBI agent hop into his car and drive away. He looked down at the card one last time before pocketing it and walking back inside his house with a sinking feeling of despair.

He'd planned to bare his soul to this woman, but the FBI showing up at his doorstep made him reconsider. As a father and physician, he couldn't be involved in anything illegal and risk losing Olivia or his medical license.

What was he going to do?

OLIVIA WAS PERFORMING her riding lessons that afternoon when she looked up and waved. Bryce turned to see Storm walking down his driveway toward the corral. She looked delicious in jeans, a baby blue t-shirt, and long, loose curls of hair rippling over her shoulders.

Too bad she belonged behind bars. He'd known this already from her introduction as an assassin, but the FBI's visit had been a keen reminder.

He glanced sideways at her as she casually came beside him and leaned on the fence. Relaxed. Not a care in the world.

"I'm really sorry about last night," she began. "I should have picked a better location than a bar to talk to you. I'm here now so we can clear the air with no distractions."

Bryce clenched his teeth before forcing himself to turn calmly toward her. He had thought about opening up to her—his and Olivia's abilities, but the FBI visit changed everything.

"I wanted to believe your claim to a higher calling and Norse mythology roots," he began, knowing he was failing to control his temper, which only fueled his frustration further. "You want to tell me why you're wanted by the FBI?" He lowered his voice at the end so Olivia wouldn't overhear. His daughter was fifty feet from a wanted criminal.

Storm narrowed her eyes at him.

"Special Agent Decker paid me a visit today," he added.

"Special Agent Decker." She bit out each word, speaking his name like a swear word.

"You know him? The FBI agent trying to track you down?"

Storm scowled. "What did he want?"

Bryce ran his fingers through his hair. "You, Storm. He wanted to know where he could find *you*."

"What did you tell him?"

"I don't know where you're hiding out."

"Hiding out?"

"Hiding from the law. You didn't tell me you were a fugitive."

She backed away from him. Her face was some mixture of hurt, rejection, and disappointment.

"Where are you going?" he demanded.

She continued to back away. "You assumed the worst. Without even asking me why an FBI agent is looking for me, you assumed it's because he wants to arrest me."

"Why else would he look for you? You told me you're an assassin. I guess all this time I didn't want to believe it. The FBI looking for you reinforced the danger you bring me. To Olivia. You're just going to leave?" he asked.

She stopped and threw her hands in the air. "What do we have, Bryce? We have nothing. You don't trust me. Most of the time, you don't really even like me. I started this relationship off wrong from the beginning, and nothing I've done has fixed it." In a defeated tone, she added, "I don't know how to fix it."

In three quick strides, he had her by the arms, firmly gripping them in his hands. Her dark hair caressed his bare arms. The fire in her violet eyes bore into him. He wanted to step into those flames and let her devour him.

"I do like you," he said. He liked how she cared about Olivia. He enjoyed hearing about her world travels and liked the way she felt in his arms on the dance floor. He admired the way she seemed like she could take on the world... and win. He liked the way she tasted when they kissed and the sounds she made when he pleasured her.

"Against your better judgment?" Storm asked.

When he hesitated, she stiffened in his arms and pushed off him.

"Will Decker is my pain in the ass brother-in-law. I'm not wanted by the FBI. I'm wanted by my family."

"You... you..."

She threw her hands in the air. "I'm still an assassin, Bryce. I still kill smudged souls. I'm judge, jury, and executioner, because I know when evil is unredeemable and when it isn't. You'll never be able to accept that. No one can."

She walked to her car, climbed in, and drove away.

He stood, watching with a bewildering sense of loss. But what had he lost but trouble?

If that was true, why did part of him want to run after her?

With rising dread and an eerie chill, he thought of Olivia's premonition.

> *Death comes this night*
> *She hunts hungry*
> *Seeks your plight*
> *Bloodshed before morning light*

Had he just averted disaster or invited it?

FIFTEEN

Storm stewed in silence as she drove down the road. She was angry with herself, not Bryce. Sure, he'd drawn the wrong conclusion about Will's visit, but who wouldn't? She had naively shared her secrets, expecting—what?—for Bryce to accept that she killed evil for a living? And what father and physician would accept a woman like that into his life?

If he hadn't believed in her or trusted her by now, he'd never accept her—what to call it?—stronger than a gut feeling, but not the strength of a premonition.

Even if he accepted what she did, maybe she did pose a threat to them by virtue of anyone who may discover her identity and retaliate. No one had in all these years, except now Will was closing in on her. Sure, he had resources others didn't, but she'd been a fool to think finding her would be impossible. For Bryce and Olivia's sake, perhaps she should make herself scarce.

Hadn't her fiancé died because she'd wanted to go to the store for snacks on game night? Did she want to be responsible for harm to someone else she cared about?

Why did I let myself become emotionally entangled with Bryce?

Her heart squeezed in her chest, threatening to implode. The pain was worse than getting bitten by a hellhound. Agonizing emotions. This was why she'd isolated herself from family, from people. The raw vulnerability of painful feelings was too much sensory overload.

If only the solution was as simple as her driving off alone into the sunset and leaving Bryce behind. But she still had to deal with the nagging sense of trouble that drove her to him in the first place. Someone was plotting against Dr. Chambers—evidenced by the cut brake line—but she didn't know who or why.

She speed-dialed a number and placed the phone on speaker.

"Hello?"

"Raine."

"Storm! I've been trying to get in touch with you. You left before I arrived on the scene of that biker's place."

"The woman is okay?"

"Yes. Protective custody until she can be returned to her family."

"Good. Now, why are you trying to reach me? Is this about Christmas dinner? Mom and Dad are already pestering me to visit." Their parents had left not-so-subtle hints in her travel blog chat boxes about coming home for Christmas. Their messages were one of the reasons she'd considered inviting Bryce along. Of course, now that ship had sailed.

"A war is coming." Raine's voice was soft and imploring. "We need your help. The council needs your help."

"I don't know."

"What's wrong?" her older sister asked.

"What's wrong is Bryce Chambers thinks I'm wanted by the FBI thanks to Will Decker."

"Oh, no."

"Yeah, *oh*," Storm shot back.

"I'm so sorry. Not knowing who you trusted, we thought it would be safer for everyone if Will didn't introduce himself as your brother-in-law. I know how you like to stay off the grid. He was doing me a favor by looking for you."

"Well, Rainbow Bright's tactic sucked." She didn't want to admit how his approach made logical sense. Still, Will would have realized how flashing his badge and asking about her would make her appear to civilians.

She'd given Will the nickname Rainbow Bright after the first time she'd met him and seen his rainbow aura. Raine had told her later how Will was a descendant of Heimdall with powers to locate people, but only those he'd met in more than a brief passing. He could also travel via the Bifröst anywhere in the world within seconds. Storm could have been an even more effective assassin with powers such as those, although she hadn't spent any time with the man, so she'd never seen the magic in action.

Will wasn't amused by the name, but Storm thought the FBI agent could use a dose of humble pie. In the limited time she'd seen Raine and Will together, he seemed to love and lavish affection on her. Storm decided she would accept him on her terms, which meant she wouldn't hold back opinions. Right now, her opinion was that he sucked.

Raine broke her thoughts. "I'm inclined to infer from the degree of hostility in your voice that you like this guy. Bryce is his name? We certainly never intended to damage a relationship you have with anyone."

"Yes, I like him." That terrible squeeze spasmed in her chest again.

"So, explain the situation to Bryce."

Storm grunted.

"You're not going to explain the situation to him?" Raine asked.

"I did explain the situation. The whole Norse mythology at-a-glance along with what I do and why. He worries I'll put him and his daughter in danger. Maybe he's right."

"You have a gift, Storm."

"A curse."

"Yes, I suppose it is both. And this is the first time I'm hearing this type of self-flagellation. Is it because of Bryce?"

"I was delusional to think I could have anything normal." She navigated the roads on auto-pilot as she drove to her apartment.

"So, have an abnormal relationship. What Will and I have isn't normal. Give Bryce a chance. Maybe he just needs time to process everything," Raine suggested.

"Not likely. I need to go. I'm getting into traffic."

"Wait. Let us help you. Let us make Will's blunder right."

Storm considered her next steps. She still sought the source of danger to Bryce. "Yeah. I'll text him and put him to work."

"Okay, but call me back soon. I miss you. We all miss you. I'm serious about needing your help."

"Sure."

When Storm had left Bryce earlier in anger, she'd wanted to cut ties with him and leave Texas. She couldn't even accept herself. How did she expect him to? No matter how many evil creatures she killed, no matter how many places she traveled, no matter how many cars she had or boats she owned, nothing filled the hollowness in her life.

Yet she couldn't abandon Bryce. She'd made that mistake once before too.

After hanging up with Raine, she drove back to her apartment. Once there, she searched for news articles about Erin's death. Among the first responders on the scene had been Dr. Wendy Cabot. Wendy had told reporters she'd hurried to her to provide first aid, but the crash victim was already dead. Storm remembered Wendy's green, toxic looking aura.

With that in mind, she texted Will for more information on Wendy. Because he owed her a favor for making Denny and Bryce think she was a wanted fugitive, Will could put those FBI skills and resources to use for her.

While she waited, Storm found bits of conversation in social media suggesting both Landon and Wendy had had extramarital relationships. None of those findings suggested Wendy had been involved in Erin's death, and none of this explained why Bryce was in danger now. If Storm shared any of this with Bryce to see if he could fit the pieces together, he'd be angry with her for dredging through his past. Just one more thing for him to dislike about her.

She needed to think through her roaming ideas. Talking through them would be better. She was still too frustrated with Raine to call her, as her sister's husband flashing around his cred pack had driven a wedge between her and Bryce. Truthfully though, his actions had only uncovered irreconcilable differences between a killer and a healer.

As Storm slipped on her black leggings and cotton top, she called Denny.

"Hello?"

"It's Storm."

"It's Saturday, clinic's closed."

"Good thing I'm not technically a client. But I could pay you overtime, if you prefer."

"Storm, when I said you could call. I didn't mean any day or time." His tone was pure exasperation.

"It's important," she interrupted. "Someone's in danger." She switched from her phone to her Bluetooth earpiece. She checked her Sig Sauer before strapping it to her waist. "A man is in danger."

"The same man from our discussion? The one with the little girl?"

"Yes."

"Danger from who or what?"

"Definitely a who," she told Denny. "I don't have many leads. Someone cut his brake line when we went to the fair. I can't find any enemies. There are no death threats, and he can't think of anyone who'd want to hurt him. I met one of his friends and colleagues, who he went to medical school with, and her aura was off."

"Her aura?"

"Yes. Wendy Cabot wasn't black and inky like a smudged soul, but sickly green. I thought perhaps she had a chronic illness—something terminal. Now I'm wondering if it's a mental illness combined with a Norse bloodline. Maybe a troll or Fossegrim—a water spirit. In any case, not something I've encountered before now. While I was digging into her past, I learned more about Bryce's wife's death. She was in a car accident. DUI." Storm locked up her apartment and walked to her car. "But it turns out Bryce's colleague was one of the first on the scene."

"If I'm to make the same outlandish conclusions it seems you have, you think Dr. Wendy Cabot is both involved in Dr. Chamber's ex-wife's death and now after him."

"Quite possible. I have Will—my FBI brother-in-law—doing a more thorough check on Wendy," Storm said.

"And in the spirit of being your sounding board, pray tell me the motive."

Storm reached her car and let out a huff. Outside, dusk was settling on the horizon of gray.

"I don't know," she admitted. "Did Bryce wrong her in some way? As colleagues, did she perceive some injustice?" she thought aloud.

"That wouldn't explain her going after ex-wife Erin," Denny said.

"Right. So, Wendy's pissed about something, but why isn't it out of her system by now, especially if she had anything to do with Erin's death?"

"Hmm, it almost sounds as though this is pure speculation without basis."

Storm rolled her eyes at Denny's sarcasm, even though he couldn't see her. She started her car and headed toward Wendy's house. "I'm not the police. I don't need enough for probable cause to snoop around. I just need to know who to be on the lookout for."

Denny sighed, and she heard what sounded like the crinkle of him sinking into his couch. "Let me try a different tactic. Based on your suspicion, you're going to investigate and surveil this woman, nothing more?"

"I would only harm her if she meant Bryce or Olivia or anyone else harm."

"You told me once you take lives to save lives."

"I see auras, Denny. I know when people are good, bad, and just plain evil. So, yeah, I take lives to save lives."

"And has your gut instinct about people ever been wrong?"

"No."

"And you've never hurt an innocent in the act of snooping?"

"No."

"Then, it sounds like you need to find out if this woman is a threat to Bryce and involve the police if she is. Perhaps even the FBI."

BRYCE WAS CUDDLING with Olivia on the couch watching a Disney movie when the doorbell pierced their tranquil moment.

Doesn't anyone call first?

He stood and told Olivia to keep watching the movie, tucking a throw blanket around her as she stared, mesmerized, at the screen of singing, dancing characters.

A woman dressed in suit pants, a vest, and a white blouse with blonde hair pulled into a ponytail paced on his porch. Behind her, the sun had set and the barn and trees were silhouetted in a sheet of gray. Her black BMW was parked in his driveway.

Bryce reluctantly opened the door. "Evening." He couldn't keep the irritation out of his voice.

She gave him a hesitant smile. Something in her oval face, nose, and the shape of her bright eyes seemed familiar.

"Dr. Bryce Chambers?"

"The one and only."

"I owe you an apology, besides the one I owe you for dropping in unannounced."

"And you are?"

"Special Agent Decker."

He cocked his head to one side. "You're much different from the Special Agent Decker I met earlier today."

"Yes. I'm Raine Decker-Thoren. The man who came earlier was my husband, Will. He's been helping me look for my sister."

"Storm Thoren." He raked a hand through his hair.

The look on Storm's face resurfaced in his mind. She'd been crushed that he'd assumed the worst of her. But some fault lay with her. She had introduced herself as an assassin the first night they met. Ever since then, her presence had stirred mixed emotions about the safety of being around her.

Raine tucked her hands in her pockets. "I'm afraid my husband may have given you the impression she was wanted by the FBI when, in fact, she is wanted by her family."

"At no point in time did Will specifically say Storm was a fugitive of the law, but I'm pretty sure he understood the implication. Why didn't your husband tell me the nature of his visit? I assumed the worst."

"We're fighting a war. We aren't in the habit of trusting anyone. It didn't occur to either of us you were—" she hesitated "—a love interest. Will realized about mid-conversation with you that you were someone of importance to her. At that point, he didn't know if she would want you to know about us. We didn't know how much you knew about us."

He mulled over her explanation. While it made sense, the situation left a sour taste in his mouth.

"Did you find her?" he asked.

"She called me, and we talked long enough for her to convey how pissed she is at us."

Bryce unleashed a bitter chuckle. She was upset with him too, so he knew how that felt.

"Why are you trying to reach her—and in such a deceptive manner?"

Raine's expression turned doleful. "We haven't seen her in over a year. And the visits have been few and far between. We took a vacation four years ago—just the three of us. Sisters. Then, I didn't see her until she came to my wedding, but her visit was brief. We follow her travel blog, but I wanted to know she's okay. She uses burner phones and blocked calls in her line of work, so we don't have any way to trace her or call her. At least she never lets us establish a routine means of communication."

"You're FBI. You can't trace her through her blog?"

"She never posts from her current location, and she doesn't post in order of the places she's visited."

"Her line of work? She called herself an assassin. She thinks she comes from Norse mythology. She's—"

"A Valkyrie."

"What?"

"We're descendants of Asgard. I need to find her because I need her to reach her potential and become a Valkyrie. There's a war coming, and I need her help." Raine shook her head. "If she confided this much in you, she must have trusted you."

Bryce felt a pain in his chest at the use of the past tense in Raine's sentence.

"Valkyries? Both of you?"

Raine took a deep breath. "Yes."

"Why did Storm become an assassin, though? Why not FBI like you?"

"Something more respectable?" Raine shot back.

"Something lawful."

Raine sighed and leaned on the edge of his porch, staring out at his property. "I'm not technically FBI. My husband is, and I'm with a facilitating agency. Anyway, it's Storm's story to tell."

"Right." Bryce's shoulders deflated.

"But since your relationship may have been irreparably damaged and you may never hear from her again, I'll tell you a little."

"Wow, you two *are* sisters."

She turned to look at him. "What does that mean?"

"Brutal honesty."

After a smirk, she faced forward and said, "Storm's fiancé was shot and killed in front of her. She's never forgiven herself for not standing up to the perpetrators."

Bryce's mouth went dry.

"Tell me, Dr. Chambers. If you had the power to see who was evil. Could you be idle or would you prevent the death of innocent humans by eliminating creatures who prey on others?"

When he said nothing, Raine said, "I need her to join me. There's a war coming."

"You mentioned that. What war?"

"Look, I need to go find my sister. You seem like a decent guy. I'm sorry things didn't work out." She started down his porch steps. "And I'm sorry Will and I contributed to the divide between you two."

"Wait." Bryce stepped toward her but stayed on the porch. "Please, when you see her again. Tell her to find me. Anywhere. Anytime. We need to talk."

Raine smiled, her brown eye softening. "I can do that." She climbed into her car and drove away.

Bryce stood on his porch for several minutes, feeling hollowed out. An ache spread through his chest as he recalled the devastated look in Storm's eyes when he'd accused her of being wanted by the FBI. And again when she'd pointed out that neither of them knew how to reconcile her calling with the danger it could potentially bring. He didn't have a solution, but if they talked again, perhaps something positive would come of it.

The faint sounds of the television rippled through the door. The movie's credit song was playing. He needed to get Oliva through the shower and ready for bed.

Another car pulled into his driveway, headlights illuminating the barn. This time, he recognized the vehicle.

"Wendy." Bryce stepped off the porch and gave Wendy a Southern hospitality hug, though he felt little warmth at her stopping by unannounced.

She wore a floral dress and an equally floral fragrance. She stepped back, flashing a sickly sweet smile, and reached into her purse.

"This is a pleasant surprise. Is Landon with you?" He glanced around her at the car.

Pain, hot and searing, jolted through him before the world went black.

CHAPTER
SIXTEEN

Bolverkr pulled into his target's driveway. Wendy Cabot paced on the porch with a body at her feet.

Skitr, he swore to himself.

She wasn't supposed to kill the physician. He needed him alive—as bait. Wendy may have hired Bolverkr to assassinate Dr. Bryce Chambers, but Helen had informed Bolverkr about her intel suggesting Bryce had taken a Valkyrie as a lover. No wonder this pathetic woman on the porch was a jealous wreck.

Bolverkr had practically salivated at the thought of killing a Valkyrie. When he'd learned this, he'd told Wendy that if she wanted Bryce dead, she would have to help incapacitate him.

So here they were.

He stalked up the steps. "What the hell is this?"

"I did what you asked," Wendy snapped, hackles raised and having apparently expected a congratulatory response. "Tasered then sedated. You can kill him now."

Sedated, not dead. That was surprisingly helpful. He needed to move the body—somewhere better to create a trap.

"And where is the child?" he asked.

Helen wanted the child dead as well—something about suspecting she was a profit. He recalled having heard Helen had been killing profits.

Wendy sniffed indignantly. "I don't know. What do I care about her?"

He glared at her. "Find the child. I'll load Dr. Chambers into the car."

"Wh-what? Why not kill him here?"

"Because I want to meet the woman he is sleeping with and kill her too."

Wendy wrinkled her nose, probably because she hadn't offered to pay for that service.

He leveled his gaze at her, daring her to challenge him. "No witnesses."

She squared her shoulders. "No witnesses." She opened the door and walked into the house.

"Olivia?" she cooed.

Pathetic, he thought. This weakling fancied she had the upper hand because he'd only received half of the payment and the other half wouldn't come until she was satisfied he'd finished the job.

What she didn't know was that money had become inconsequential once he'd learned he would get to kill a Valkyrie.

Wendy Cabot was already a corpse. She just didn't know it yet.

No witnesses.

Nausea struck Storm as she was driving toward Wendy's house and pain speared through her like a gut punch. A flash of golden light strobed in front of her before quickly fading.

"Bryce," she gasped. She swung an illegal U-turn and headed toward his home.

Gunning the V10 engine, all 602 horses roared as the wheels effortlessly gripped the road. She didn't slow until she reached his driveway. His flood light burst on as she came to a halt near his house. Bryce's truck was parked near the barn, and no other vehicles were in the vicinity. The sun had set, and a faint breeze rustled the grass.

She cut the engine, knowing the element of surprise was gone because of her loud approached. When she slipped out of the car, she listened for the sounds of intruders.

Silence.

She crept onto the porch, avoiding the boards she knew creaked. As she was about to pull her gun and peer in through the window, a horse neighed. She froze, listening.

A sniffle sounded.

She turned and focused on the animals in the pasture. Laying on the back of Faith was a small lump.

Storm trotted down the porch stairs and toward the little girl. "Olivia?"

She sat up, wiping her eyes. "Storm?"

When Storm arrived at the fence, she stepped up one rung and vaulted over it, reaching for the girl. Olivia threw herself toward Storm.

She caught the girl in her arms and hugged her close. "What happened?"

"I don't know. Some people came. I was watching TV, and Daddy was on the porch. My movie finished, so I went to the front door. Daddy's friend, Wendy… she wasn't right. She shot Daddy. I opened my mouth to scream, but nothing came out. So, I ran away."

Fresh tears spilled from her eyes as Storm carried her toward her car.

"I've got you. Nobody's going to hurt you, Olivia."

Shot? The thought sickened Storm. She hadn't seen any blood on the porch, and moving a dead body didn't seem like something Wendy was capable of, so Storm suspected he was still alive. But in what condition?

"I'm sorry, Olivia. I'll get him back. I'll take you to your Granny's and then go get your dad."

Olivia buried her face in Storm's hair. "I ran away. You wouldn't have run away."

I did though, once, Storm thought. She'd run away when the man she loved was attacked.

Not today.

Not ever again.

"You did the right thing, baby girl. Remember the day I got bit by the snake?" Storm asked.

"You saved me from the snake," Olivia said.

"That's right. Well, that's what I'm going to do for your dad— save him from a different kind of snake."

"What are you going to do if it bites you?"

She bared her teeth. "I'm going to bite it back."

She stole the booster seat out of Bryce's truck, situated Olivia in her Audi, apologizing that she didn't have a back seat to put her more safely into. As she drove toward Maddie's house, she tried Raine's phone, but no one answered.

Next, she called her brother-in-law.

"Hello?"

"Will, it's Storm."

"At last. Did Raine find you?"

"She came to find me?" Storm asked.

"She went to Dr. Chamber's house to find you and to apologize to him."

"Shhhoot." She corrected her language at the last moment in front of Olivia.

"What happened?" Will demanded.

"Bryce is missing from his house. Can you get a location on him?"

"Let me focus. I'll call you back. At this number?"

"Yeah."

The connection ended.

When she arrived at Maddie's, she hopped out of the car and

asked Olivia to sit tight for a minute. Her mind churned with what her next move would be to find Bryce.

Maddie came outside, drying her hands on a towel, even before Storm knocked.

"Storm? This is a pleasant surprise, but Bryce isn't here."

"I know." She gestured to her car and Maddie's eyes went wide. "Bryce is missing." She didn't want to say abducted because she suspected Maddie's first reaction would be to call the police. Although when Olivia told her what happened, she probably would alert authorities, but maybe Storm could get a head start. She would be faster and more effective without cops in her way.

"Missing?"

"Can you look after Olivia while I find him?"

"He would never leave Olivia without telling me. Is he in some kind of trouble?"

"Yes. I need to go find him. Can you take Olivia?"

"Of course, of course." She seemed to pick up on Storm's urgency as she shuffled to the car.

Olivia climbed out and into Maddie's arms as Storm sat back in the driver's seat.

"Call me!" Maddie shouted after her.

As Storm drove away, her phone rang. "Will, I just dropped off Bryce's daughter Olivia at his mother's. What did you learn?"

"Bryce is at a health clinic. Not a great-looking part of town. I'm seeing he's alone and tied up. Do you want me to fetch him?"

"Could be a trap. No one else is around?"

"Not that I could see, but it was dark."

"Is he injured?" she asked.

"Didn't look like it."

"Okay. Fetch him. Watch your back. Get him to safety, and let him know Olivia is okay."

She sped, only minutes away from the clinic now. "Let me know when you have him."

Bryce woke with his hands clasped together behind his back with duct tape. He bolted upright and looked around the room. Pain coursed through his entire body, settling in his shoulder, back, and hips. His temples throbbed as he shook his head and blinked, trying to clear his vision.

Memories of earlier that evening hit him. Lying on his porch, completely incapacitated by Wendy's stun gun, he'd overheard her phone conversation with someone.

"I have him here. Come do the job I'm paying you for... Well, I'm tired of waiting... What do you mean, plans have changed? I'm making the plans." She had paced, using the gun to scratch an itch on her head. "Okay, but I can't move him by myself... Fine... Yeah, I said fine."

The last thing Bryce remembered was praying for Olivia to stay safe when Wendy injected something into him, a sedative no doubt, something she easily would have kept at her office to give in small doses for minor procedures.

Where is Wendy now?

Bryce looked at the couch he sat on, and his gaze roamed the tables and check-in desk in the dark room. Why had she brought them to his clinic? And where was Olivia?

Desperate fear spiked his heart rate. He would kill Wendy if she harmed one hair on his daughter's head.

One step at a time.

First, he needed to escape.

He sucked in a deep breath and let it out slowly, formulating a plan.

"God, I'm an idiot." He leaned his head back and looked at the ceiling. Storm had been right all along. She'd said he was in danger, evidenced by someone cutting the brake line in his truck. Instead of listening to her, he'd accused *her* of being the danger, or bringing the danger, or both.

He eased to the edge of the couch and let his feet hit the floor. With his feet bound, he could hop over to his receptionist's desk where scissors sat in the top drawer, but if he fell on his face, there would be no catching himself with his hands tied behind his back. He opted instead to slide on his butt, pushing with his feet.

The friction of his jeans on the worn carpet made the work slow. "I should have trusted Storm," he said to himself. If he hadn't upset her to the point of leaving, she might have still been at his ranch when Wendy had arrived. "Okay. Self-berating can wait. It's currently counterproductive."

When he reached the desk, he glanced at the door one more time. The clinic entrance was silent. "This is the part where she busts through the door and saves me? Not likely. She doesn't know you've been taken, and even if she did, you pissed her off into next Sunday."

Wobbling, he managed to stand, backside facing the desk, so that his finger could rummage through the drawer for scissors he couldn't see. His fingertips found some thumbtacks, paperclips, and paper edges, which all inflicted minor injuries. He swore but persisted in his search.

He thought about how he'd misjudged Storm. She'd been wonderful with Olivia at the fair and protected her from the snake.

Olivia.

For all his worry about Storm being an assassin and fearing her skillset, that was the part of her he wanted most right now. He needed her but had no way of reaching her.

He had to free himself of these restraints and take control of the situation.

A half dozen paper cuts and sharp pricks later, he found the cool steel of the scissors. Easing back down to the floor, he used his toe to bump the rolling chair out of his way and slid under the desk.

With one edge of the scissors, he sawed the duct tape on his wrists, knowing his life and maybe Olivia's depended on him escaping.

CHAPTER

SEVENTEEN

Will called back. "We've got a problem. I did another room view of the clinic in order to watch for traps before I went in—"

"Trap?" Storm asked, stomach clenching.

"No, but Bryce is gone."

"He's been relocated?"

"No. When I use my powers to hone in, I'm still sensing him in the clinic. I just can't see him. I can go back and do a thorough search with the lights on, but I thought you should know first. If I start turning lights on and calling his name, I might find him. We might also miss the opportunity to capture whoever kidnapped him."

"I'm pulling in to the parking lot now. If he's still here, I'll find him. Meet me here, but first, can you check on a civilian? The husband of the woman who abducted Bryce could be in danger or hurt if she's snapped." Storm rattled off the address from memory of when she'd first looked into the couple. "Check on him, and then join me at the clinic."

"On it."

"Where's Raine?"

130

"She's with me now."

"Hey, Storm," Raine said through the speaker.

"When this is over, we're going to have a discussion about you giving me orders," Will said.

"Sure thing, Rainbow Bright."

"The two of you—" Raine began in exasperation.

Storm didn't hear the rest of their words because she disconnected the call as she exited her car. Rolling her shoulders, she felt the comforting weight of her Sig. Her stomach gnawed on itself with worry over Bryce.

Danger.

She honed all of her senses on her surroundings as her muscles tensed for conflict. She didn't back down from a fight, from a challenge. Never again.

What are you going to do if it bites you?

I'm going to bite it back.

WHEN BRYCE HEARD the front door creaking open, he halted his efforts to cut the duct tape. The awkward angle made the process slow. He focused instead on creating an illusion of himself still tied on the couch exactly where Wendy had left him.

The light flicked on. Illuminating the room. Through a small hole under a desk where wires ran through, Bryce could see Wendy standing in the reception area.

"Where's Olivia?" Bryce demanded, projecting a voice from his illusion.

"I have no idea," Wendy replied.

Fear riveted through Bryce like a pinball. Olivia was too young to be left home alone, and if Wendy hadn't found her, she could be anywhere on the farm—alone in the dark. Conversely, his daughter knew her way around the barn and the property. Given Wendy's apparent psychotic break, Olivia might be safer alone at the ranch.

His alternative self glared at Wendy. "Why are you doing this?"

She snorted. "Of course, you don't know. Clueless Bryce Chambers. Always clueless."

"Enlighten me," he demanded. He started sawing his restraints again.

"You should've just accepted my offer," Wendy said.

"Your offer?" he asked.

"I offered myself to you, and you turned me down."

"Jeez, Wendy. That was years ago. You were married, and I'd been recently divorced." He remembered Wendy coming on to him.

She'd arrived at his apartment in the city on a night when Olivia was with her mother. Wendy had worn a skimpy red dress and slurred something about chemistry between them that didn't exist. Bryce had sent her home in a cab.

They'd never spoken of the event, so he'd assumed she'd experienced an appropriate amount of mortification on a sober morning after and chose to bury the memory of her actions. Had she been stewing all this time?

Hell hath no fury like—

"That didn't stop Erin," Wendy sneered. "She was screwing my husband long before the two of you separated and divorced."

Bryce frowned and slowed his sawing. He hadn't known that about Erin and Landon. He'd suspected Erin of infidelity, but he'd had no concrete proof. He certainly wouldn't have thought Landon capable of that type of betrayal. They'd known each other for years. Bryce felt Landon's stab in the back like an ache down to his bones. As a physician working eighty hours a week, Bryce hadn't had time to spy or snoop, so, yeah, apparently, he was clueless.

"Hah!" Wendy shouted.

Bryce heard Wendy pace. Was she waiting for something? Someone? Perhaps the person she'd talked to on the phone.

"Where's Landon?" He tried to ignore the pain of his body cramping in the small space under the desk. Sweat dripped into his eyes.

"Landon's gone." Her voice held a finality that chilled Bryce's bones.

"Gone like Erin is gone," she continued. "The two of them can rot in hell together. First, I thought I'd get back at my cheating husband and your wife by sleeping with you. But Good Ol' Boy Bryce wouldn't have it. I thought killing Erin would solve this festering problem. For a while, it did. Landon turned to me in mourning, and you shriveled into obscurity. But Landon always had to drive to bumfuck hole in the wall bars to hang out with his buddy Bryce. His guilt made him feel sorry for you. So I had to keep seeing you and being reminded of Erin. Then you found someone who made you *happy*." She spat the last word out as if a bug had flown into her mouth.

"I didn't even tell you about Storm before you sabotaged my breaks."

"Yes, you did. You told Landon you were taking Olivia and a date to the fair. You can't be happy. You don't deserve it," she said, a sneer in her voice. "The brakes didn't take you out like they did Erin. But that's okay. I've made other, more definitive, arrangements."

Bryce's mouth went dry. "Wendy, what've you done?"

"I hired someone." The tone suggested she was smiling as she spoke the words.

The front door swung open, banging the wall behind it with a loud crack. Bryce chanced a glimpse through a small hole in the desk meant for running wires. A figure filled the space and ducked to enter the clinic. He looked like a giant—perhaps Death himself—shrouded in black with a bluish hue to his skin as if he was fresh from a frigid hell. With eerie dread, Bryce knew this was the blue Frankenstein's monster Olivia had drawn earlier.

"You're finally back," Wendy said.

"Your husband is dispatched," he said. "Where is the Valkyrie?"

"The who?" Wendy stared at him.

"This man's lover?" he gestured to Bryce.

"Oh, Storm. She hasn't shown up yet. Maybe I can have him call her on his phone."

That won't work, Bryce thought. They'd never exchanged phone numbers because he'd been too much of a donkey's ass to ever ask. He also didn't need Wendy frisking his illusion and discovering his current form on the couch wasn't flesh and blood.

"Don't bother," the man said. "She's a Valkyrie. She will find him."

Through blurred thoughts from the lingering sedative, Bryce tried to piece together events based on what he'd overheard earlier.

Wendy had orchestrated this man to kill him, but somehow now he was also being used as bait to catch Storm.

And damn if the blue monster wasn't right. Storm would come for him if she knew he was in danger.

His head throbbed from the effort of holding the illusion.

But where was Olivia?

STORM CIRCLED THE MEDICAL OFFICE, scouting for dangers inside and outside. At this time of night, no lights should have been on, but the receptionist area glowed through the window. The light was dim enough Storm couldn't discern figures from her vantage point, but she'd seen Wendy enter, so Storm knew there were at least two people in there.

She finished her perimeter sweep. No sentries outside. Why would there be? Wendy had no idea what she was up against. She wouldn't know Storm's skillset. No one knew she was J-7.

If Wendy lay in wait with only herself and her hostage, she was woefully unprepared. If she had harmed Bryce and converted her putrid green aura to black, then Storm would have no hesitation in sending her to her death.

A colossal figure emerged from a truck and stomped toward the front door. With a powerful kick, he sent it flying open. This was a new and unexpected development.

After creeping along one exterior wall, she hovered beside the open door where the man had entered. Muffled voices emitted from within the building. Whoever spoke was just inside the clinic, probably in the front waiting room.

Storm shuffled around to the back door and picked the lock. Fortunately, it was a simple pin-and-tumbler, but she made a mental note to discuss the security of his clinic with Bryce. Not that it mattered too much if gang members were going to splinter his doors with crowbars and Frost Giants used their massive boots.

As she crept down the familiar hallway, past clinic rooms, she heard a deep male voice and Wendy's feminine voice.

"I hired you, Bolverkr," Wendy snapped.

"But you failed the adjustments made to our agreement. We don't have his daughter. And we don't have the Valkyrie." The man's voice was sinister and deep.

When Storm peeked from the hallway near the receptionist's desk, she could see the entire room. Wendy appeared ghastly with dark circles under her eyes on a face stiff like plaster. Her lips were drawn in the same perpetual grin Storm had noticed in the bar on Friday. Tonight, however, by the dim clinic light with Wendy sporting a gun in her hand, the look made her appear demonic.

Bryce sat on the couch, looking as though his hands were bound behind his back. Storm did a double take when she glanced behind the desk where Bryce was crammed, staring at her with wide eyes.

How was he in two places at once?

Unbelievable.

Bryce's aura, she realized. He was Vanir and apparently possessed the power of illusion. This must be what he'd wanted to share with her at the bar before she'd had to leave.

From under the desk, he jerked his head, clearly wanting Storm to untie him. She shook her head. There wasn't time or a way to do so undetected.

Words materialized into the air in front of him.

OLIVIA?

Realizing this was another of his illusions, she mouthed to him, "*Safe.*"

He pursed his lips with a grateful look, squeezed his eyes shut, and nodded.

Storm turned her attention back to the kidnapers. Wendy stood with her gun pointed at the floor as she poked a finger at the man she'd hired. Bolverkr was as tall as a basketball player with a wide, square body and shoulders, and a sharp-angled head, nose, and jaw. Surrounding him was a dark blue, frigid aura, wafting like dry ice.

Frost Giant.

By all appearances, Wendy had hired a ferocious hitman, and Storm's blood ran cold as she sensed his ruthlessness.

Bolverkr shot a hand out and wrapped long, meaty fingers around Wendy's neck. Her surprised scream was cut short by his massive vice-like grip squeezing her. She brought her right hand up to fire the gun, but the assassin twisted his wrist and snapped her neck. When she went limp, he tossed her aside like a rag doll.

Swifter than Odin's six-legged horse, Storm bolted from the hallway, weapon drawn. She fired, knowing the aim was true—center mass, just left of the sternum to hit Bolverkr's heart.

The giant grunted, took a step back, and then lunged for her.

Impossible.

He should have gone down.

Spinning, she dodged his swinging wrecking ball of a hand and took aim to fire again, this time at his head, but he slammed his weight into her, taking both of them onto and over the receptionist's desk with a loud clatter. She fell to the floor, her breath woofing out of her.

The blue beast crashed to the floor beside her. "Valkyrie," he sneered. "Does your blood taste as sweet as you smell, Asgardian?"

She rolled away from him, but the space was finite, and she wouldn't be able to move out of reach of his massive arms. She brought the gun up, this time to shoot him anywhere she could hit flesh and not whatever body armor he was wearing.

As she squeezed the trigger, agony exploded through her left ribcage. Her vision blurred from the pain as she struggled to breathe.

Scrambling to her feet, she shoved away from the assassin, who seemed momentarily stunned by the bullet in his leg. The room spun while cold sweat dripped down her face. She shuffled backward until she hit the wall, which gave her the support she needed to keep upright.

Bolverkr stood slowly, his large, square shoulders filling the room as his massive head blocked the overhead light.

Storm clutched her side, feeling the knife buried there. She was still alive, so it hadn't penetrated at the right angle to reach her heart. Yet she could still die of blood loss, or the Frost Giant could finish her.

Bryce appeared, swinging a steel hole puncher from off the desk and smashing it into Bolverkr's head. The giant grunted and wavered before punching Bryce square in the chest, sending him crashing into the desk chair and onto his back.

Too busy trying to breathe, Storm had no time to react. Bolverkr's enormous hand closed around her throat. She thought of Bryce. When this Jotun finished killing her, he'd finish the job by killing the man she loved.

Her neck seared with agony at his frigid touch. She'd never met a Frost Giant descendant, but she didn't have to meet one to recognize one.

When she tried to raise her right hand, she realized the gun was no longer there. She must have dropped it when he'd stabbed her.

With a feral grin, Bolverkr yanked the knife out of Storm's side as he held her immobile with his other hand. Hot blood gushed from her wound, tumbling down her side like rolling lava. She would have screamed in pain, except no air was moving in or out of her crushed larynx. Her vision darkened at the edges, then rippled in rainbow colors before vanishing all together.

A gunshot rang out as Storm's world faded into darkness.

EIGHTEEN

Bryce carried Storm into one of his exam rooms, ignoring the pain in his bruised chest and back from Bolverkr's blow. After flicking on the light, he set her down on the table. Yanking out the extension, he raised her legs.

"Hold pressure here," he instructed Raine.

Storm's sister holstered the weapon she'd just used to shoot the enormous assassin and followed Bryce's orders. She and her husband, Will, had simply magically appeared inside a rainbow in time to help Storm.

"He's getting away," Raine said.

"If we're going to save Storm's life, you're going to have to let Bolverkr get away. Will, I need you to grab the saline and IV tubing in that cabinet."

The FBI agent followed his instructions. Bryce barked for more supplies as he cut Storm's shirt around the stab wound. Inspecting the area, he noted a single, smooth wound directly between her ribs. He felt her pulse—weak and thready.

Will expeditiously laid out the requested supplies on the counter

—saline, IV tubing, IV supplies, chest tube kit, sterile gown and gloves, gauze, and tape.

"Will she be okay?" Will asked.

"She's in shock," Bryce answered.

"She can heal herself," Raine said.

"That might be part of the problem." Bryce leaned over to start an intravenous line on Storm. "She's already sealing off her wounds, but a few liters of blood and air trapped in her pleural space will keep her left lung collapsed and may also strangulate the major blood vessels on that side. I need to insert a chest tube. She also needs a blood transfusion. Call for an ambulance. Tell them the situation."

While Will walked down the hall to call, Bryce hung the saline bag and tightened a blood pressure cuff around the bag to force the fluid quickly into Storm's veins. He needed the IV fluid to keep her blood pressure high enough to still perfuse her major organs.

After setting up his workstation on a tray, he donned sterile attire and slathered her left chest with chlorhexidine to cleanse the area. Maybe a sterile technique was superfluous for someone who could heal herself, but he would take the steps he'd been trained to do.

He made an inch-long incision and swept his index finger inside, feeling the pleural cavity. Unconscious, Storm didn't even flinch. Warm blood and air gushed out. He slipped the chest tube in and held it in place as blood drained into a suction canister he'd placed at the bedside.

"What can I do?" Raine asked.

She looked distraught at the sight of her sister's blood on the floor but didn't retreat. They were a tough pair.

"Pump that cuff up again. I want to get that bag of fluid into her and then hang another."

She pumped up the cuff. "Now what?"

Special Agent Decker reappeared, and he halted at the doorway, eyes wide. "Oh, shit. That's a lot of blood."

Bryce continued his instructions to Raine. "When the blood stops flowing, I'll ease the tube out. Ideally, this would be connected to suction and I'd get an x-ray before removing it." Ideally, he'd have Storm at a level one trauma center right now.

"No x-ray machine here?" Raine asked.

"No."

She bit her lip.

"Can you slip on a pair of gloves and hold the tube?" Bryce asked Raine.

She pulled on a clean pair of gloves from the nearby box and gently took hold of the tube. "You're so calm."

Bryce tore off his gown and snapped off his gloves. He might be calm externally, but deep inside, his emotions tore at him. Storm had saved his life. Again. He couldn't stand the thought she might die in his clinic and they would never have that reconciliatory conversation.

And where was the damn ambulance?

He put his stethoscope to her chest and listened to her breath sounds. Her left lung had re-expanded. He peaked over at the tube.

Raine's eyes followed his every move. "It stopped draining," she said.

He came around to Storm's left side and clamped the tube. "You're going to ease it out. One inch every five minutes and on her exhalation only. I'll intermittently listen to her breath sounds and make sure the lung doesn't collapse again."

A half hour later, Bryce had another liter of fluid coursing through Storm and the chest tube out of her. Her breathing was slow and restful, and her color was improving. Her healing abilities were beyond unnatural. He'd never seen anything like it.

His clinic looked like a trauma bay, with blood and supplies strewn about the room. The ambulance still hadn't arrived.

Raine was picking up soaked gauze and opened packages.

Bryce turned to Will Decker, hands balled into fists. "You didn't call for an ambulance."

"No," he told Bryce. "I knew you could fix her, and then her body would do the rest. I've seen Raine heal from catastrophic injuries. If anyone witnessed what you did as Storm healed, there would be questions and probing. It's better to keep our existence a secret. Although, when I saw all of that blood, I thought I might have made the wrong judgment call."

"She just needs time," Raine agreed.

Bryce wondered if Storm being on death's door was something Raine had witnessed before tonight. He was still pissed at Will, though he could see the man's logic. Now that he considered Will's powers, the man could have just transported Storm directly to a hospital, but Bryce supposed that, too, would interfere with keeping magic a secret. Bryce's medical training would always drive him to seek a higher level of care, but what could an ambulance and hospital have done for Storm? Like the snake bite, an encounter with non-supernatural humans would only raise questions.

"Did Storm tell you she dropped Olivia off with your mother before coming here?" Will asked him as he lingered outside the treatment room.

Bryce collapsed in a chair. "Thank God. Storm had mouthed to me that my daughter was safe, but I still didn't know where she was."

Will typed on his phone as he eyed Storm from across the room. "Is Storm responsible for the carnage out front? The dead woman?"

"No," Bryce replied, throwing away the last of the gauze. "The assassin, Bolverkr, hired by Dr. Wendy Cabot killed her."

Will shook his head. "Killed by the very assassin you hire. That has to be the biggest dose of karma. I'm sorry to tell you we found Landon Cabot dead at home."

Bryce nodded. He'd already suspected Bolverkr had been doing that deed while Wendy waited for him at the clinic. It pained him to think his friend had died and at the hands of a brutal assassin.

Bryce cleared his throat. "After the man killed Wendy, Storm tried to take him on. She shot him twice, but I think he was wearing a body armor vest."

"I shot him in the head and the asshole still got away," Raine added. "He was a Frost Giant. The biggest I've ever seen."

"This isn't the end," Will noted, still texting with someone on his phone.

"You're right." She took off her gloves, spritzed clean with hand sanitizer, and stepped into her husband's arms. "The team's on the way?"

"Any minute now." He pocketed his phone. "I've spent the last twenty minutes out front convincing local PD that we're handling the situation of reported gunshots."

Bryce pondered if the FBI was whom will had been texting. "The FBI is coming here?" he asked.

"Yes. I need to get back out front."

Will must have called them when he was supposed to be calling for an ambulance. Bryce still hadn't decided if he wanted to thank the man for his faith in Bryce's ability to save Storm or punch him in the face for taking the risk.

"By the way," Will added, pausing, "Storm isn't wanted by the FBI. She's not even on their radar. My connections tell me Interpol has her as a person of interest, but only by her handle with no knowledge of her true identity." He left.

Raine gave a heavy sigh. "You should also know that Will ran Bolverkr in the system after you first said his name. The Frost Giant has been a wanted murderer for over a decade." She shuddered.

"Frost Giant?" Bryce asked. They kept throwing that term around.

"I'll let Storm explain the lineage."

Bryce scrubbed a hand through his hair. "I get it. Asgardian sworn enemies, right? That's why he went red with rage when he saw Storm."

"The connection, and the fact that she shot him," Raine said.

A shot that should have put him down, Bryce thought. Even with a bullet resistant vest, he should have at least been crippled with pain for several minutes.

"I should have done more to help her," he berated himself.

"A human against a Frost Giant?" Raine asked skeptically.

"I'm an illusionist. But, uh, rusty. I mostly don't use the magic." He thought back to when the gang members had attacked his clinic. He hadn't used his powers in so long, it hadn't occurred to him at the time that he could have created an illusion of police arriving or something equally as alarming or frightful and run them off.

"Oh, Vanir bloodline." Raine brightened.

"I guess. This is all a bit new to me."

"Storm can see people's auras and guess their bloodlines. I wonder if she knows what you are."

Judging by the surprised and hurt look on Storm's face when she saw him under the table twenty feet from the illusion of himself, she hadn't known. He'd wanted to tell her, but everything snowballed out of control.

"What happens to Storm when the FBI comes here?" he asked.

"If she'll let them, the FBI will question her, as they will you, as they would any civilian. She'll be fine."

"If she doesn't let them?"

"Will can run interference for her," Raine said.

"What am I supposed to tell the FBI?" Bryce asked.

"My husband will take your statement. Just tell the truth. Wendy kidnapped you, and Storm came to the rescue. Maybe just leave out the part where she calls herself an assassin."

STORM BLINKED HER EYES OPEN. She knew this couch, this room.

Bryce knelt beside her—a head of disheveled hair, a grin on his lips, and a look of relief in his eyes. "You gave me a scare."

"You and me both." She felt ragged, like she'd tumbled through the River of Wisdom at the base of Yggdrasil and been rung out to dry.

"Here, Raine said you would need this." He handed her a plastic cup filled with water. "Although, you got a few liters intravenously before I took out the IV."

"Thanks." She took the water and drank. "Judging by your expression, you did something heroic and saved my life."

"Raine arrived—via the rainbow bridge, it seems—and shot Bolverkr. A bullet to the head like that would have killed a normal human, but it only scared him off. She saved your life first. Then I did."

"The Frost Giant?" She pieced together his words, but her brain felt fuzzy.

Bryce's expression fell. "His name is Bolverkr. Apparently, he's a wanted assassin."

"Seems I recall having a knife in my side and couldn't breathe. Did you do something about that?"

"Yeah. I might have patched you up. In my clinic. *Again.*" He feigned annoyance as the corners of his mouth turned up.

Her lips quirked. "You should have charged me for services when you had the chance."

Bryce chuckled.

Storm looked down at the white t-shirt she wore. She plucked at it and gave Bryce an expectant look.

"Your shirt was ruined, and your leather jacket will need scrubbing to get the blood out. Your present attire is courtesy of Agent Decker."

Storm nodded and looked around the room. FBI agents were tagging and bagging samples.

A warm hand slipped into hers. "I thought I was going to lose you." Bryce's words were a dry whisper as he leaned closer.

"You couldn't be so lucky," she tried at a joke again, but he didn't laugh this time.

"Don't ever leave, Storm. I misjudged the situation. I understand what you bring to this world." He laid his head on her chest and closed his eyes.

She ran a hand through his thick brown hair, feeling a swell of longing for him. Never had a man bared himself like this to her. Never had she let her own vulnerability sweep her away.

"Say you'll stay," he said.

Stay.

Images of the Frost Giant flashed through her mind. She felt like the cold fist that had been around her throat was now around her heart. Dropping her hand, she pushed to her feet, fighting off a wave of vertigo and nausea.

She needed space and isolation to finish healing and to think. She'd opened up to Bryce in a way she hadn't opened to anyone in a decade. She'd wanted his acceptance more than anything, but now that he was asking her to stay, she had an excellent reason to leave. Putting a hand to the pain in her side, she felt the bulky dressing.

He leaned back and stood with her. "You shouldn't move so soon."

His tone of physician's authority grated on her.

"What do you know about my healing and my world? From day one, I've been honest about who I am. You are part of my world, but you pretended not to be or to understand. You're just hiding who you are, whereas I accept who I am." She knew she unjustly lashed out at Bryce when her real frustration was not being able to have every-thing she craved—love, family, and safety for them all.

"I didn't understand how Olivia and I are part of these Norse bloodlines. Now I do. I was going to tell you."

She lowered her voice. "I know. At the bar, I think. And the inter-ruption is on me." She walked toward the back exit of the clinic, scooping her blood-crusted jacket up off one of the chairs. She intended to slip away from the commotion of agents up front as they took photos and talked to Will and Raine.

Bryce rushed to her side. "Storm—"

She paused. "You're safe. Olivia is safe. That's what matters." The gnawing sensation she'd had with the need to protect them had subsided, at least for the immediate future, replaced by a hollow ache at the way events had unfolded. The emotions were too much, too raw. She couldn't endanger the people she cared about. "I was a fool to think I didn't bring danger to you and Olivia. You can't be around me."

"You're wrong." He grabbed her arm just as she reached the back door.

She jerked away and whirled on him. "That thing out there isn't finished with me, so your concern the first time we met is justified. You might actually face danger by proximity to me. Your worst fear, remember? I'm granting your wish from the first day we met. I'm out of your life."

She didn't slow as she marched outside into the night, clutching at the pain in her side, even if it didn't compare to the pain in her heart.

NINETEEN

Bryce sat on the couch of his indigent care clinic, holding his head in his hands. He'd given his statement, and the FBI had cleared out. After that, he'd called his mom and talked to Olivia, assuring her he was fine and Storm was well.

Well and gone.

He looked around at the now empty room. He'd first met Storm in this place, and it was where he'd lost her. The poetic symmetry sickened him. He had no way of reaching her.

"That bad?"

Bryce looked up to see Raine standing in front of him.

"She really lives up to her name." He rubbed the back of his neck. "She showed up in my life, all thunder and lightning, then vanished in the wind."

Raine gave him a soft smile.

He sighed and leaned back on the couch. "By the time I realized we needed to be together, she'd already made up her mind to leave."

"I know you care about her, and she wouldn't have *stormed* out of here if she didn't care about you."

"I can't convince her to come back if I don't know how to find her."

"We'll help you. I need to find her too."

"Right, because a war is coming."

"Exactly," Raine said. "I hope Will can help us. Although, amidst the emergency, he didn't spend time in close proximity to her so I don't know if he can find her with his Heimdall powers or not."

"I need to go see my daughter."

"Will and I can take you."

"Don't trouble yourself. I can take a rideshare." Bryce wanted to be alone with his self-pity.

"Not a chance, cowboy. With the Frost Giant still out there, you and your daughter need protective custody until he's found."

With a sinking feeling, Bryce wondered how long that might take. "You're right." He put his head back in his hands, feeling utterly defeated.

When the FBI cleared out of Bryce's clinic, only Will and Raine remained.

"Ready?" Will said.

"I guess."

Will frowned. "Uh. Raine told me how my intrusion caused a rift between you and Storm. I can see you care deeply about her, and I didn't know that at the time. I mean, the longer we talked on your porch, I sensed you cared about her, but I didn't know if the feelings were mutual or how much she'd told you about the shadow world. I'm sorry about misleading you."

"Apology accepted."

They walked outside to Raine's BMW. When she stood beside them and held her husband's hand, Will placed his free hand on Bryce's shoulder. The surrounding space lit in shimmering rainbow colors so bright, Bryce blinked to adjust his eyes.

When the luminous colors dissipated, he was standing at his

ranch house near his truck. Will had brought him, Raine, and the car. Dolly and Faith's heads snapped up, and they trotted in a small circle on the other side of the fence, tails and ears at attention.

"That's one hell of a way to travel," Bryce said.

"Thanks. Let's exchange numbers so we can stay in contact," Will said.

After they traded numbers, Raine pocketed her phone and said, "We'll follow you to your mom's house and wait outside until the protection detail arrives."

"Thank you." Bryce climbed in his truck and started the engine.

Although he was exhausted, worry gnawed at his insides. He'd lost Storm, possibly forever. Gone into the night like the first time they'd met. On top of that, a crazed killer giant was still on the loose. And Olivia's visions were back. His life was in turmoil, and he couldn't help but feel that if Storm came back, he could make sense of it all.

He drove down the darkened roads feeling the weight of loneliness mixed with bone-deep exhaustion.

After parking, he slid out of his truck and walked to his mom's porch. He waved farewell to Raine and Will, who parked on the neighborhood street and remained in the car. With a knock, he let himself inside the house, entered the security code, and reset the alarm.

His mom stirred from the recliner where she'd evidently been napping, waiting for his return. He waved at her as he dropped his keys and phone on the counter before walking quietly to Oliva's room. When he opened the door, he peeked inside. Seeing her sleeping peacefully eased his mind. Closing the door, he crept silently back down the hall.

Maddie tossed off the throw blanket and blinked, bleary-eyed.

"Hi, Mom." He walked over and hugged her as she stood. "Thanks for watching Olivia."

"I'm glad you're safe. I've been worried."

Rightfully so, Bryce thought. And the worry wasn't over.

"I can reheat supper or fix hot chocolate, and you can tell me what's going on." Her tone held no room for negotiation.

He owed her an explanation. Rubbing his neck, he said. "Just the hot chocolate. Thanks."

Five minutes later, they were seated at the table, steaming mugs before them.

He settled in and started at the beginning. "Erin and Landon had an affair." Landon, who was dead now, according to Will Decker. Bryce hadn't yet processed his best friend's betrayal and death. "I'd no idea, but Wendy knew. She killed Erin."

"I thought Erin died in a car accident."

"Wendy admitted to cutting her brake lines."

Maddie gasped, putting a hand over her mouth. "And your brakes were cut the other day."

"Yes, Wendy was the perpetrator in that as well." The story was unbelievable, even without Frost Giants and magic, which he opted to leave out. "She hired an assassin to kill me—that's how out of her mind she was. Storm saved me."

"Storm's okay?"

"She's okay—physically, anyway. Emotionally, she hates me." He raked a hand through his hair.

"Why would she hate you?"

"Not hate. That's too strong. We're at odds. I haven't been entirely cordial. When the brakes were cut, I accused her of bringing danger into our lives because I didn't know about Wendy at the time." He shook his head.

After that, he'd accused her of being wanted by the FBI. All of this reflected how he wasn't willing to accept the danger she might bring to him and Olivia. Considering tonight's events, he was re-thinking everything. He and Olivia were part of Storm's world. She might be the very protection they needed.

Maddie reached across the table and patted his hand. "Good communication can mend any situation if hearts are invested. Just talk to her."

He let out a humorless chuckle. "I was such a jerk, I never even asked for her number."

"You don't have any way to reach her?"

"No, I—" he thought about how Raine said Will would help. "I have her brother-in-law's number."

"There you go." His mom smiled as if reaching Storm was as easy as a phone call.

The problem was that Will and Raine didn't have Storm's number, either. They'd had to track her down through him. Bryce took a sip of his tea as he felt a new resolve taking hold of him. He could ensure he was part of their efforts to find her again and then win her back... somehow.

"She also has abilities." Bryce swallowed. "I know we never talk about mine and I don't use my illusions, but Storm can heal herself and she's one hell of a fighter." He could still see flashes of her fighting Bolverkr. Sure, she'd been beaten, but she would have killed any normal man with the way she'd fought. "I think she can help me make sense of where my magic originated."

"Sounds like she's your people." His mom reached over and patted his hand. "You'll find her again."

BOLVERKR'S HEAD STILL POUNDED. One day had passed since his confrontation with the Valkyrie. He'd had her in his grasp until other people had magically appeared. He didn't know if the woman he'd stabbed still lived. Surely not.

He'd barely escaped with his life from a head shot, but Frost Giants weren't so easily killed—thick skin, thick bones. The bullet had embedded itself in his skull, and he'd had to pay some street medic cash to dig it out. That and the one in his leg. He was left with two bandages and a migraine that wouldn't quit—as if the Midgard serpent had wrapped around his head and squeezed relentlessly.

Still, Bolverkr had to finish the job.

Helen.

Son of an Asgardian asshole, he swore.

He called her because he must.

"The job is finished?" she asked with no preamble.

"Partially," he said, thinking the dark-haired Valkyrie had probably died after he'd escaped, but the physician's daughter remained and now he had the blonde Valkyrie who'd shot him to kill. "I seem to have stumbled across a little conglomerate of light magic. They ambushed me."

"Explain."

"Two Valkyrie. I killed one. I was shot but managed to escape."

"What about the girl?"

"Still alive. Not for long. I know where the physician lives. I will plot my next move." Since he wasn't in any shape for a confrontation, he would start with reconnaissance.

"You will keep me informed every step of the way."

"Yes."

CHAPTER

TWENTY

Storm lay on the deck of her yacht under the afternoon sun at the Houston Yacht Marina. The November ocean breeze was cool but not cold. Still, she wore her leather jacket she'd thoroughly cleaned to ward off the chill of near death she still felt.

While the rest of the country celebrated Thanksgiving, she was alone with her thoughts. She replayed the fight with Bolverkr in her mind as the ocean breeze swept around her, assessing what she should have done differently. Done better. She'd never had such a crushing defeat. She wouldn't have survived if Raine and Will hadn't shown up, followed with Bryce's medical expertise. Maybe working alone wasn't her best option anymore.

One thing the Jotun had said as he was talking to Wendy stuck in Storm's mind: "You failed… We don't have his daughter." Later, when Storm had already decided to leave, Bryce had said, "I didn't understand that Olivia and I are part of these Norse bloodlines."

Olivia and I.

What powers did the girl have that a Frost Giant would want to get his hands on her? And when would he try again?

Storm tugged her phone out of her back pocket and texted Raine

153

through an anonymous chat app, *Thank you for putting security on Bryce and his daughter. I'll let you know when I've dealt with the Jotun.*

She had driven by Bryce's house to check on him and seen the FBI vehicles. With Will and Raine protecting Bryce and Olivia, Storm was free to hunt down the Frost Giant.

The reply from Raine came swiftly, *Of course. But let me help you.*

Storm stared at the message. Raine had saved her life, and she was grateful, but Storm worked alone. Always. Until now. She couldn't simultaneously protect Olivia and take offensive measures against Bolverkr. She couldn't work alone and protect the people she cared about.

The Jotun might have been injured, but he wouldn't seek standard medical care, so she couldn't trace him through hospitals. Furthermore, he hadn't stayed off the radar this long by using his real name and credit cards. She would have to use the same channels people used to hire her as an assassin in order to find him.

Bolverkr had called Storm a Valkyrie, and she wondered what he'd seen to make him think so. She was no angelic warrior. She was an assassin. Even if she only eliminated smudged souls, she still took payment. She wasn't philanthropic, although she wasn't idle if she came across evil—such as Bone Crusher from the other night.

Nevertheless, her lifestyle choices could put Bryce and Olivia in danger despite her claims earlier to the opposite. She wasn't untraceable, evidenced by Will having found the people with whom she'd spent time. The thought of avoiding him caused physical pain, but what choice did she have?

She took a deep breath. At the end of the day, what mattered was that he was safe from Wendy, and the protection team Raine set up would keep him and Olivia safe from Bolverkr. Raine could fill Bryce in on the Nine Realms and bloodline details since Storm blundered her opportunity to do so.

Raine, who has a far nobler cause.

Her sister had tried to recruit Storm into the Shadow Guardians when Storm had made an appearance at her wedding. Word in the shadows was that the Guardians were legitimately helping people—protecting the innocent, eliminating threats, and working to undermine Helen.

Storm had plainly told Raine that day that she wasn't joining some Norse cult. Truth be told, Raine had looked amazing and alive and in love that day. Storm had wondered if this Shadow Guardian group had helped create this glowing version of her sister. Then again, probably all brides radiated that way. No, her aura had definitely grown stronger each time Storm had seen her.

She was happy for her sister, even bought her a BMW as a wedding gift. But she wasn't ready to work with others as a team—didn't really know how. She doubted she would ever belong with anyone, anywhere.

Yet, the Frost Giant thought she looked like a Valkyrie. Storm wondered if he saw auras the way she did—the way she'd seen Bryce had something special within him. She couldn't see her own aura, but maybe others could.

Raine, *We need to talk.*

Talk? Storm had failed miserably talking to Bryce and somewhere along the way only succeed in becoming entirely too attached to the physician.

Denny had been right from the beginning about the danger Bryce and his daughter had no business being involved in. Storm should probably tell him as much. Maybe the psychologist would have suggestions on how to stop the ache in her chest at cutting ties with Bryce.

Not knowing how to reply to her sister, she slipped the phone back in her pocket.

Storm drove to Denny's house. She had lain low for two days until she'd fully healed from being stabbed, strangled, and emotionally shaken. But the hunt for the Frost Giant needed to resume. To do that, she needed a clear head.

As she pulled into Denny's drive and parked her Audi, she saw the psychologist move a curtain aside and glance at her.

She exited the car, walked up the steps, and rang the doorbell.

He answered without delay. "You're ringing doorbells now." He looked her up and down, probably noticing she was wearing all black again.

"I'm learning boundaries," she said.

He leveled his gaze at her. "Except that you came to my house instead of my office."

"I'm not here for a session. I'm here to say goodbye. Thank you for helping me. I won't bother you anymore."

"Okay. Okay." He stepped back from the door. "Just come in a minute. What happened?"

She didn't budge. "I tried something new." She swallowed. "I tried to form relationships, but I'm rustier than I thought. And you were right, people shouldn't be a part of my violent life—least of all a father and his daughter."

Denny gave her a pitying look she instantly disliked. He gestured at his foyer. "Please come inside. I have a comfortable couch here too."

Narrowing her eyes at his uncharacteristic hospitality, she walked through his front door and followed him to the living room. What happened to constantly pushing her away? She began to think she liked his exasperation and irritation better than pity.

He scrambled to tidy books and magazines and potato chip bags even as she entered his living room. He had a large flat screen TV, two couches, a rocking chair, and a recliner. Bookshelves lined one wall, filled with Star Wars figurines and vintage photos of the actors and actresses starring in the earlier movies.

No sooner had Storm sat on his couch than a shimmering, translucent rainbow column appeared in his living room. Will, Raine, and Bryce appeared, teleporting directly into Denny's house.

He scratched his chin. "Never going to get used to that."

"You told them I was here." Storm pushed to her feet and glared at Denny.

He nodded. "It's called an intervention, Storm. Will told me all about the Norse bloodlines, and while it's a bit much to digest and I think all of you need therapy, it's hard to refute the supernatural when someone magically appears in your clinic."

"Hear us out," Raine said to Storm.

"All of us," Bryce added. He turned to Denny and offered a hand. "Bryce Chambers."

"Denny Smith. Licensed and certified psychologist and newly minted betrayer of Storm's trust."

"Thank you for calling Will," Bryce told Denny when they released hands.

Denny cleared his throat. "I'm going to go make some beverages. I'm thinking alcohol may help this conversation move forward." He disappeared into the kitchen.

Everyone stared at Storm like they half expected her to bolt. Their worried expressions were filled with a bottomless compassion.

"Where's Olivia?" Storm asked Bryce.

"My mom's house—with a security team. She misses you."

A lump formed in Storm's throat. She sat down in one of the chairs, intentionally avoiding the couches where the others could crowd her. They looked suspiciously like they all wanted to hug her.

The three of them piled onto the couch, their eager looks radiating love. Storm felt the walls she'd spent a decade building dissolving like ice in warm liquid.

Denny set a pitcher and drinking glasses on the coffee table and then sat in a rocking chair. "Long-island iced tea." He shifted his weight, seemingly unable to decide if he needed to rock or sit still.

"Who goes first?" Storm asked.

"I'll go first," Raine said. "I know how you can defeat Bolverkr, and I need you to join the Shadow Guardians. We can't fight the coming war without you."

"What war?"

"First, let's start at the beginning."

"The beginning?" Storm asked skeptically.

"How about we start with you telling me what you already know about the world in which we live—the real world?" Raine asked.

Denny poured tea and passed around glasses. He took a long gulp from his before sitting back down.

Storm nodded, rubbing sweating palms along her black jeans. A summary would help everyone start on the same page. "Much of what I learned came from dreams and the Dark Elf underworld— fragmented pieces I assembled over the years about a hidden under-current of magic that has survived thousands of years. After Ragnarök, Midgard—Earth—was all that remained. Survivors lived here, and over the millennia all the races mixed. Some the demonic blood lines have enough evil that they manifest dark tendencies if they're too concentrated and combined with destructive behavior. Some combination of the genes they manifest and the exposures shaping their lives has the potential to make them irredeemably evil."

She shifted her weight in the chair. "Those are the ones I've been killing for the last near decade. Contract kills. Meanwhile, you work for some super-secret organization—you called them the Shadow Guardians—and Will is legit FBI."

Raine set down her glass of tea, leaned back, and crossed her legs. "I'm a Shadow Guardian under an international organization known as the Council of Mjölnir. We try to stop violence from Dark Elves, Frost Giants, Midgard Serpents, and others. Sometimes within the legal system, sometimes not." She glanced at Bryce. "Storm, Sky, and I are sisters, all with Asgardian blood lines. Each of us has different gifts."

"Like the ability to heal?" Bryce asked, glancing at Storm.

"That is one all three of us have. Storm has the best gift for seeing auras, and she's the best at combat. I have stealth. And Sky has powers of perception."

"Does Sky need to be here for this?" Denny asked.

Both Raine and Storm shook their heads.

Storm said, "Sky stays safe from the violence we deal with."

Denny gave a contemplative look, making Storm feel as though she and Raine were overprotective of of their sister.

"And Will can transport," Denny said, prompting the discussion before taking another sip of the Long Island Iced Tea.

"Yes. He can locate people and transport." She adjusted her gaze back to Storm. "We have these gifts for a purpose."

And here's the sales pitch, Storm thought.

Storm had her purpose—assassination of evil. But she understood Raine hadn't taken the time to hunt her down for a tea party—or just Christmas dinner. She needed help. Storm's help. And Storm needed to accept that she, too, needed help.

Raine placed a hand on Will's thigh. "Evil is amassing an army. There's a war coming. One side comprises mixed bloodlines, many of whom have been protecting hubbles—" at Denny and Bryce's confused look, she explained, "—uh, HBL or human bloodlines. We call them hubbles. The opposing side will be an army of Frost Giants, Dark Elves, Fire Giants, Midgard serpents, and the undead."

"Undead?" Bryce sat up straighter.

"The leader of the dark forces is Hel," Raine continued.

"Hell?" Denny had been quietly rocking up until that point.

Storm shook her head. "Hel was Odin's daughter and ruler of Helheim—the underworld of Norse legend. But she has to be dead like the rest of them." She looked to Raine.

"Yes. Today, she's Helen—great, great, great, whatever descendant of the original monster. And there are rumors she's breeding the darker bloodlines stronger."

"If the Council of Mjölnir has so much insight and power, why not eliminate this Helen before the battle ever begins?" Bryce asked.

"That's what they want to do. What *we* want to do." Raine stared at Storm. "And we need an assassin to do it."

"You want Storm to kill Helen?" Bryce swallowed.

"Well, we have to find Helen first. And then, yes, but not alone. We'll help her."

"Who's we?" Bryce asked.

"All the Shadow Guardians. There are a dozen of us on every continent."

"All super warriors," Will chimed in, "like Raine and Storm, though not as powerful."

"Are you one of them?" Bryce asked.

"Like Raine said, I have my gifts. I don't sit on the sidelines." There was a mild challenge in his voice, making Storm wonder if they expected Bryce to take some role in all of this.

Storm shifted to look at Raine again. "So, what are the stakes if we fail?"

"Apocalypse," Will answered matter-of-factly.

"Naturally." Denny grunted, his face going pale.

Raine sighed. "Yes. Death and devastation."

"When is this war supposed to take place?"

"I don't know precisely when. Will and I have been studying prophetic works from Vanir but haven't found specifics."

"Vanir?" Denny asked.

"The Vanir bloodline from Vanaheim. They were prophets, sorceresses, and magicians," Storm explained, casting a glance at Bryce.

She took a long drink of the beverage, letting everything they discussed wash over her. "Bolverkr first. I'll help you, but I need to eliminate him first."

"Storm, you almost died," Bryce protested.

"I don't leave a job undone. The woman who hired him may be dead, but you're still his contract kill. What if *he* doesn't leave a job unfinished? And he obviously wants Olivia for something. Hence, the FBI protection on you. If he doesn't come after you two, he'll certainly come after me."

Bryce paled as his eyes widened.

"I'll be better prepared next time," Storm said.

"Better than bullets?" Bryce asked.

Raine leaned forward and addressed Bryce. "Yes. She'll be better prepared."

Storm's brow furrowed. "You know something about fighting Frost Giants that I don't?"

"No, but I know a dream walk will take your fighting abilities to the next level."

"What the hell is a dream walk?"

TWENTY-ONE

When conversation about Shadow Guardians, bloodlines, and dream walking wound down, Bryce's head spun. He'd hidden his illusion gift for so long he hadn't considered it was part of a larger, unseen world. He faced the realization now with a new clarity. No one had discussed his role in all of this, but he would be by Storm's side. For the safety of his family and Storm, he wanted to see them win this war.

Everyone stood, and Denny cleared the table of drink glasses.

Storm turned to Raine. "So, dream walk, take down Bolverkr, then I'll join your cult."

Raine shook her head. "The Shadow Guardians are part of an organization. Not a cult."

Storm shrugged at the semantics. "Meh."

Bryce turned to Storm. "Can we talk?" He glanced around the psychologist's living room. "Not here. My place?"

"Yeah. Sure. I'll drive. I'll meet you at the car." She disappeared after Denny.

Will clasped a hand on Bryce's shoulder. "You got this," he said with encouragement.

Bryce nodded. "Thanks for coming to get me before you came here."

"No problem. We're all in this together, and relationships make us stronger, be that friendship or something more."

Bryce hoped Storm felt the same way. He went outside and waited by her car—facing the road, naturally. When she joined him, they both climbed inside the vehicle. She started the engine and pulled out of the drive.

"Landon's funeral is tomorrow," he said.

"I'm sorry about your friend."

Bryce thought about Will's words of encouragement—'you got this.' His tone had been much more sincere than anything he'd heard from Landon in the last several years. "I think I lost him a while ago and didn't realize it."

He shifted in his seat. "Now that I've found you again. I don't want to lose you."

"My life brings danger to others. That hasn't changed."

"I know. But you saved me. Saved Olivia. She has magic too. She has premonitions."

Storm stared at the road ahead. "I was afraid I was too late to save you. I thought I'd failed. Again."

"Again?"

She shifted in her seat. "James and I took a break mid game night to make a convenience store run for snacks when a few punks were raiding the place. I knew the gunmen were damaged bloodlines —*smudged souls.* But I did nothing to help James when they attacked. For sport." She swallowed. "They were killing him and laughing about it."

Bryce tried to imagine Storm a decade ago with no training—a terrified young woman.

"When James told me to run away, I did. I left him there to die alone and in pain." She pulled into his driveway, pulled a U-turn to face toward the road, and parked.

"You can't blame yourself for what happened." Bryce didn't

move to get out of the car.

Still staring ahead, she continued, "After quitting college, I traveled the world in search of answers. What did these auras mean? What were the dreams my sisters and I share? I learned our origins within Norse mythology, and I learned how to fight. Determined never to be a victim again, I made it my mission to stop smudged souls and prevent them from hurting others. I made myself judge, jury, and executioner."

"As a doctor, that's difficult to stomach, but I'm not sure I can claim I'd have taken a different path if I'd walked in your boots. You see auras for a reason." He took her hand and leaned over the center console to look deep in those violet eyes. "Maybe that reason is so you can be a vigilante. It's not as though you can haul these creatures into the nearest police station and tell them to lock them up because their aura is off."

She nodded.

"Raine told me what you did for that woman kidnapped by the Dark Elf. Makes me wonder how many dozen lives you've saved for every smudged soul you've eliminated."

"I only take a job if it involves stopping a smudged soul—a Dark Elf usually, or the occasional dishonorable dead. Sometimes, the person who hires me turns into the job. I'm still an assassin. I've still been paid for the work I've done."

"Maybe you'll need that money to buy the resources you'll need to find Helen."

"Maybe."

"Stay with me," he said, not caring how desperate his tone sounded.

"The danger I bring—"

"We'll talk through it more. Tonight. Stay with me." He leaned his head down, placing his forehead on hers and closing his eyes. "Stay."

A soft hand touched his cheek. "I'll stay."

His pounding heart swelled in his chest. Moving quickly before she could reconsider, he hopped out of the car and scurried around to the driver side where Storm was just standing.

Bryce pulled her into his arms, ignoring her initial surprise and hugging her close.

"I'm sorry for how I treated you."

"I'm the one who ran away. I pushed you away," she said, relaxing into the embrace.

"My judgment was harsh." He held her a moment, relishing the feel of her, before stepping back. He pulled out his phone and sent a quick text to his mom that he could pick up Olivia in the morning, then they walked toward his house.

"Your judgment was justified based on what you knew of the shadow world, your perspective as a father, and your role as a physician."

Maddie replied, *I'll bring her home.*

Bryce replied, *Thanks.*

She arched back to look up at him. "Nothing's changed. I still bring danger by proximity. Probably more when I join the Shadow Guardians."

"Maybe. Probably. But I can't turn my back on what we could have together. What we could be to each other. I understand there are risks, but I want to give a relationship a try."

When they reached the porch, he tugged Storm into his arms, wanting to feel her body close to his again. She molded to him. Leaning back, he raised his hands and held her face as he stared into her luminous eyes, sparkling with desire.

"Storm." He crushed his mouth against hers as he fisted a handful of her hair. Need flared in him.

She matched his fervor, plunging her tongue deep into his mouth as she pressed her body against his.

He pulled off his shirt and wrapped his arms around her. Pulling her to him, he kissed her again, those succulent lips escalating his arousal.

In a warm, sensual haze, they backed into Bryce's house, tearing clothes from each other and barely breaking from the kiss as they made their way to his bedroom.

STORM DIDN'T WANT to be alone anymore. Isolation hadn't been the same barrier it once was between her and the world since her first night with Bryce. Every moment spent with him showed her a future she'd thought she could never have. But now that he wanted to explore what their future together might be, she was acutely aware of how the danger in her life meant she couldn't have a long-term relationship. Not without putting Bryce in danger.

In his arms and with the touch of his lips, rational thought escaped her. Every touch of his lips and tantalizing fingertips sent waves of pulsating heat through her. Slowly, with his intense gaze fixed on her, he eased her shirt over her head.

She didn't have patience for slow. Stepping back, she pulled off her bra, before stripping completely naked. Her body zinged with anticipation. She felt simultaneously like she was floating on air and grounded in a place she belonged.

"You are so beautiful." He skimmed his hands down her hips. "I want to savor you." He pulled her against his bare chest and pressed his lips to her neck.

"I've been wanting you again since our first night together. I don't want slow."

His deep, sweet chuckle reverberated through her. "Okay, Darling. You win. But next time—slow." He whispered, "So slow you'll be begging for more."

She shivered in anticipation.

He stepped back and took off his underwear, and she stared at the mouth-watering bare manliness of all of him.

'Next time' he'd said so naturally, like there would always be a next time and always with her. So simple.

He smiled then pressed his body and mouth to hers. The kiss was long and deep. Still kissing, they moved onto the bed, bodies entwining like they couldn't get close enough.

After he slipped on a condom from his bedside dresser, Bryce stepped forward to take her in his arms again.

He moved his lips down her neck to her shoulder, pressing kisses so sublimely sensual her whole body pulsated with arousal.

"Ready?" he asked.

"For you," she said dreamily.

"For us," he said, and the entire ceiling transformed into a starry night filled with colorful nebulae.

She gasped at the glorious illusion of twinkling colors. "It's beautiful."

He hovered his body over her, slid down, and suckled her breasts, his right hand caressing between her thighs. Her body felt drenched in pleasure and need. Reaching for him, she pulled up until he eased inside of her, and she arched up toward him.

"Storm." He wound a hand through her hair as he pressed his body against hers, rhythmically sliding in and out of her. He buried his face in her neck, kissing and caressing. "Can we spend the night together?"

"All night."

In his arms, she could forget the outside world and the obligations looming over her. Tomorrow she could be lonely again, but tonight she had the comfort of his embrace.

The friction built as they moved and bloomed until she cried her release. Bryce followed with his own groans of pleasure, still rocking into her, while she floated in the nebulae of Bryce's illusion.

Storm lay in Bryce's arms, satiated and sublime. His love-making for the last several hours had vacillated between tender and tumultuous —like he was both claiming her and surrendering to her. She drank in every heated movement and lingering touch of his fingers and lips as if she'd been starving for them.

Calm now and staring out the window at the shadows of night, she considered how danger lurked in the darkness. Somewhere out there a Frost Giant assassin wanted her dead. He wouldn't be the last, and none of them would hesitate to use Bryce and Olivia to get to her. Then there was the matter of Olivia's powers and what that meant. On the bedside table, a candle flame flickered.

A small shudder coursed through Storm. "We have to protect Olivia. A few years ago Helen was targeting prophets. Raine stopped her assassin, but we need to keep vigilant in case Helen starts trying to eliminate them again." She bit her lip. "We know Bolverkr was after her, but he was hired by Wendy and I don't think she cared about Olivia one way or the other. That raises the possibility that Helen is also involved here."

Bryce's throat bobbed in a swallow. "You're suggesting the goddess of darkness—or her descendent—wants my daughter dead?"

"It's one explanation. There might be another." She couldn't think of an alternative though.

He ran a hand through his hair as his brow furrowed.

"I'll do what I can. I'll eliminate Bolverkr and work with Raine to bring down Helen and end the shadow war." After that, she didn't know what the future held for them, or for anyone.

"I didn't understand the origin of my illusions. You're right. I've been hiding who I am," Bryce said, trailing fingers lightly over the curve of her hip.

"It's okay. I shouldn't have snapped at you before about hiding them. I understand why you would. You have a lot to lose if hubbles discovered your supernatural abilities."

"I'll help in any way I can—with keeping Olivia safe and with the shadow war."

THE NEXT MORNING, Bryce woke and made coffee. While it stewed, he stepped into the cool morning air and fed the horses, passing by Storm's sports car. He smiled to himself. They'd spent the night making love, which had been even more amazing than the first time. He was learning what she liked and what damn near tipped her over the edge.

He'd wanted to secure a commitment from her to stay with him long term, but the heat of passion wasn't the time. He could tell she was still reserved, still thinking he and Olivia were safer without her than with her. The Frost Giant targeting them seemed to have raised an awareness of the danger to others her role might incur that she'd previously thought impossible.

But he'd only just won her back. Perhaps one day he could convince her to think about staying. There was no rush. He wasn't going anywhere, even with this impending war. He would stay with her and help in any way he could, as promised.

His commitment to her and the war meant drastic life changes, but he'd been through radical changes before when he'd started the free clinic. Besides, knowing Olivia was a target already altered their lives. Helping Storm would be different for both him and Olivia, but he and Storm would communicate on how best to handle it.

Noise from the swinging porch door caught his attention, and he turned to see Storm emerge, two coffee cups in hand. He smiled and waved, enjoying the way she smiled back with beaming affection.

But she'd gotten dressed, dammit.

She'd done the right thing, he admitted to himself. He'd told her his mother would bring Olivia back home this morning—with her protection detail in tow. He would tell Olivia about his feelings for Storm, but his daughter didn't need to know her father had had a sleepover.

Will and Raine had put two FBI agents on his daughter at all times, under the guise that this was all protection from the assassin Bolverkr. Still, the manpower and womanpower made Bryce wonder how much influence Will and or The Council of Mjölnir had within an organization like the FBI.

Storm handed him a cup of coffee as he slipped through the fence toward her.

"Thanks."

Her violet gaze roamed up and down his body. "Do you always feed the horses shirtless in jeans? Because I could get used to seeing this every morning."

His core heated. Every morning? Maybe she was thinking a little more long term.

"Usually." He sipped his coffee with a wink. "For you, always."

She grinned, showing those dimples he loved. "I need to take this dream walk. After that, I need to see a dwarf about a weapon. Do you want to come with me?"

"I'd love to. Tell me when you need me. Olivia can stay with Mom and the guards again." He was nervous whenever Olivia was out of sight, but the sooner he helped Storm attain what she needed, the sooner they could eliminate the Frost Giant threat.

"Apparently, the shop is in New Jersey. I'll text Will and see if he can give us a lift there and back."

"Perfect." Bryce leaned over and gave her a quick kiss on the lips. "So was last night."

"Agreed."

He opened his mouth, planning to assess Storm's feelings about how permanent she thought their relationship was. Even though he'd just told himself he would be patient, the sight of her had him wanting to solidify their future a bit more. But the tires of his mother's van crunched on the gravel drive as the vehicle headed their way.

Storm glanced from the van to him. "I know you need to ease our relationship news to Olivia slowly. Tell me when to stay or go. I won't get upset."

Relationship. So at least she understood they were in one. But for how long?

Cool your spurs, Cowboy.

"Thanks. Oh! And I need your number before you go anywhere," he quickly added.

Olivia bounded out of the minivan and toward him, her overnight backpack bouncing. "Daddy!"

He set his mug on the fence post and scooped her into his arms. "Hey, sweetie. Did you have fun?"

"Uh, huh." She hugged him before squirming away and toward Storm. She wrapped her arms around Storm's neck such that the woman had to take her in her arms so Olivia wasn't sprawled between the pair of them.

"Oh, hey, there," Storm said, obviously surprised and enjoying the girl's affection.

"You came back."

Storm chuckled. "Yeah, I'm like a bad penny that way."

"More like our good luck charm," Bryce said, thinking of how she'd taken Olivia to safety and saved him at the clinic.

Maddie joined them. "Good to see you again, hon'."

"Hi, Maddie. You too."

Maddie glanced between Bryce and Storm. "Hope you'll stick around a while."

Bryce's mom had commented on his morose mood in Storm's absence, and she could probably see now his overflowing happiness with the woman back in his life.

Storm shifted Olivia in her arms. "Yeah. A while."

Her eyes averted to the ground, and Bryce knew he had more work to do to convince her she was a right fit for his family.

TWENTY-TWO

When Bryce went inside to talk to Olivia about her day and change clothes for an afternoon ride, Storm leaned on the porch, reflecting on how her life had drastically changed. She'd told Maddie she would stick around for a while, but was that best for Bryce and Olivia? Probably not once the threat to them was over. She knew she was sending mixed messages to Bryce, something she would sort out how to remedy later.

Raine arrived in her BMW, parked, and slid out of the car. "Hi, Storm. It's really nice to stop by and see you relaxed on a country porch. Did you and Bryce make up?"

"And then some." She sipped her coffee before setting the mug down on the railing.

When Raine reached the porch, they hugged briefly. "He really cares about you."

"Feeling's mutual."

"Are you ready for your dream walk?"

Storm motioned for her sister to follow her off the porch, walking along the perimeter fence of Bryce's property. "If it's going to help me defeat the Frost Giant and one day, Helen, I'm ready. What do I need to do?" Dry grass crunched beneath her boots.

"Take a little walk alone. If Will and I are interpreting the Noble Prophecies correctly, you're looking for a waterfall."

Dolly and Faith ambled over to them. Both women paused and stroked hands on the horses' foreheads.

"Where do I find this waterfall?"

"I don't think where you start the walk matters so much as where you end up."

"Mysterious much?"

"I think the waterfall finds you."

"Uh, okay." Storm rubbed along Faith's neck.

"And watch your back. Helen telepathically inserted herself into my dream walk and threw me off course. We'll have Will monitor your whereabouts, but it's not without risk."

"So, just another day in the life of an Asgardian?"

Raine smirked her agreement. "After that, we'll get you set up to see the weapons maker."

"What weapon did you get?" Storm asked.

"Buy. What weapon did I *buy*?"

"Buy?"

"Yes. You need to be prepared to pay when you arrive. I bought this collapsible spear thing." Raine gestured to a baton on her belt.

"Show me."

Raine took several steps away from the horses and pulled the baton off her hip. With a flick of her wrist, she extended it before a spear head emerged—one long tapering blade flanked on both sides by smaller ones.

"Wicked." Storm grinned. "Wow. Aren't you a badass?" With a sobering realization, she considered how she and Raine needed to spar if they were going to fight the forces of darkness side by side. Fighting each other would help them learn each other's strengths and weaknesses.

Raine looked back and forth at her weapon and Storm, making

Storm wonder if she had the same thought. She collapsed the spear and situated it back on her hip.

"Let me see your gun." Storm jutted her chin at the holster over Raine's vest.

Raine handed her the Glock 19. Storm felt the weight of it. Light. Fifteen rounds.

"You like it?" She handed the weapon back to Raine.

"It's functional. And it's standard for FBI, which is what I pretend to be half the time even though it irritates Will."

"Will has the same weapon?"

Raine holstered the Glock. "He likes the 17. Bigger and two more rounds. Not that the magazine size matters anymore. His gun is enchanted to never run out of bullets."

"Handy."

"What's your flavor?"

"I like my Sig 226."

"Respectable."

They walked in silence for several minutes around Bryce's property.

"You also need to get fitted for protective clothes," Raine said.

Storm nodded. "Is that why you and Rainbow Bright are perpetually dressed in suits?"

"Yes. Our suits are equipped with uru nanoparticles. And Will really hates that nickname, you know?"

Storm grinned. "I know."

Raine shook her head and tugged at her vest. "These threads are bullet resistant. I have vambraces too."

"I can see how that would complete the look."

"You don't have to get a navy suit. Brok can reinforce any outfit you want."

"Good. I have no intention of looking like an FBI agent," Storm smirked. "Hopefully, by the time I've finished running all these errands, I'll have a lead on Bolverkr."

"We're searching too," Raine said, stepping into line beside Storm as she resumed walking along the fence.

"Can Will's rainbow magic find him?"

Raine chuckled. "Don't let him hear you call it that. It's the Bifröst. For it to work, he needs more than a passing minute in close proximity to the person he wants to track down. That's why you were so difficult. If you'd been sociable at the wedding, he would have been able to get a bead on you. Once he'd met Denny and spent time with him, we revisited him, revealed our magic to him, and convinced him to call us when you came by."

Storm was glad they'd found her, even if their success unnerved her and shook the pride she'd taken in considering herself un-trackable.

She thumped a fist along the wooden beams of the fence as she walked. "Thank you for the protective detail you've been putting on Olivia."

"Of course."

"Sometimes I wonder if we'd be safer moving her to an entirely secure location, but uprooting a little girl from her friends and even her grandmother doesn't seem right."

"Agreed. I think we can keep her safe with the rotating team we're using."

"I'm grateful. For everything." She placed a hand on Raine's shoulder. "Thank you for tracking me down."

Bolverkr watched his laptop screen as he flew his drone over the physician's property. Four cars—two of which were standard issue government sedans. Protection detail. Not a problem.

Two women emerged from the ranch house—one blonde, one brunette.

Bolverkr snarled.

The Asgardian warrior still lives!

He hadn't expected her to survive his stabbing. No ordinary human would have. Impossibly, she seemed fully healed. Could Valkyries heal themselves, or was this someone else's magic?

When she cocked her head to one side, he quickly flew his drone out of sight. Judging by the security, they were anticipating his attack, but they didn't also need to see him spying on them.

He tapped his fingers on the controller as the contemplated the situation. Two Valkyries. At least one of which possibly had accelerated healing abilities, evidenced by how healthy she looked sashaying about after he'd stabbed her in the chest. The other had transported magically into the clinic and shot him.

He landed the drone in his truck and turned it off. After he set the remote control down, he picked up his laptop and scrolled through photos he'd taken. Two women. Similar cheekbones and oval faces. Must be related. Sisters?

He thought about how fast the slinky brunette had been. If the other was as skilled, he couldn't risk taking them both on at the same time.

His vision blurred, and the pain of his headache forced him to close his eyes. If only he had the Valkyrie's healing powers. But he didn't, and he needed to heal before confronting her.

Rest.

Heal.

Then confrontation.

He would have to be patient for an opportune moment when the Asgardian was alone. After that, he would be unencumbered to kill the physician and his daughter.

When his phone rang, he knew it was Helen. She would want answers. Then action.

TWENTY-THREE

Remote.

Raine had dropped her off in nowhere West Texas.

After two days of hiking across the plains, Storm's clothes, skin, and hair were covered in a fine layer of dirt. She tipped back her canteen and let the last drops of water drip onto her tongue. If she didn't find this elusive waterfall soon, she'd die of dehydration.

She pushed herself harder. She hadn't walked all this way to die. She needed answers.

Ahead, the sun's rays beat against the flat, dry landscape, creating rippling waves along the horizon. Like a gentle breeze across a lake. Fortunately, she'd taken this walk in early December and not in the heat of summer.

Licking her lips did nothing to relieve their dry, cracked surface.

A rock structure emerged into view, growing larger as she approached. A mixture of smooth and jagged twists and turns of reddish brown plummeted into a darkened crevice.

Shade.

She could use a few hours of shade before continuing. The crack looked large enough to squeeze through. She reached for her knife in case she needed to defend herself against other creatures using the rock formation for shelter.

Her hand came up empty. Right. She'd only been allowed clothing and water for this spiritual journey. What good was finding divine guidance if she was gouged and eaten by a bobcat in the process?

Or if Helen inserted herself as she'd done to Raine, Storm had no way of defending herself.

The rock crevice and shade beckoned—wild animals be damned. She squeezed through, instantly feeling the cool air and... moisture.

Blinded by darkness, Storm stumbled deeper into the cave as her eyes adjusted. By the dim light filtering through tiny cracks, she made her way over the rocky floor toward the sound of trickling water.

The tiny waterfall cascading from a rock cliff twelve feet high was a welcome sight. It collected in a shallow pool of water. She cupped her hands under the falling stream, brought the liquid to her dry lips, and indulged her thirst. The cool water felt sublime trailing down her throat. As she filled her canteen, she glanced around. She wasn't violating sacred ground, was she? Surely this tiny trickle of water wasn't *the* waterfall she was supposed to find.

And what was the source of this water?

The faint sounds of men rollicking in conversation and laughter had her craning her head closer to the water to listen more intently. She couldn't discern words, but the boisterous noise came from *behind* the waterfall.

After securing her canteen on her waist, she eased behind the flowing water and squeezed through another crevice. No wonder she was supposed to starve for two days; there were tiny holes to force herself through.

The crack yielded to an enormous room with thirty-foot high ceilings supported by golden beams and decorative arches. The ceiling was painted in endless battle scenes of barely clad men and women clashing swords and spears. Mounted calvary fought

Dökkálfar—Dark Elves—seated on red-eyed beasts. Valkyrie atop winged horses battled hollow-cheeked, gray-skinned, living dead riding yellow-toothed wolves. The image moved and writhed like a video in slow motion.

Stretching before her, the festive dining hall was filled with long tables overflowing with plates of food and mugs of ale as burly soldiers drank and spoke of battles long forgotten.

Storm walked through Valhalla, unseen by this illusion of grandeur but amused by the hearty laughter. When she reached the end of the long rows of tables, she felt eyes watching her. A throne, elevated at the end of the room, glittered gold where a man and woman sat.

As Storm approached, she took in their fine embroidered clothes, smiles that wrinkled the cheeks and eyes, and heads of white hair. Odin wore a patch over one eye, while Frigg wore a necklace of gold with an intricate pendant of Yggdrasil that seemed to shimmer with swaying branches.

Storm looked for weapons but saw none. This may be an illusion of her remote ancestry, but danger could hide anywhere. Not to mention that every tale of mythology and religion—Norse, Greek, Roman, Egyptian, Muslim, and Christian—were filled with trials, tribulations, and trickery instigated by gods.

"Odin, King of Asgard, and Frigg, Queen of Wisdom." Storm greeted them formally but without subjugation. They were not *her* king and queen, nor was he a true deity. Ancient man may have deified Asgardians because of the powers they possessed, but magic and nobility did not create a god. Furthermore, these images were that of long ago time, and Storm didn't worship the ghosts of her ancestors.

Odin smiled more broadly as the eye not covered with a patch crinkled in delight. "Storm Thoren. We've been awaiting your visit."

"Then you know why I'm here." Looking around, she added, "At least, I don't recall dying in battle to earn a place in Valhalla."

Frigg spoke, her voice a melodic, silken tone. "You are not dead, only in a dream. All who dream walk come for knowledge. Wisdom is all that can be gained from a place such as this."

"Okay, but just so we're clear, I'm not giving up an eye or an appendage to gain knowledge."

"Some of us have earned wisdom without such a sacrifice." Frigg's eyes glinted as if Odin's loss of an eye was perhaps an unnecessary part of his search for knowledge.

Odin chuckled, a deep rumbling that was nearly palpable. "No such demand shall be required. And you have already drank from the well of Mimir."

"Oh." Storm felt the moment slip into awkwardness. "That was *the* well. I didn't mean offense by taking without asking."

"Don't fret, child," Frigg said. "Your journey here was the ask."

"I need knowledge on how to defeat a Frost Giant."

"You need to seek the weapons maker, Brok Waldorf. He will fashion you knives of uru. Indestructible metal."

"Knives?" Knives implied an intimate fight, and Storm had been hoping next time to keep her distance and avoid Bolverkr's meaty, vice-like hands. "Not bullets? I live in the twenty-first century." She would even take a long spear, like Raine's.

Odin arched a visible brow.

"Okay, knives." Maybe she could get enough of them to throw them at Bolverkr and kill him from a distance.

"Your husband, Bryce, will need a magical tattoo which will enable him to form a defensive shield. He will need this in addition to his illusions when you're fighting side by side."

"He isn't my husband."

Frigg rolled one shoulder. "Not yet, perhaps."

Storm opted to change the subject rather than argue about her ability to be a wife and what that would mean to Olivia. She hadn't even decided if she would stay with him once the immediate threat was over.

"My sister also mentioned asking about Helen. Rumor has it the descendant of Helheim is plotting something apocalyptic."

"Raine is correct," Odin said. "Helen gains power daily."

"How can we stop her?"

We. The Shadow Guardians. She wasn't working alone anymore.

"By the power of three," the Queen said.

"Three? Three, what?" Storm felt a sudden urgent angst as the tables and the men in the great hall began to fade from view.

"Three sisters by blood. Three brothers by bond. Three couples' destinies."

On the wall behind them, the number three glowed golden. Beneath it, a mural of a battle scene played, complete with moving characters. Fire and ice. On one side, jagged ice-covered mountains pierced a pale sky. On the other, black, billowing smoke rose from a volcano. Bodies of the fallen littered the ground. Six people—three men and three women—stood on one side, their backs to the room as they looked out over the carnage.

"When?" she asked.

As the scene faded, blackness surrounded Storm.

"Two years." Odin's voice faded.

"Two years? Why can't we stop her now?"

No answer.

If Helen planned to mass forces and attack in two years, why not eliminate her now as Raine wanted? Storm never worked within the confines of the law or anyone's rules; she didn't have to follow some absurd destiny now.

If this Helen woman was prophesied to plan global catastrophe, Storm could find her—or Will could—and if Storm didn't like what she saw, she wouldn't lose sleep over turning Helen into primordial goo. Why wait two years if something could be achieved with less bloodshed in two months? Or one month?

"One more thing." Odin's voice reverberated through the darkness. "You are enough, Storm Thoren."

"What does that mean? I thought I was taking this dream walk because I wasn't enough. I got my ass kicked by a Frost Giant because I wasn't enough."

Frigg explained, "Odin speaks of your inner soul, Valkyrie. You seek to fill the void in your life with violence, a count of lives saved, and financial wealth. You are living life from the outside in. You need to live life from the inside out. You cannot fill your cup with good deeds, blog likes, and money. You must start by knowing you are enough. Your pain makes you feel hollow. You must fill it with emotion. Fill it with love. Start with love of yourself."

Storm looked around as her eyes once again adjusted to the dim cave as she stood alone, blinking away tears. She hated the way their words struck her like an arrow of truth. She wasn't ready to face that empty void, or the simplicity of how to remedy it.

She thought of the hollowness within her she'd fought to fill all these years since James' death. To avoid that empty feeling, she'd always occupied her time—a mission, planning a mission, training for a mission, writing her blog. She avoided the quiet moments because those were when she was reminded of her hollowness. Reminded of how all her efforts couldn't fill the void of feeling like she wasn't enough ever since she'd failed to help James.

Frigg was telling her she had to accept who she was, flaws and all. *Hell's bells.* That was harder than killing a Frost Giant. Storm's chest constricted as a tear fell. She'd been running from her past, present, and future as she filled her time with distractions.

With a shaking hand, she wiped her eyes. "I'll just show myself to the door." Her voice echoed along the cave walls. As she moved toward the small crevice of light, her head spun. She needed food, but she had a two-day walk back to civilization, unless her brother-in-law locked in on her location and brought her back.

She squeezed through the crack as the blinding sunlight of white and yellow scoured her eyes. Squinting, she stepped out from the rock, but couldn't find sure footing. She stumbled forward and, weakened, started to fall.

She caught herself with her hands, landing unexpectedly nearly upright on a smooth vertical surface. Looking in front of her, she saw a reflection of herself. She gasped at the realization she was surrounded by mirrors. Some made her look elongated, others contorted, and others stocky. Unlike the fun she'd had in such a room with Olivia at the fair, this place had a dark and insidious feel to it.

Was this part of Odin's message? Storm's life was one of reflection, deflection, and projection, like these mirrors. Nowhere in here was her true self, but that was the point, right? She looked outward instead of inward. Inward was emptiness... until she loved and accepted herself as she was.

From the darkness within the mirrors, a woman stepped into view, skin as pale as moonlight and dressed in a gown so black it seemed to have been woven from the shadows of hell. She had a narrow nose and prominent cheekbones, with large obsidian eyes framed in dark lashes and crowned with thick, arched eyebrows.

"Helen," Storm bit out her name.

This hellish fiend had been behind so much death and destruction over the years. The woman moved in the shadows and situated her pawns across the world to do her bidding and inflict suffering. For the first time, Storm had a face to go with the reputation. Her fury flared at the sight of the sneer on Helen's blood-red lips and the gleam of gloating triumph in her eyes.

"Valkyrie." Her voice, thick with a German accent, dripped with disdain. "There are two of you, yes? I sensed the other when she was making her transition to enlightenment as well. If you seek words of wisdom, I can give those to you. Surrender to me, and I will show mercy to you and the ones you love. Defy me, and all will suffer the painful consequences for years to come—as your flesh slowly burns and heals again and again until you beg for death."

Storm discreetly eyed the mirrors as she spoke, unable to tell which image was the real Helen. If she could break one, she could use a shard as a weapon.

Buying time, she said, "I'm going to need a bit more information before I make a decision. How about you tell me where to find you, and we'll sit down and discuss the terms of your surrender to me?"

Despite the calm in Storm's voice, her heart jack hammered as fear and adrenaline pulsed through her arteries.

She was trapped.

The mirrors surrounding her all contained some version of Helen either staring at her, picking at her nails as if this meeting was beneath her, drinking a reddish substance that looked suspiciously like blood from a goblet, or slashing a sword through what looked to be innocent bystanders in a shopping mall.

To make matters worse, Storm was unarmed save for her cantina of water, but even if she wasn't weak from two days of dehydration and starvation, she didn't have the strength to impale a blunt object through the goddess of death. Storm had good hand-to-hand combat, but she had no idea what Helen was capable of. Unaccustomed to this overwhelming vulnerability, icy fear prickled Storm's skin.

"Your decision, then, is not one of surrender?" Helen asked.

Storm cocked her head to one side. "Yes, I absolutely accept your surrender."

Helen's lip curled in fury. "Enough games! Insolent Asgardian." She raised her hands and flicked her wrist while extending her fingers outward.

With the motion, every mirror shattered, imploding into the center of the small room where Storm stood. A thousand tiny, razor-sharp blades sliced into her skin. She dropped to her knees and covered her head in a dual protective gesture and as the only move she could make while pain seared every nerve ending on the surface of her body.

"Now you die in agony."

CHAPTER
TWENTY-FOUR

"Okay, Pumpkin, Granny's going to be here any minute. I've got you all packed, and you'll be back here tomorrow."

"Storm will be back today?" Olivia wore a burgundy shirt and leggings with her pink boots.

Bryce washed the breakfast dishes in the sink. "Yeah, she should be back today." He kept his tone light even though he worried about Storm's absence.

Storm had left yesterday morning, and according to Raine's experience, the excursion would last for one to two days. Storm had told him Helen had inserted herself into Raine's dream walk somehow. What if the goddess of the underworld threatened Storm's safety when she was unarmed and vulnerable?

He appreciated Storm sharing this possibility with him, but the knowledge something could go wrong had him on edge.

"I like Storm," Olivia said.

Bryce smiled at his daughter as he bent down and kissed the top of her head. "Me too. How do you feel about me spending time with her?" He dried his hands and slung the towel over his shoulder.

"I think she makes us both happier."

"I can't argue with that." He just needed to convince Storm to stay long term.

When he heard a car engine, he hoisted up Olivia's overnight bag and walked her to the front door. The girl bounded down the porch stairs and into the arms of her grandmother while two men in suits stood on either side—her protection detail. They were simultaneously reassuring of his family's safety and a reminder of how they were all still in grave danger.

Waving goodbye, he watched his mother and daughter drive away with the security detail close behind. Raine's BMW pulled into the driveway next, and Bryce lamented how his quiet, secluded piece of land had been anything but quiet and secluded since the fight with Bolverkr. Normalcy was no longer a word capable of describing any part of his life.

Bryce waited expectantly while Raine and Will got out of the car, hoping they had some news of Storm.

"I thought we could all be here when Storm returns and ask her the details of her encounter with the dream walk," Raine said as she stepped onto his porch.

"Please, come inside." He stepped aside, noting Will seemed a little more intense than usual.

"Can I get you something to drink?" Bryce asked when they were all indoors.

"No, thanks," Raine said.

Will shook his head. "I'm good."

Bryce crossed his arms. "You don't seem good. You seem tense. Which is making me tense. Does this have something to do with Storm and her dream walk?"

"What did she tell you to expect?" Will asked.

"We're edgy is because at the end of my dream walk, Helen somehow inserted herself and..." Raine's voice trailed.

"Helen almost killed her," Will said flatly. "I only found her, half-dead, because of my magical location abilities."

The hair on Bryce's neck stood on end. "Storm mentioned there would be danger involved."

Raine said quickly, "Will has been monitoring her activity, and she vanished, which is entirely expected. We think that's when she entered the dream world."

"But you're here and you're edgy, so what else happened?"

"Nothing else has happened," Will said, his tone a little too placating for Bryce's comfort.

Raine added, "We just thought the three of us should be together if something does happen."

Will nodded. "I'm going to work on trying to get a read on where she is and as soon as she resurfaces from the dream walk, we'll be ready to get her home safe."

Bryce couldn't swallow down the lump in his throat. He'd spent the last thirty-six hours fretting about her while simultaneously telling himself he was over-reacting. Now, seeing both Will and Raine nervous, he was worried again. He moved his half-full coffee cup to the sink. He didn't need any caffeine now that his nerves were shaking.

Will cleared a spot on Bryce's living room floor, moving the pink table and stuffed animals who'd last been part of her tea party, and sat. He folded his legs and closed his eyes before strumming on an invisible guitar.

"Now what?" Bryce asked.

Raine gave him a sad smile. "Now we wait."

Bryce paced in his kitchen, trying to give Will some space, but he couldn't focus on anything while he was worried sick about Storm. He tried to distract himself by paying bills and cleaning his house, but the silent waiting was just unbearable.

"I don't understand the premise," he told Raine. "Is something like this really worth the risk?"

"It's meant to be a leap of faith. Reaching, connecting, and learning from our ancestors gives us a new strength to take our abilities to the next level."

"But somehow some crazy woman who we think will be the source of the apocalypse can find out about this and inject herself into the dream?"

"Yes. I don't know how Helen knew I was in my dream walk. She obviously has potent powers to be able to both know about my dream walk and interfere with it. I've wondered if maybe it's because we are interconnected in these prophecies."

"And Storm is written in these prophecies?"

"Yes. Three sisters. But also their significant others."

Will spoke, startling them both. "Bryce, will you come over here and see if you can give me a stronger connection to Storm? I'm sensing something, but I can't get a firm lock on her."

Bryce settled down on the floor across from Will, mimicking him and crossing his legs.

"Need your hands." Will extended his.

Bryce hesitated, readjusting his seated position.

"Look," Will began, "I get that this is all a little new and weird for you. I don't go around holding other dude's hands, and I don't even know if this will work. But I'm struggling to sense Storm, and I'm hoping your feelings for her will give me an extra jolt."

Bryce set his hands in Will's. "Do I need to do something in particular?"

"Just think about her. Anything about Storm."

"Why didn't you do this with Raine to find Storm long ago?"

"I need to first have my own connection. I could probably use Raine or you right now, but I feel like you'll feel better having a role in bringing Storm home."

"Yes, I appreciate that."

Bryce closed his eyes, willing to try anything if there was a possibility Storm was in danger and needed help. He pictured her the first time they'd met at his clinic, dressed in all black like a burglar with matted hair and kicking the ass of the clinic robbers as easily as if she was washing her car or taking out the garbage. He envisioned her walking up his driveway in blue jeans and boots, full of color and life and hope. He saw her at the fair, smiling and talking to Olivia. He saw her fighting the blue beast, all vicious warrior woman, ready to take on the world.

By storm.

"The hell? No idea where we are."

Bryce opened his eyes to see mirrors surrounding him and Will. They both scrambled to their feet on high alert, Will pulling his gun and Bryce wishing he had one.

"Holy shit," Will gasped.

The blank mirrors filled with a view of Storm crouched on the floor, arms covering her head as shards of glass swirled around her in a miniature twister. In every mirror, the whirlwind settled as, behind her, a tall woman in a black dress stalked her, flashing a dagger raised in one hand. The glint of deadly metal winked at Bryce.

His heart rate spiked at the site of Storm bleeding and about to be stabbed. They were too far away to reach her on foot in time.

Will spun in a full three-hundred-sixty degrees with his gun drawn. "Which one?" His voice rose an octave in panic.

Which image was the real image? And if Bryce guessed wrong, Storm would die by that encroaching dagger. Bryce was an illusionist. If he could create one, he could spot the real one. He was reminded of Olivia's hidden pictures puzzles.

What was different?

"That one." He pointed. Only one had blood on the shards of glass on the floor and the faint shadow of both women.

Will fired.

The gunshot unleashed a deafening roar, and the wicked woman in black jerked like she'd been struck.

She looked in their direction—surprise, shock, and madness all etched on her beautiful porcelain face, and hissed before spinning away into the darkness.

Bryce ran to Storm and crouched down. "I've got you, sweetheart." He wrapped his arms around her. "Will, get us out of here." His voice was harsher than he'd intended, but Will looked like he wanted to bolt after Helen when they needed to get Storm to safety.

A hand dropped on his shoulder and the world shimmered in shades of red, oranges, and blues.

TWENTY-FIVE

Strong arms hugged her.

"Storm?"

Looking into Bryce's eyes, she grinned. He was haloed in the colors of Will's transportation magic along with his own bright aura. "There is a gorgeous man at the end of a rainbow. Better than gold."

"Is she delirious?" Will asked.

"Around Bryce? Always." She looked around as the exterior of his ranch house came into focus and the rainbow colors faded.

Will and Raine crowded around them.

"What the hell happened?" Raine demanded.

"Helen," Storm croaked. "Does it look bad? Judging by your reaction, and my pain level, it must look bad."

Bryce's shirt was splotched in patches of blood. Her blood.

"You look like someone attacked you with a cheese grater," Raine said.

Storm grimaced. "Well, it sounds gross when you put it that way." She accepted her sister's joke because she knew she wasn't dying. She had no internal injuries, even though the pain was intense.

"It's not fatal, but we need to get this glass out of her." Bryce eased her down on the hard, wood planks of his porch, not a shred of amusement in his voice. His eyebrows were pinched together with worry.

Storm bit back a groan from the chards on her back digging into her flesh.

"Olivia?" Storm asked.

"My mom's."

That was a relief. Storm didn't need to give the girl nightmares with her current appearance. She also didn't think she'd ever enter another fun house of mirrors at the fair. Damn Helen. Storm's happy memory with Olivia was now tainted with the demon's horrific actions.

"Tweezers?" Will asked.

"First aid kit in the pantry and tweezers in the bathroom." Bryce motioned to Raine, who took his cue and grabbed a cushion off one of the rocking chairs. He used it as a pillow and gently laid Storm's head on it.

"Grab a horse bucket so we have something to drop the glass into," he told Raine.

Storm's whole body was one giant, oozing, pulsating lump of pain. She wanted to play the strong heroine, but she whimpered at the first shard of glass Bryce pulled out with his thumb and index finger. Will returned with supplies, and Bryce took the tweezers.

"This is torture," Raine said, returning with the bucket and setting it beside Bryce.

"It'll be worse if we try to dig it out of healed skin later," Will noted.

"Should we do this at Bryce's clinic?" she asked. "She needs something for pain."

"I don't have pain meds at the clinic. I can work faster right here, rather than moving her. Moving her will cause more pain."

Raine stroked Storm's head. "We need Sky. Will, will you get her?"

"Yeah."

Out of Storm's peripheral vision, rainbow light shimmered. Bryce pulled another sliver of glass from her. A tear slid down her face.

"I'm so sorry, sweetheart," Bryce said.

"Do what you have to do," she told him, closing her eyes.

Five agonizing minutes and ten pieces of mirror later, Will returned with Sky, who was carrying a basket full of jars and tinctures. She wore a bright yellow dress and sandals.

"Oh, son of a six-legged horse! Storm! What happened? Will said you were a little scraped up! This isn't a little." She knelt down, red hair falling in her eyes as she sifted through her remedies.

"You should see the other guy." Storm wet her lips. She was so thirsty.

"Really?"

"No. Helen pulverized me, and I didn't get one lick in. She was unscathed except for Will's bullet graze."

"More than a graze," Will grumbled.

Storm grinned. Getting a rise out of Will took her mind off the pain. She'd been too busy cowering in pain to know where Will had hit Helen, only that he'd fired his gun. Since no one was singing *Ding Dong the Witch is Dead*, she assumed the she-demon was still alive.

"You'll heal. We'll patch you up." Her younger sister could always summon a cheerful voice, no matter the situation. Sky opened a jar of something that smelled like jasmine.

Glancing at Bryce, she added, "Hi, I'm Sky."

"Bryce. I'd shake your hand, but mine are currently covered in your sister's blood, and I need to keep working."

"You do you, cowboy. I'm just going to ease some of the pain." She knelt down by Storm's head. "Raine, you can apply a drop of that lineament to every wound—with or without glass protruding from it." She laid hands on Storm's temples. "As for you, the trouble-making middle child, it's really good to see you again. I hope you'll stick around. I'm going to sing a little Nordic ballad and take the edge off.

> *"Where dragons' breath meets the frost*
> *There's a cold wind to swallow the lost*
> *In the dreary early morning hours*
> *There's a whisper of souls devoured."*

Her voice in song flowed like liquid satin, and Storm instantly relaxed. She barely registered Raine dribbling oil on her or Bryce plucking out the glass. If she focused, she could think about how Sky was doing something telepathically to disconnect her from the pain beyond just singing a melancholy song. Because that required too much effort, Storm gave herself over to the relief.

An hour later all the glass had all been removed, and Storm stood in a hot shower watching her blood wash down the drain.

How were they going to defeat a woman with so much power? Now, more than ever, Storm was glad she wasn't alone in this fight. Still, the Frost Giant had to be dealt with first.

After she'd toweled off and dressed, Sky burst into the room, wrapping Storm in a hug.

Storm winced, still tender from the healing cuts, and set aside the towel she was using to dry her hair and smiled. "Hey, Sunshine."

"Oh, my stars, I've missed you! It's so good to see you, especially now you're not bleeding everywhere. Are you back for good? How are you?" Sky's jubilant voice and strawberry scent brought back so many memories, but the red rings around her eyes betrayed tears she'd shed.

Storm had rarely spoken to her since Raine's wedding. Sky was such an open and giving person that Storm found her own emotions harder to control around her. Now she was emotionally healing from her past, and perhaps she would be better able to handle her sorrow and joy. She'd bared everything to Bryce, who seemed to lift a weight from her.

"I'm better, Sky. I'm better."

The redhead pulled away to look at her sister. She gasped. "You are better! I'm not saying that just because of my powers of perception. I can hear it in your voice and see it in your eyes."

Storm picked her towel back off the bed and began drying her hair again. "I'm joining Raine."

"Yeah, yeah, get to the part where you tell me about that hunk of muscle who was working on you on the porch."

"Bryce Chambers is a physician and illusionist, and this is his place. He has an adorable daughter. She's under Shadow Guardian and FBI protection for her premonitions."

"Uh, huh? And what sort of emotional entanglement have you got going on here?" She gestured at her with a zig-zagging finger. "On a scale of one to ten? One being you could take him or leave him, and ten being Odin himself couldn't separate you two. I see he's madly in love with you already."

Storm pursed her lips. "Ten. I'm definitely a goner when it comes to Bryce and Olivia."

It's going to hurt when I have to leave, Storm thought.

"What? Why?" Sky asked.

Of course, her sister had picked up on her thoughts.

Storm set her towel down and picked up a brush, tugging through the snarls. "All this time I thought I was so clever. So hidden. But that Frost Giant used Bryce to bait me. His original target was Bryce, but somehow he learned about me. Even Will and Raine were able to track me through my contacts. All that to say they aren't safe around me."

"Mm. I believe your logic is flawed."

"What do you mean?"

"Cat's out of the bag on your secrets, right? First of all, you saved them so you can't claim they're safer without you. Now that they've been targeted, they need you more than ever. If you care about them at all. You can't cut and run."

Storm swallowed.

Was Sky right? Could Storm keep the love she wanted so desperately?

"Of course I'm right." Sky's smile lit the room. "And you're in love. I'm so happy for you."

"There's still work to do. I have a Frost Giant to kill, and then there's the goddess of the underworld."

"Pfft." She waved a hand. "There will always be demons to slay. Love is what makes those hardships endurable. Besides, Helen is clearly a bully." Sky looped an arm through hers, escorting her out of the room. "The others are waiting to hear what happened. Can Helen even be a goddess of something that no longer exists? Talk about clinging to the past."

Storm smiled at Sky's rambling, and she was still smiling when she joined the group in Bryce's living room.

"Did you see that touchdown pass?" Will was saying.

"I can't wait to see the Cowboys-Packers game," Bryce said.

They stopped talking about something that sounded suspiciously like sports as she appeared.

Bryce stood, relief flooding his amber eyes. He walked to her and kissed her cheek. "Feeling better?"

"Yeah. Thanks."

He gestured for Storm to sit on the couch and brought her water and a bowl of fresh cantaloupe. The sweet smell reminded her she hadn't eaten in two days. As she ate and drank, she told Bryce, Raine, Will, and Sky about her encounter with Odin and Frigg.

"Knives?" Bryce frowned. "No silver bullet? No arrow dipped in holy water?"

"I know, right?" Storm sighed. "I guess knives are better than wooden stakes."

"I guess." Bryce rubbed his chin. "Does it have to be you?"

Storm swallowed a bite of melon. "It does. The Frost Giant has to be stopped from harming any more innocent people, and I'm not about to send someone else into this kind of danger."

Bryce took her hand and held it. Storm suspected he was thinking about how she'd nearly died in her last skirmish with Bolverkr, followed by Helen's insta-shred magic. But she'd been unprepared both times. The next time she confronted the Frost Giant, she wouldn't underestimate him.

And she wouldn't be alone.

"I don't think I'm meant to do this by myself. Any of this." She glanced at Bryce.

"What do you mean?"

"Frigg told me there is a tattoo you need to get which will provide a protective shield you can summon at will."

Sky's eyes lit up. "Do you remember Jake Folkvar? He had an energy shield. Avery told me it comes from a tattoo on his back."

"I remember Jake." Storm recalled the Shadow Guardian. He was the only other one she'd ever met and only because several years ago Sky had roped the two of them into helping Jake and Avery while the three sisters were supposed to be on vacation.

Storm asked Raine, "Do you know how to reach him for Bryce? I need to know who the tattoo artist was."

Raine withdrew her phone and sent a text message.

Bryce arched an eyebrow. "Do I get a say in this tattoo?"

All three women shrugged, as if to say, 'not really.'

A few moments later, Raine's phone dinged in reply. "He said to ask Brok for the woman's number. Apparently, she changes it and moves locations frequently to avoid detection."

Storm nodded. "Seems our next stop is New Jersey. I need to see a dwarf about a weapon."

BRYCE LAY UNDER THE BEDSHEETS, basking in the feel of his naked body against Storm's. She'd given him yet another scare today.

He hated to think of the pain she'd been through, the pain she had yet to endure. He couldn't shield her from any of it, and to attempt to do so would be an insult to everything she stood for. For his part, he could be a source of pleasure for her. He could be her shelter from the storm. And when the occasion called for it, he could fight with her.

"We could have this," he dared suggest. "Nights in each other's arms. A few moments of daylight together."

"I shouldn't be here, Bryce. I'm indulging in a fantasy I can never have. I'm afraid it's at the expense of both our hearts."

"I know you think you need to leave after you deal with the Frost Giant, but I disagree. Don't leave."

In the dim light of predawn in his bedroom, she looked up at him. "You saw Helen today. Saw how powerful she is. What if she decides to trap you or Olivia in a mirrored cage for being a part of my life—a Valkyrie destined to resist her?"

He stroked a hand along Storm's thigh. "I saw a powerful woman yes. I also saw a scared and broken one in Helen. Fear drives her anger, which means she knows you and your sister have it in you to destroy her."

"I feel..." she swallowed. "I like how I feel with you—like I am this better person you and my sisters think I am. Like the fates think I am. Like Odin and Frigg think I am. But I also feel selfish for contemplating staying with you when that may not be the safest decision for you and Olivia."

"I think the safest place is by your side. You're skilled. You're powerful. And I want to help stop a psychopathic descendant of a goddess who thinks of world domination."

"You're meant to help."

"You alluded to that when we were in my living room."

"Odin and Frigg said you would fight by my side."

"Ah, well. There you have it. We're meant to be a team." He kept his tone light, as he could feel the hesitation in her willingness to accept he was meant to fight with her.

"How about we take things one day at a time?"

"Frost Giant first?"

"Yes."

He worried she would kill Bolverkr and vanish with Raine to seek out Helen, leaving Bryce alone. How did he take a woman so conditioned to moving from one mission to the next and convince her a relationship was worth the time and effort and risk?

He pulled her leg up to drape it over his hip as he pressed his body, his erection, against her. Leaning in, he nipped at her ear.

"I'll take you one day at a time."

TWENTY-SIX

The next day, Will transported Storm and Bryce to the driveway of a rundown home. Rusted shells of cars squatted in tall grass. A KEEP OUT sign sat askew on a stake in the ground.

The dull thunk of hammering resonated from a wooden workshop to the right of the house. Storm gauged the distance between her and the workshop. The overgrown grass could obscure hazards —mines or trip wires. One of her instructors had always pounded into her the importance of knowing her surroundings. He would catch her racing through an obstacle course and shout, "You just stepped on a mine! Start over!"

Who used mines? Her work didn't take her into war zones.

Yet.

But she understood the premise: be mindful of your surroundings.

Will cast his gaze about the place with an amused grin. "This place is even more rundown and hazardous looking than last time. Call me when you're ready for me to pick you up."

"Thanks," Bryce told him.

With that, Will vanished.

"I'm not sure I'll ever get used to his way of travel," Bryce commented.

Storm smirked. "He could make a fortune. *The Rainbow Taxi Express.*"

Bryce shook his head with a grin.

"Follow me." Storm picked her way through the tall grass—careful and alert—with Bryce close behind, following the noises emitting from the workshop. They both wore blue jeans, Storm in a sweater and her leather jacket to ward off the New Jersey winter frost and Bryce in a wool coat.

A thin glint of light caught her eyes. "Tripwire," she said. She wondered what it triggered but had no intention of finding out.

When they reached the front door of the workshop of faded and wrapped brown and gray wood, she noted the stone slab in front of it was slightly raised.

"Pressure plate," she said, stepping to the side as Bryce stepped to the opposite side.

"Triggering what?" Bryce asked.

She looked around, not seeing anything above them that could fall. It wouldn't detonate a bomb, as that would risk injury to the property owner and his shack. "Perhaps it's some type of warning system."

She knocked loudly on the door while keeping off the pressure plate. The hammering stopped, followed by cessation of classical music which had been playing.

The door swung open and the muzzle if a .357 magnum protruded. Storm side-stepped, grabbed the wrist of the short man holding the gun and twisted.

"Ow! Okay! Okay! Uncle!"

Storm wrenched the gun free and looked down at the short and very hairy dwarf. "Brok Waldorf?"

He squinted at her. "You must be a Thoren," he grumbled, rubbing his wrist.

She gave him a slight scowl. "Storm Thoren. You pull guns on all your clients?"

"Didn't know who you were," Brok said.

"If you had a phone, we could have called ahead. Alternatively, you could even have an online website to schedule visits in this modern day and age."

Ignoring her combined suggestion and insult, his eyes darted around her as if ensuring she and Bryce were the only guests. After ushering them inside, he glanced around outside again.

"How did you get past my booby traps? Are you some kind of wraith?"

"Funny thing," she said. "The meaning of booby trap is something that makes a person look like a fool—a boob. I'm neither a fool nor a boob."

Brok grunted his agreement.

She set his gun down on one of his many countertops while her eyes roamed the room. Weapons. So many weapons. She felt like a kid in a candy store seeing all the swords, axes, batons, and morning star clubs. No guns, though, except the one Brok had pulled on her. The only weapon not for close quarters fighting was a crossbow. In the middle of the room was an enormous telescope-looking device which extended into the ceiling.

"This is Bryce Chambers," Storm said.

"Afternoon." Bryce tipped his head. "Why all the precautions?"

Brok snorted as he looked up at Storm. "I'm the blacksmith making weapons for the three Asgardians and their mates predicted to prevent the apocalypse. I'm not popular in some circles. Since helping your sister, Raine, I've been attacked three times—two Dark Elves and a hellhound."

"Hellhound?" Bryce asked.

Storm rubbed at her left forearm, recalling the time one of those had bitten into her. "Hel's shapeshifter wolves," she told Bryce.

"Sneaky bastards," Brok added. "Descendants of Fenrir with sworn allegiance to the goddess of the damned."

"My knowledge of the undercurrent fantasy realm barely scratches the surface," he told Brok.

Storm picked up a battle-ax and felt the weight in her hands.

Bryce touched fingers to a spearhead. "Any special tricks to killing hellhounds?"

Brok grunted. "The trick is knowing what they are. They're perfectly human looking, right up until they transform and tear you to shreds. But it's not like you have to use silver bullets or anything. They're mortal like the rest of us. Just strong, fast, and mean... with really sharp teeth." He shuddered as if recalling his dreadful encounter.

"So, how does this work?" Storm asked. "I pick a weapon?" Maybe she could pick something other than the knives Odin and Frigg had suggested.

The dwarf scowled, plucked the ax from her grasp, and returned it to the spot on the wall. "This isn't a Wal-Mart."

Bryce smirked. "You're right, we would've had a much friendlier greeting at the door."

Brok grunted, which she decided was probably his version of a chuckle. He led her past bright, hot embers in a fire pit and toward a row of knives.

"Mistilteinn," he said.

"I thought Mistilteinn is a sword," Storm said.

"*Was* a sword." He turned to Bryce as if a teacher to a pupil. "Hrómundr Gripsson—a warrior under the Danish king Óláfr—raided King Þráinn's barrow. Hrómundr fought and defeated Þráinn, who was guarding his treasure hoard as a draugr—living dead. Hrómundr took the treasure—including Mistilteinn—and went on to kill more people with it. Fast forward to the Ragnarök and the weapon is lost."

He turned back to Storm. "It turns up in an archeological dig five years ago and yours truly snatches it off the black market. I used the pieces—six pieces—to make six knives. Added handles and coated them in Asgardian ore. Uru. Never needs sharpening. Perfectly balanced, although I recommend not throwing them unless you're sure you won't miss. If you miss, they're going to imbed in whatever they hit—brick, metal, concrete—and you won't be able to pull them out and resume your knife fight. Well, you are a Valkyrie, so maybe *you* will be able to retrieve it... but not in a hurry."

Mesmerized by the flawless, silver beauties, she picked up one shining object and spun it in one hand. "These will work against a Frost Giant?"

"Oh. Is that your next target?" His bushy eyebrows raised.

"Yes. And his grip is like being held by a sub-zero vice, so I'm not thrilled with the prospect of a close proximity fight." But maybe she'd be willing with these sleek weapons in her hands.

"You survived a fight with a Frost Giant?" Brok's tone held awe, but Storm wouldn't discuss the details of her failure with a stranger, so she narrowed her eyes at him in response.

He cleared his throat. "I guess you did, since you're standing here. Yeah, the knives are effective against Frost Giants. Their hide and bones are tougher and stronger, but they're still mortal. And they can't heal the way you and your sisters can."

She eyed the oversized dwarf. He was a wealth of information. She would have to remember that for future assignments.

And what did those look like? A war was coming—a pre-apocalyptic battle, according to some. One that had Storm abandoning her lucrative assassin business to become a Shadow Guardian in order to take down Helen before she could incite war.

The decision had been easier than expected. All Storm had to do was imagine the destruction reaching the people she cared most about—her family, Bryce, and Olivia.

"How much for the knives?" She reached into her jacket and withdrew a stack of cash. "And Raine told me you make nanotech clothes?"

"Yeah. You want a suit like the Deckers? Very *Men in Black*." He closed up the knife set in a wooden case.

"No."

He looked her up and down. "Leggings, shirt, and leather jacket?"

"Yes. And the boots."

He turned and scratched something on a Sticky Note. Peeling off the paper, he handed it to her. "There's the total and the address to the tailor. Once you're measured, it'll take five to seven days to finish the clothes. That sum includes nanotech amplified clothing for your friend."

Bryce turned his attention away from the knives on the table. "Me? Do they come in blue jeans?"

"Uh, yeah." Brok shrugged. "We can make that happen."

"Bryce needs a weapon," Storm said.

Bryce lifted his eyebrows in pleasant surprise. "I'd like that."

They hadn't discussed him fighting, but she wanted him to be prepared—if nothing else than to be able to protect his daughter and himself.

The dwarf scratched his beard. "I did a gun enchantment for Will Decker. Along with a sword. I could do that. What's your genealogy?"

"Vanir," Storm answered.

He looked Bryce up and down, eyes settling on his cowboy boots. Snapping his thick, grimy fingers, he grinned. "I've got the perfect thing."

From under one of his cabinets, he withdrew a case and pressed his thumb to the sensor. Nothing happened. He scrubbed the grime off his fingerprint and tried again. The lid popped open. He withdrew a thin, golden lariat.

Bryce hooked a thumb in his jeans and cocked his head to one side. "You want me to lasso and hog tie the bad guys?"

"Oh, ye of little faith. This is fashioned like Gleipnir."

"A what now?"

"Gleipnir. The silk ribbon that held Fenrir—Helen's fiendish wolf. The material is stronger than iron chains."

"Uh. Okay," Bryce consented.

Brok held it out for him. "When you don't need it immediately available, you can wrap the rope and wear it as a belt. When you go to use it, it will be activated by your Vanir powers."

Bryce took it, running the thin rope through his hands. "Does it make people tell the truth?"

Brok scowled. "Probably will if you squeeze them hard enough. But, no, this isn't Wonder Woman's Lariat of Truth."

Bryce flicked his wrist and spun the looped end in a small circle. The lasso glowed golden. "Wow. Thank you."

"Yeah, yeah." Brok waved a hand. "Knock it off before you hit my workshop weapons with that thing." He shook his head, grumbling, "Damn bull in a China shop."

Bryce fumbled with the rope, trying to figure out how to turn it into a belt.

"Thanks for all your help," Storm said. "One more thing. I met a Vanir a few years ago with a tattoo that gave him the ability to throw up an energy shield. I'd like to get one of those for Bryce. Do you know who does them?"

Turning, Brok scratched another note down, peeled it off, and handed it to Bryce. "That's the phone to set up an appointment with the tattoo artist."

"How does a tattoo create a force field?" Bryce asked, raising a skeptic eyebrow as he secured the rope, which seemed to have braided itself in place through the loops of his jeans.

Without his powers activating it, the lariat was gold but not luminescent. Storm noted how the color was similar to his aura and the gold flecks in his eyes.

Brok snorted. "Magic runes and enchanted ink. How else would it work? Of course, it doesn't work for just anybody. You have to have a strong Vanir bloodline for the magic to take."

TWENTY-SEVEN

Bryce ran a hand along the corded rope as Storm called Will for a pick up to take them to the tailor. After the fitting, they had Will lift them to the tattoo artist's shop. It was located in a strip mall in downtown Los Angeles. Will dropped them off in the alley, rolling his eyes when Storm thanked him for the taxi service.

"So Storm got knives. What did you get?" Will asked Bryce.

He gestured to the belt on his jeans. "A lariat stronger than iron chains."

"Very cool."

"What about you?" Bryce asked. "Brok said he gave you a sword, but I haven't seen you with one."

Will glanced around the alley before reaching one hand behind his back and pulling a long, gleaming sword from out of thin air... almost thin air since the space behind him briefly glowed in rainbow colors.

"Wow." Bryce took the sword and hefted the weight of it.

"It's a replica of Heimdall's sword. I keep it stored in a locker in the Bifröst."

"Handy." Bryce handed the sword back. "Don't suppose you keep a cold beer in there?" he made a gesture of looking behind Will.

Will chuckled.

"Tempting." Will slipped the blade back into the Bifröst. "Call me when you're ready for extraction." He disappeared again.

Bryce followed Storm around to the front of the building with its cracked, graffiti-covered walls. The shop—*Alfheim Designs*—was wedged between a pizza place and a nail salon. Storm carried her box of knives in one hand, keeping the other free out of habit, Bryce had observed, in preparation for danger.

Storm, apparently extremely determined for him to have a tattoo which he hadn't even mentally prepared for, reached the front and opened the door without hesitation. He liked the idea of a magical shield to protect Olivia, but were they certain this would work? Was he a powerful Vanir?

As they entered, the smell of incense wafted toward them. A woman in baggy clothes approached. She had long black hair on one side and the other shaved. Her ears, nose, and eyebrows sported too many piercings to count. Hindustani classical music, heavy with sounds from the sitar and tambura, filled the small shop.

"I'm Anka."

"Storm and Bryce," Storm said. "I called ahead."

Anka nodded. "You're one of the Valkyrie sisters everyone's talking about?"

Storm shrugged. "So they tell me."

Bryce wondered if Storm had called when she'd stepped out during his fitting with the tailor.

The tattoo artist turned toward Bryce. "Shirt off. Sit in the chair." She gestured to the seat with the high cushioned back where his chest would rest.

Not so big on bedside manner, he thought.

He hesitated for a moment. Was he really doing this? Glancing at Storm, he could see the worried look on her face—like he might refuse and deny the protective shield she thought this body marking would bring. If this shield could be used to protect Olivia, then it would be worth the pain of a thousand tattoos.

Pulling off his shirt, he sat, chest pressed to the cold pleather cushion and back exposed. Anka set to work, cleaning the skin before commencing the inking. He grit his teeth, listening to the high-pitched hum of the tattooing pen. He felt the color draining from his face, and a thin sheen of sweat coated his forehead.

"How big is it going to be?" he asked, realizing that was something he should have inquired about before starting.

"It will be centered on your back. About half the skin will be inked." Anka paused to put earbuds in place and resumed working. Apparently, she wasn't accepting any more questions about her work.

"Can I get you anything?" Storm asked, pacing and obviously uncomfortable with Bryce in pain, even if it was for his own good.

"A tranquilizer," he squeaked.

"That bad?"

"Getting kicked in the chest by a horse hurts less." He exhaled, trying to breathe through the pain. "After the things you've been through, I probably seem weak, cringing over a tattoo."

"Not at all."

"Is the penetrating chest wound the worst injury you've ever had?" Bryce asked.

"The only life-threatening one. The bullet in the shin was painful. I had a wolf mangle my forearm once. That wound took longer to heal."

"A wolf?" Bryce asked.

"Fenrir bloodline. Hel's hounds. They're shapeshifters."

"The shapeshifters you and Brok talked about? From human to wolf?"

"Yes."

"How many of those are loose in the world?"

"I've no idea. Most of them aren't actually evil by nature. They're controlled by a compulsion to serve Helen though. I didn't know that when I fought them initially."

"So they may be innately good, but they have to serve their master when called upon? That's awful."

"I'm told some embrace the relationship and others dread the days she calls them to service."

"I repeat. Awful."

"Well, we hope to end that. End Helen and we set them free. Along with anyone else under her control. Theoretically."

"Can you tell which ones are redeemable based on their aura?"

"Hellhounds? No. I see a bluish-purple aura, nothing distinguishing good versus evil."

He glanced up at her. "You're on this crusade to benefit other people—because clearly you could choose to only look after yourself and you don't—yet you don't seem to fully believe you and your sisters are the chosen Valkyrie."

She walked to the counter nearby and fidgeted with one binder containing design images. "Maybe we are. Maybe it's too much responsibility to dwell on. I've been reading the Noble Prophecies Raine talked about. There is no prophecy saying we win. And if we fail, Helen and her creatures will take over Midgard. She'll enact genocide on the entire human race and any breeds who don't serve her purpose."

"To think we've coexisted for thousands of years since Ragnarök, and it's all coming to a head now."

"Helen has been driving the shadow war for years. Before her, the conflict of good bloodlines fighting the bad was mixed in with the rest of mankind's wars."

"What do you mean?"

"Dark Elves would pick a side while the light would balance it out."

"Now it's come down to a single battle."

"If you believe the prophecies, yes."

"You know an awful lot about this for someone who's been trying to stay aloof."

"I know all about the shadow world. Doesn't make me any less of a loner. Until now. Now, I can see the importance of not working alone. Now, I'm hoping Raine and I can stop Helen before it comes to that single battle."

He grimaced when the artist inked near his spine. "You think you can thwart the prophecy?" he asked, tone teasing. His limited experience with Olivia's prophecies was that they'd all come true.

"Shouldn't we at least try?" She ran a hand through her hair. "If we are the chosen ones, that means I'm on that battlefield with my younger sister, who has no experience fighting monsters. I'm on that battlefield with you. I can't bear the thought of the people I love hurt and possibly dying."

Bryce reached out a hand and held hers. "Speaking of protecting others, Olivia has a birthday this Sunday. I previously sent out invitations to a dozen parents to host a party at my house. I'm thinking I should cancel for safety reasons. Not put anyone at risk."

Storm gasped. "She'll be devastated."

"It's the safe play. I wasn't able to reserve everything I wanted for her anyway."

"What if we're all there—me, Raine, Will? Two Asgardians and a Heimdall descendent. We can't make it any safer than that."

Bryce considered and thought of Storm's premonitions about danger. "If you sense anything, we'll call it off?"

"Absolutely. Now, what did you mean by reserve everything you wanted?"

"I was hoping to get a bouncy house and a princess."

"Reserve a princess?"

"Yes. She wanted a princess theme. All the guests—the children —will be dressed as princesses, and she wanted a character princess, like Snow White or Moana, for entertainment." He wouldn't get an actress on short notice now. "Olivia will be disappointed."

Storm leaned on the counter, brows knitted in thought. "So you need princess characters and some activity stations?"

"Yes," he said, voice muffled as he scrubbed hands over his face, silently chastising himself for forgetting the details of arranging the party.

"I'll cover the princesses and a face-painting booth. You can do a magic show."

"What are you talking about?"

"My sisters and I will play the part of your characters."

His mouth dropped open. "No. I can't ask that of them, of you. You're warriors, not princesses." He flinched, hoping that didn't come across sounding as an insult. As remote descendants of Thor, maybe they were both.

Storm grinned. "Sky and Raine would enjoy playing dress up if it meant bringing a six-year-old happiness on her birthday. We were little girls once, too. Besides, it will let us stay close without looking like security or—Odin forbid—FBI."

"I don't know what to say. That would be amazing."

"I'd say you need to conjure up a magician's outfit and choreograph a little stage show."

TWENTY-EIGHT

Bryce sipped his coffee as he moved aside his curtain windows in the kitchen. He was still simultaneously uncomfortable and reassured with the presence of the FBI camping outside his house. They had a trailer parked on his property for staying the night. During the day, they swept the perimeter hourly. Olivia had asked about the new people, and Bryce had explained how they were here to keep bad people from coming after both of them again.

Storm came up behind him and slid her arms around him. "Are you tender?"

Now, he was already comfortable with her presence in his house. He set down his coffee cup and wrapped his hands around her, loving her in his space.

"Not bad." The new tattoo mostly itched. Anka had instructed him to wait to attempt to use the magic for twelve hours, which meant today was the day for tryouts.

Storm pressed gentle lips to the back of his neck in a kiss.

"Any word on the Frost Giant?" Bryce asked, instantly regretting the question as Storm pulled away from him.

"I've got feelers out on the Dark Web. No pun intended. But nothing yet. If I get word back, there's a possibility it's him setting a trap."

"Then we'll need to be ready for anything." He settled his hands on her hips.

"Are you going into the clinic Monday?"

He pulled Storm close, needing her in his space. "No. I can't run it until I know Olivia is safe. Maybe after Bolverkr is dealt with. I don't know. I hate to leave all those patients without healthcare access. There are other indigent care clinics, but they have to drive farther and most have trouble affording the price of gasoline."

"We'll figure it out," she said.

He pressed his lips to hers. The more she stayed with him and the more they talked, the more Bryce felt like she intended to stay long term or was at least adjusting to the idea. He wanted to press her about it but opted to give her time.

She wriggled against him. "Now, show me some magic."

He arched an eyebrow. He wouldn't mind getting frisky again with Storm, but Olivia was home, sleeping in her own bed. Olivia— whom he had switched to home schooling between himself and his mother until he felt safe for her to be in public again.

"Can you make the tattoo work?" Storm asked.

"Oh, right." That was the magic to which she was referring.

He took a deep breath, feeling her shapely body against his, and focused on the runes on his back. With his mind, he called to them.

Instantly, a golden orb formed around the two of them.

"Wow." Storm rotated her head to inspect it without letting go of him. "You're a natural."

He marveled at his new creation. "I can feel the boundaries on all sides. I can make it bigger or smaller."

"Can you now?"

He grinned at her sultry tone. "I'll need some practice to get a feel for how fast I can erect the barrier and how much force it can withstand."

Bolverkr's fist? he wondered. *A bullet?*

"I'm stoked about having something more than just illusions. This feels incredible."

"Worth the pain?"

"Worth it."

She smiled. "I like it. I like the peace of mind knowing you can throw this up and protect you and Olivia at any time."

And you, he thought. Storm was a warrior, but she might need his shield one day, too.

On Sunday morning at one o'clock, the cars rolled down Bryce's driveway. Parents and princesses poured out of vehicles. Everything was set. Bryce was in awe at how amazing Storm and her sisters had been. Amidst all of their responsibilities, they'd taken the time out to make his daughter's birthday special. With all of them present, Will had given the FBI the day off.

Soon, Storm would hopefully have a location on Bolverkr. Raine had also put out a BOLO through the Shadow Guardians for him. And of course, Will and the FBI already hunted him. By the time he surfaced, Storm's armored outfit would be finished.

Will, Raine, and Storm had set the stage... literally. They had built a stage in his pasture where Bryce could perform his magic tricks as part of the party. Sky had set up booths. One where she would do face painting and another where Raine would make balloon animals. Will ran the food stand. Bryce couldn't believe what they had done for him. For Olivia.

Sky wore a princess outfit of The Little Mermaid. She had the matching red hair and blue eyes for the perfect look. Raine was dressed as Cinderella in a blue gown with her long golden locks up in a twisted bun, and Storm was Belle from *Beauty and the Beast* in a yellow gown.

He had rented a Doctor Strange outfit from a local costume store.

It didn't quite match the princess theme, but at least it was a popular, recognized character. He'd even tacked on the facial hair to complete the look.

Will wore his usual suit and attended the food booth where people had their choice of hotdogs or pizza.

The first hour was spent with guests arriving, stacking their gifts on a table, and exploring the different booths. When faces were painted, hands were filled with balloons, and stomachs were full, Bryce took the stage.

"Princesses, parents, Texans, lend me your ears!" he boomed.

Even as they gathered, he started with his illusion—card decks hanging in the air, rabbits jumping out of hats, and writing names in the air with vibrant neon letters. Next, he pulled out his Gleipnir replica and spun it, the golden glow inducing 'ohs' from the crowd.

He gauged Olivia's reaction—pure delight. She had opted to dress like Princess Leia because she wanted to wear a light saber and a blaster. With her side buns and the face painting of REBEL WARRIOR in pink, she looked absolutely adorable.

When he tried to get too fancy with the rope, he tripped himself up, which a dozen little girls found hilarious. He finished his magic show with a small fireworks display. He danced around, pretending to dodge the miniature explosions that were going off sooner than he intended. Since they were illusions, they were harmless. The crowd erupted in laughter at his antics.

As he was leaving the stage, he saw his mother heading toward the house. She was in charge of the ice cream birthday cake and was probably on her way to retrieve it from the freezer and light the candles. Right on time.

Life was perfect.

When he caught sight of Storm, she was frowning with one hand to her stomach as she looked at Sky. Sky was biting her lip while looking back-and-forth between Raine and Storm with wide-eyed worry.

The hair on Bryce's neck rose as he took long strides toward Storm. He caught a quick glimpse of Olivia playing with other girls. "What is it?"

Storm was walking toward Sky, as was Raine. "I don't know."

As soon as they were within range of hearing Sky speak, the redhead said, "Everyone needs to get out of here. Something's coming."

Bryce needed no other explanation than the obvious danger everyone sensed. With worry spiking his heart rate, he scanned the cheery crowd of kids and parents. He was about to find out just how big of an illusion he could make. He summoned everything he had, rolling in dark storm clouds from the horizon as he pulled in the sensation of wind whipping through the crowd and the rumbling sound of thunder through their ears.

"Storm's coming," he announced. "Sorry people, we have to shut down the birthday party." Even as he spoke, he kept his concentration on the magic and walked over to Olivia.

The threat of rain on tiny shimmering dresses and face paint was enough to get the parents in high gear. They fled to their vehicles with balloon animals squeaking and high-pitched girls shrieking as if they might all melt under the impending threat of rain.

He scooped Olivia up and in a soft voice said, "I'm sorry, pumpkin. We have to get everyone out of here safely."

"I'm scared, Daddy."

"I've got you."

Raine, Storm, and Will took up sentry-like positions on the perimeter with eyes scanning the landscape and looking for threats. Raine held a baton in one hand while Will looked ready to pull his gun from his holster. Bryce was thankful Will hadn't drawn in front of the other parents. Sky kept her cheerful attitude and sing-song voice goodbyes to everyone while she passed out the goody bags of trinkets and candy to guests as they rushed away.

Bryce glanced at the table where the cake sat, still covered in its box. It was missing candles, and he suspected that was what his mother had trotted back to the house to retrieve, oblivious the party was drawing to a close.

He could carry the cake back into the house, but he didn't want to separate Olivia from the Thoren sisters and the strength of their protection. He stood with Olivia in the field, watching and waiting, astonished at how these women were ready to protect him and his daughter with their lives as easily as they had been willing to help him host a birthday party.

When all the other parents and children were gone, taillights in the distance, Bryce dropped the illusion. The clouds above vanished, and the wind ceased.

The sisters and Will clustered back toward him to regroup. Will reached a hand behind him as if he was going to scratch his back. Instead, rainbow colors briefly shimmered behind him, and he pulled his long sword with a gold handle out of thin air.

Bryce did a double take at the surrounding scene—an FBI agent dressed in a suit holding a sword, Cinderella holding a spear, and Belle—aka Storm—with knives in hand. Princess Leia clung to his leg.

"What's next?" he asked.

"I can move everyone to safety," Will offered.

"My mother's in my house," Bryce said. "We have to get her too."

"Look out!" Sky cried.

Bryce saw nothing, but instantly had his shield around the six of them. A deafening explosion of heat and flame rocked the world. He felt weightless, like floating then falling through a fiery hell.

His vision blurred, and he fell to one knee under the strain of maintaining the shield as Olivia screamed.

A hand touched his cheek. "He's okay, baby," Storm told Olivia. "We're all okay."

He blinked watering eyes open, holding the shield, which was keeping billowing fumes from engulfing them. His ears rang, but he knew the shield had kept most of the noise of the explosion out as well, or they would all be enduring ruptured ear drums.

Trying to stand, he gazed at the clearing smoke to see that the six of them were surrounded by a crater in the earth. He fell back to his knees as his world went black.

CHAPTER
TWENTY-NINE

When Bryce collapsed and passed out, Storm caught him. The shield flickered and faded as he slipped into unconsciousness.

Son of a hellhound, she silently swore.

"Við hamri Þórs!" By Thor's hammer, Raine gasped.

Sky took Olivia in her arms as the girl sobbed. "Your daddy's going to be okay. He's just tired." Her voice sounded edgy and as fearful as Storm felt. Storm hoped Sky was right and Bryce hadn't damaged himself saving the rest of them.

Will and Raine held each other, looking around at the crater.

"Did someone just throw a damn missile at us?" Will fumed.

"Language, honey." Raine tilted her head toward Olivia, who'd buried her face in Sky's red hair over her shoulder.

"I was controlling my language. I've a few more choice expletives that are more appropriate for nearly being incinerated. Look at this radius. Fifty feet. I bet it was an AGM-114 Hellfire."

"What in the world?" Maddie was walking unsteadily toward them, across the pasture, holding candles in one hand and a cake knife in the other, her hands shaking.

Olivia raised her head. "Granny!" She let go of Sky and ran up the embankment of the crater, soiling her white robes but not stopping until she'd reached Maddie. She threw her arms around her leg.

"Bryce collapsed. He's alive," Storm called to her. She would give him a few minutes to wake up. If he needed longer, she would need Will's help to carry Bryce to the house.

"That was some incredible magic," Sky commented, looking at Bryce.

"Yeah. I didn't know it would hold up against a bomb." Storm stroked a hand over his face. She gently tugged off the stuck-on goatee.

"We need to get everyone moved while we regroup," Will said. "We can go to my cabin or Usha's ranch."

Raine nodded. "Let's do your cabin. Start with Storm and Bryce. Come back for the rest of us. While you're getting them settled, I'll talk to Maddie. Explain what I can."

Storm shook her head. "Olivia needs to come with us. Bryce will lose his mind if he doesn't see her safe with his own eyes the minute he regains consciousness."

Raine and Sky walked away and climbed the embankment as Storm took one last look around at the devastation. The blast had leveled the barn, but fortunately, the horses were far out to pasture. Bryce's house, a good distance away, still stood. The blast had shattered the windows, but those could easily be replaced. There'd be no coming back here until they dealt with Helen. She had attacked Bryce's home and nearly killed them all.

Helen or Bolverkr? Or both?

Storm had no intention of waiting for some prophetic war in a land of fire and ice to take place. She would do everything in her power to find Helen and end her now.

First order of business was to find a new home for Bryce and Olivia, one they couldn't be traced to.

Next on her list was to locate and destroy Bolverkr.

Then, take down Helen.

Bryce woke to a headache in a living room he didn't recognize.

"Sorry to plop you on the futon. Raine and I have moved into the cabin, but we're still furnishing," Will told him.

"Daddy?" Olivia wrapped her arms around his neck.

"Hey, pumpkin. You okay?"

"Storm says you saved us."

He sat up, embracing Olivia with one arm and rubbing his temple with the other. He looked around to see Storm sitting cross-legged beside the futon on the hardwood floor. She was still wearing the Belle outfit, but her hair was in tangled tufts.

"Damage report?" he asked her.

"Your house will need some repairs, but it's still standing. Fortunately, Maddie was inside the house so she's okay. Unfortunately, your barn is in shambles, but the horses were in the far pasture, so they're okay. No one was injured."

Bryce breathed a sigh of relief.

Raine leaned against one wooden pillar. "That was an impressive shield. I've never seen anything so powerful. I hope I never have to again."

"Bryce?"

He swiveled to see his mother sitting in one corner of the living room. "Mom? Are you okay?"

"I'm shaken up."

He shifted Olivia so she was sitting in his lap. Above him were large beams in a high, vaulted ceiling. Taking in the rest of the room, he saw Sky sitting on the stone fireplace beside Raine.

"I'll explain as best I can." He glanced at Storm who glanced at Olivia. Yes, his daughter needed to stay for this conversation. He hated it, but she'd been targeted for her abilities and needed to hear the danger even if it was beyond comprehension.

Bryce launched into what he knew of bloodlines and the fallen

Nine Realms. "I'm an illusionist. Both of you already knew that, but I also have a magical shield. Olivia is a prophet."

Sometime during the conversation, Sky sat beside Maddie and offered a hand to hold. They'd only just met today, but Sky's gesture seemed to ease some of his mother's angst.

"We need to get you off the grid," Will said.

Raine nodded. "No clinic. No cell phone."

Bryce understood what they were saying, but the transition seemed impossible. He had a little money from Erin's death years ago, but not enough to live off of indefinitely. "I have to work. I have a mortgage and mouths to feed. And what about my mother?"

"I'll cover expenses," Storm said, as if it was so simple.

He thought about her car, her clothes, and the cash she'd produced at Brok's. Didn't she say she also owned a boat? Maybe it was simple for her. They'd never discussed finances.

Storm added, "Odin said the war is in two years. Your hiding will be temporary."

Two years maximum he understood, unless Raine and Storm found Helen sooner. Two years was a long time for Olivia to stay isolated. He would have to make arrangements for someone else to run the clinic entirely, or a lot of patients would be without that care.

"Did you say Odin?" Maddie asked.

Storm grimaced. "I met him in something called a dream walk."

"Maddie can stay with me," Sky offered. "I have a guest room, and I've already established protection around my house."

"Protection?" Bryce asked.

"Magic symbols to create an invisible barrier against evil entering. My house and our parents' house."

Raine and Storm exchanged looks of mild surprise.

"What?" Sky shot back at the pair of them. "I'm not helpless, you know."

"That leaves finding a place for Bryce and Olivia," Will said.

"I'll handle that," Storm said.

Bryce was about to ask where that was and if he had any say in the matter when his phone dinged with a message.

He withdrew it from his pocket and read the text. His blood chilled. "It's Bolverkr. He wants to set up a meet with Storm. Tonight."

THIRTY

Bolverkr perched in a tree, waiting for his victim. Lightning split the sky overhead as Storm walked onto the deserted soccer field. He had seen the front moving through on his weather app, but he'd be finished with her before the downpour started.

He'd thought he'd wanted hand to hand combat, and was disappointed Helen had ordered a drone strike. But after seeing the two Valkyries and their families survive, he opted for a distance kill instead.

Besides, what were the odds she would come alone when she could enlist the help of her sister? Perhaps the dark-haired Valkyrie would have fought him in solo combat if Helen hadn't sent a bomb and declared an all-out war on the warrior woman. Such an act was devoid of any honor. The Asgardian probably thought he had committed the attack, and her retaliation would come in the form of the full force of her arsenal. He was prepared to face an ambush.

His invitation for their final confrontation had been clear—a match to the death.

Valkyrie vs Frost Giant.

After he killed her, the physician and his daughter would be less protected. He could eliminate them, though he may have to target the blonde sister first. He would sort that out next. He hadn't told Helen her Hellfire had failed. After he killed the Valkyrie and her sister, he could report his success. Enraging the she-demon now could only incur her wrath, which few were known to survive.

Dark clouds gathered overhead as the wind swirled in air charged with electricity. Another flash of lightning illuminated the field and bordering trees. The gusty breeze whistled through bare limbs.

He lined up the site of his Blaser R-93 Tactical. The Valkyrie stood directly in the crosshairs of his sniper rifle, waiting for his arrival on the field. She wore a tight-fitting, all black outfit with her long hair swirling in the wind.

Alone.

Still, he wouldn't risk her having her own sniper poised in a tree to shoot him when he appeared on the field. He hadn't lived this long by being a fool.

On a satisfied exhale, he squeezed the trigger and the shot split through the night air, cracking like fresh thunder.

The Valkyrie crumpled onto the field, unmoving.

STORM—THE real Storm, not the illusion Bryce had created who now lay dying on the field—waited at the base of the tree. She had been stalking through the woods and honed in on Bolverkr when he'd fired. As soon as the Jotun's boots crunched on dry ground, she sprang around the trunk with knives drawn.

She sliced into an arm and a leg, one with each knife, before sliding out of reach of his massive flailing arms.

He snarled in outrage.

"Coward," she said as she prepared her next strike.

He wore the same vest, protecting the vital organs of his torso. If she was going to put this beast down, she would have to target his femoral, brachial, and carotid arteries.

"You couldn't face me on the field?" she demanded. "Had to take me out from a distance?"

"I thought I smelled your stench too close for that to be you on the field," Bolverkr said with a sneer.

"Still. Kind of a dick move."

"I prefer clean kills, but I didn't want to risk you ambushing me." He tossed his rifle case to the side and pulled out a knife of his own, a twelve-inch monstrosity.

"Like the bomb you sent after my family." She lunged toward him, swinging.

"Helen's order, not mine."

They fought, blades clashing, mixing blows and blocks with careful footwork. Storm was pleased to see she was faster than him this time, and the dream walk seemed to have given her extra strength as well. She'd have to credit Raine's cult for guiding her to the well and illusion of Valhalla. The armor-woven clothing kept her free of nicks from his knife.

When Bolverkr's hand lashed out to grab her throat, a move he seemed fond of, she thrust the knife up, burying the blade in his wrist before twisting it. She felt it grind against bone and tear through tendons.

He roared in agony and jerked his hand back before ramrodding his fist into her chest.

The blow sent her stumbling several feet backward, knocking the wind out of her. She went down to one knee momentarily, now out in the open soccer field.

Lightning flashed, illuminating the sky in deep violet, and the downpour began.

The Frost Giant lunged at her, leading with his knife even as blood poured from his other wrist.

She sprang to her feet and blocked. His every strike had more force—more rage—behind it, and she was grateful for the extra protection from Brok's uru nanoparticles. She was a little slower in her defensive and offensive moves because of the blow to her chest.

At his next swing, she spun into him, trapping the hand with the weapon between her arm and torso. With her other hand, she thrust the knife into the soft, exposed flesh of his neck.

His mouth gaped wide before twisting into an angry snarl. Despite his injured wrist, he uppercut a fist into her abdomen. The blow loosened where she'd trapped his other arm.

Vision blurring from the pain of his punch, she ripped her knife back out of his neck. As she stumbled backward, he jerked the arm holding the blade back, slicing into the unprotected flesh of her hand.

She cried out, feeling warm blood ooze from the wound before mixing with the down-pouring rain.

To her surprise, Bolverkr advanced on her, even as blood poured from his neck.

Shit.

He's harder to kill than a damn bull.

She must have hit a vein instead of an artery, which meant a slower death for him. It also meant he could use his extra sixty seconds of life to kill her in her weakened state.

He was still advancing as she retreated to regain her composure and catch her breath. He reached for the handgun strapped to his thigh, but before he could raise and take aim, a gold whip zipped through the air. Bryce's rope looped around the gun, and he yanked it from Bolverkr's slippery grasp.

A bolt of lightning jetted from the sky, striking the ground between Storm and Bolverkr. The Frost Giant shrank back in surprise, giving Storm the seconds she needed to attack. She dove between his wide stance, cut into his Achilles tendon, and brought him to one knee.

He teetered for a moment before toppling over, the last of his circulating blood spilling onto the field and diluting in the rain.

His body sunk into itself as if suddenly dehydrated and freeze-dried before it dissolved all together in the rain.

Bryce rushed to her side.

"Where's the worst of it?" he asked, helping her to the ground.

"Left hand. It'll heal."

He slung his medic bag off his shoulder and pulled out several thick dressings. Raising her hand, he swore at whatever he saw there before applying pressure. "You've had worse. You'll be okay."

"Thanks for the lasso and lightning assist," she croaked out. Because of the lack of heat from the bolt that had landed between her and Bolverkr, she'd known it was one of Bryce's illusions. The distraction had given her time to pounce as the giant hesitated, not wanting to get electrocuted.

"You looked like you needed a distraction."

"I did."

"We make a pretty good team," he said, rain dripping over his hair and down his handsome face.

"Damn right we do."

THIRTY-ONE

Storm relished the warmth of Bryce's hand as he held hers. They'd eaten dinner and gotten lost in conversation—travel, Olivia, medicine, and Norse mythology.

He smiled, his face radiant by the candlelight. "Good first date?"

"Wonderful first date. Your lasagna was phenomenal."

"Good enough to add to your travel blog?"

She chuckled. "I'm going to keep this one to myself. I don't want a bunch of people showing up at your ranch house asking to taste your lasagna."

He laughed.

"That was not a metaphor, by the way."

She had supplied the ambience, and he had brought the food. She'd worn a navy dress with a frilled collar while he'd worn slacks and a button-down shirt. His golden lariat was around his waist as a belt.

He leaned back and looked around the room. "So, this is your yacht."

She looked at the spotless indoor dining area. A few months ago she'd made peanut butter and jelly sandwiches here with a small, frightened girl. "This is mine. The owner decided she didn't want the boat and certain memories that accompanied it, so this was her form of payment."

He stood up and pulled Storm into his arms. "Thank you for being my date."

In the background, Adele quietly sang "Make You Feel My Love" on the radio.

"Well, you had a fair point. We should go on at least one date before you meet the rest of my family."

Bryce began swaying with her to the music. "It feels so good to have you in my arms."

"I've mostly wanted to stay in them since meeting you."

When he leaned down and kissed her neck, she drew in a sharp breath. Desire flared through her.

"I'd like you to stay. With me. With Olivia."

She closed her eyes. "There's a war coming, haven't you heard?"

Bryce drew back and carefully looked at Storm's expression. "Then what do you want?"

"Helen won't stop coming for your daughter. I want to keep the two of you close. Not me staying with you, but you staying with me. This boat isn't under my name. She can't find you here. It means home schooling Olivia—or rather, boat-schooling her. Just until we can stop Helen. I had Sky put wards on the boat to help keep it protected."

He nodded. "After the bomb, I've been wondering how I was going to protect her. I appreciate the team Raine has had on her, but that's not sustainable. The boat is a good idea. Not ideal for raising a child and too socially isolated, but fortunately only temporary."

"Temporary," she agreed, though they didn't know if the duration was in months or years.

"Will you visit often?" he asked. "I'll be miserable if I have to go months at a time without seeing you while you hunt Helen."

Storm bit her lip. "How often is too often?"

He pressed his lips to her collarbone. "I'd take you every night."

"Rainbow Bright has his transporting abilities. The three of us are teaming up. He can bring me home every night and pick me up in the morning. Unless we have work specifically taking place at night or are in a different time zone."

Bryce smiled. "I'd like that. I'd like waking beside you and enjoying a cup of coffee before you head off to work, fighting demons. I'd join you, but I won't leave Olivia."

"I know. I love you, Bryce."

"We're going to make this work. After we win the war," he wriggled his body against hers, "do you think you'll still do your travel blog?"

What would the future hold? She'd never made long-term plans. She felt she belonged for the first time in a very long time. She had her family back with her sisters and Will, and now she had a new one.

"I'd like to settle. I've spent over a decade traveling, as if staying on the move would somehow keep the pain of the past from catching up to me."

"Settle on, say, a ranch with weekend boat rides in the Gulf? Maybe sleep under a roof with a man who makes killer lasagna? Maybe forever?" He shook his head. "I'm sorry. Too soon. I'm pushing for a commitment, and we're so new to each other. Don't answer that question. Let's just enjoy this moment." His arms tightened around her.

She lay her head on his shoulder. "I only see a future with you, Bryce." She arched up toward him, pressing her lips to his.

She would never tire of the feel of this man's body against hers. Their mouths collided, softly at first but quickly exploding into burning need.

"Ever made love on a boat?" she asked between kisses.

"No."

"Me neither."

"I'd take you anywhere." He kissed his way down her neck and across her collarbone.

There were too many clothes between them. She unbuttoned his shirt, feeling his muscles flex beneath her.

"I'll never tire of this. Of us. Of the feel of you," she said.

He reached around and unzipped the back of her dress. "I'm glad you wore something easy to slip out of. I've been envisioning stripping it off you since I first laid eyes on it."

"Have you now?" The outfit slid off her shoulders and down to the floor.

"Wait," she said hoarsely. She reached up and unclasped her necklace with the engagement ring and set it on the table.

"Storm, you don't have to do that."

"I know. But I'm better." She walked to him and placed a hand on his cheek. "I'm ready for whatever is next with you."

Reaching around once more, he twisted the hooks of her bra to disconnect it. She slipped out of it, watching his eyes widen with lust as he lowered himself to caress her breast with his tongue. She gasped and fisted a hand into his hair.

He worked a hand lower, his mouth higher, and she opened up for him—mind, body, and soul.

"I'll never tire of this either," he said.

"You're wearing too many clothes," she said breathlessly as his fingers stroked her.

He chuckled. "So I am."

By the time they reached the bed below deck, they were both naked. He covered her with his body, kissing as his hands roamed—kneading and caressing. His tongue worked over every sensitive part of her until she was gasping her release.

"That was incredible," she said, feeling divine.

He left for a moment to slip on a condom before he was back at her side. He added an illusion of them surrounded by floating clouds.

"I think we should repeat all the positions of our first night together," he said as he eased inside of her.

She gasped, digging her fingertips into his hips.

"Okay." She was certain she'd agree to anything when he was overloading her senses with pleasure like this. "I want you."

As he moved and slid deeper, they gave themselves over to each other and the magic they felt in the ecstasy of passion when they merged.

EPILOGUE

"Oh, heavens me! You came. I just knew you'd come. Wyatt, didn't I tell you yesterday our baby Storm will come back?" Ida's red and green dress blew in the breeze that swept around the country home.

Wyatt smiled, hands tucked into the pockets of his khaki shorts under his Hawaiian shirt of abstract palm trees decorated in Christmas lights. "Raine did call saying she was bringing Storm over."

Storm took turns hugging her parents, her mother taking a long embrace, which she didn't mind. She'd deprived herself of hugs for a very long time. She'd worn a red dress with a green scarf while Bryce had sported dark brown slacks and a white button-down shirt with his cowboy boots.

When Storm stepped back, Raine and Will took turns hugging their parents. Raine wore blue jeans and a forest green blouse with a red beaded necklace. Will also wore jeans but with a red sweater. Sky hopped in next for hugs, wearing a vibrant green dress that accentuated her red hair.

Meanwhile, her parents habitually looked like they were about to take a tropical vacation or perhaps had just returned from one.

Storm realized her mother was looking expectantly at her.

"Mom, this is Bryce Chambers. He's my..." she hesitated. Was he her boyfriend? She wasn't sure she could say the word, not because she wasn't devoted to him, because she was, but she hadn't had a significant other in so long and the term boyfriend sounded so juvenile compared to what she felt for Bryce. "We're together. Permanently."

Beside her, Bryce chuckled. "For as long as she'll have me." He extended a hand, but Ida was having none of it. She stepped right into him and hugged him.

"I don't know if you had some part in bringing my baby back to me. Some part in healing her. But I believe you did. You and her sisters. Thank you all."

"All right, Ida," Wyatt said. "You're going to scare him off if you keep that up." His voice was all amusement and adoration.

She pulled away to straighten. "Well, just look at them," she told her husband. "His love makes her happy, doesn't it? Okay, okay, enough of that." She waved her hand in front of her face and moistening eyes.

"Who is this adorable creature?"

Bryce smiled. "My daughter Olivia."

Olivia wore a sparkling red dress with her hair in a braid.

"Charmed," Ida said, shaking her hand.

"And this is my mother, Maddie."

"Yes, we met at Sky's house the other day. How are you?"

"Well," Maddie said. She'd worn jeans and a silver top with sequins.

"Dinner is just about ready," Ida said.

They took their seats at the table, Storm marveling at the simple pleasure of family. She was back in the house she'd grown up in, surrounded by family who loved her and whom she loved. They had welcomed her back so simply. Just that quick, the world was as it should be. Of course, there were still monsters lurking in the darkness who needed to be dealt with, but these people were as much a part of her as her Valkyrie side.

Around the table, they took turns relating stories from childhood. Three sisters riding horses. Raine and Storm sneaking out of the house to see their boyfriends. The time they'd set half a field to flame with Fourth of July fireworks.

The food tasted delicious, and Storm felt amazed to be back at home with all of her family, new and old.

A fork clattered onto a plate, drawing everyone's attention to Olivia. With a distant look in her eyes, she stood on her chair. Her voice rang in a deeper, otherworldly tone.

> *"Three by three*
> *By the faith of the tree*
> *Face the demon she.*
> *Rain bleeds*
> *Storm screams*
> *Sky shatters."*

When she collapsed, Bryce caught her. He was pale with worried brows.

"Oh, my," Ida gasped.

Sky stood by her side, one hand resting on her shoulder.

"Is she okay?" Storm crowded close to Bryce's side, feeling Olivia's forehead.

"It'll pass," Bryce said in a shaky voice. "She'll need something to write with," he added.

Ida and Wyatt rushed to the other room.

Raine and Will exchanged worried glances. "We've read those words before," her sister said. "They were part of the Noble prophecies."

Bryce set her gently back in her chair as Olivia blinked her eyes open. "Are you okay, sweetie?"

"I'm okay," she said with a smile. "Is there pie for dessert?"

<<<THE END>>>

ANKA'S ORB

Bonus novella

When a man introduces a mysterious Norse relic to Anka before his untimely death, she realizes the power within the orb must not fall into the hands of darkness. With the help of Denny, a human with ties to the shadow world, she sets out to retrieve the magical device before it can be delivered into the hands of Helen.

Can they track down the orb before the goddess of darkness secures it, or will the forces of evil have it within their power to end the world?

CHAPTER
ONE

When the bell to Anka's store chimed, signaling the opening of her front door, the scent wafting in struck her, overpowering the Moksh Agarbatti incense burning on the counter. She wished she'd closed early rather than deal with the next customer.

Sweaty biker looking for his next tattoo? Or maybe a homeless person had wandered in off the street, looking for a handout. Hank had been lingering in the alley ever since she'd bought him a muffuletta from the sandwich shop on the strip.

Pushing out of her seat in the back room, she scratched her small diamond nose ring and walked toward the front.

A haggard-looking man she didn't recognize stood just inside her shop. His brown skin had a waxy appearance, and his sunken brown eyes stared into nothingness. Dreadlocks hung down to his shoulders to meet a tattered *Star Wars* T-shirt of the earlier cast posing for action. Baggy pants draped over what she suspected were thin legs and tapered down to sandaled feet. In his left hand, he held a gold ball.

He stared directly at her with those hollow eyes, not gazing around her tattoo parlor the way a prospective customer might. Maybe he was a homeless man, but Anka would be surprised if Hank let another person in his territory.

Before she could ask what he was doing in her store, the man collapsed.

Shock and worry replacing her annoyance and angst, she hoisted herself on her cash register counter, pivoted on the smooth leggings over her butt, and dropped to the floor.

Rushing over, she crouched beside him. "Are you hurt?"

In lieu of an answer, he thrust the orb in her direction.

She batted his hand away. "Let me see where you're hurt. I'm going to lift your shirt." She didn't notice any blood on his clothing. Perhaps he had some type of medical condition. Hypoglycemia?

She raised up his shirt and gasped at the sight of bruises over his chest and abdomen. Internal bleeding then.

She thrust her right hand into the air, palm facing the opening to the back office, where her mobile phone lay on her desk. The device flew across the room, into her hand, and she faced the screen toward her, unlocking it with facial recognition.

Before she could dial 911, the man's hand shot out and gripped her forearm. Startled, she let out a soft cry.

"Keep it safe," the man said through gritted teeth as he thrust the orb in her direction once more.

"Okay, okay. I'll take it, but you have to release me so I can call an ambulance for you."

"No time. I'm Dune."

Because the gold ball was now in her face, she had no choice but to take it. She grasped it with her left hand as she turned back to the phone in her right, and as soon as her fingers closed over the cool metal, power from the orb pulsed through her. Whispered magic called to her, tugging gently at her telekinetic abilities, coaxing them to be used. She'd never felt anything like it.

In awe, she stared down at the powerful relic. The smooth,

polished gold glinted under the fluorescent lights of her shop. Carved into the metal were Norse runes.

"What is this?" she asked the man.

"Odin's Orb," he croaked out before his eyes rolled back in his head.

Dropping her phone, she felt for a pulse. His waxy skin was moist with sweat, and nothing bounded against her fingertips on his neck. Glancing at his chest, she saw no rise and fall. Turning again to her phone, she started to dial for emergency services. She needed to call them and then start CPR.

The door chime sounded again, and she jerked her head up, hoping for help, but instead, slinking into her shop were three gray-skinned abominations dressed in black tattered clothing. She went absolutely still as her blood turned to ice.

The power of the orb called to her once more. Tugging, pulling again at her powers. The way a puppy might tug the end of a rope, wanting its master to play.

The intruders' sunken black eyes fixated on the orb in her hand. There was no escaping this. She was outnumbered—three undead against one unarmed Asgardian with embarrassingly weak tele-kinetic abilities.

Simultaneously, the three humanoid creatures launched them-selves at her. Acting on instinct, she squeezed her hand tight over the orb, invoking her telekinetic abilities. The power rushed out, pouring over and through her in a split second before bursting out of her. In the blink of an eye, the three undead fell to the floor, their rib cages folded in on themselves, crushing the organs in their chest cavity.

Panting and horrified, Anka scooted back from the destruction she'd caused. She couldn't stay here. The undead were, well, not living, and, therefore, killing them by crushing their heart and lungs would probably only slow them down. She scampered to her feet, still clutching her phone in one hand and the orb in the other, as she raced toward the back door of her shop.

Anka burst through the rear entrance, shoving her phone in the back pocket of her black pants. She needed to reach her car and drive somewhere safe. The undead didn't have driving skills. It was her understanding that they rose from their earthly graves, did Helen's bidding, and then rested once more until called upon.

Suddenly something hard collided with her side. As the impact knocked her to the ground, agony flared through her right hip. Stars swam through her eyes as the pain intensified. She blinked watering eyes to see the dirty concrete of the alley behind the strip mall. Looking up, she panicked.

Five undead surrounded her.

One held a metal pipe, which she expected was the weapon her throbbing hip would forever hate. Another demon bent over and scooped up the orb she had evidently dropped when she'd fallen. Without the magical device, escape wouldn't be as simple as crushing the ribs of her attackers.

If she didn't think of something fast, she would be dead, just like the poor man on the floor of her tattoo shop. He'd been the last person before her to hold the orb. She wondered how many more had fallen in its presence.

She stretched out a hand, trying to call the orb to her.

It jerked in the creature's grip until another demon stomped on her hand, and she screamed in pain.

The undead with the blunt instrument brought the pipe over his head to bring down another crushing blow to her body or head, but before it could strike, a blur of metal plowed into him.

She gaped as Hank let go of the careening shopping cart he had just rammed into her attacker. He bent over, picked up the metal pipe, and when he stood, began swinging it at the undead closest to him who'd attacked Anka. Metal crunched into the brittle bone of the creature's jaw.

"Get out of here!" Hank yelled to her.

She pushed through the pain in her hip and her throbbing hand, managing to clamor to her feet. "Come with me," she pleaded to Hank.

He was no match for these monsters. Perhaps he could strike a debilitating blow to a human, but that would only slow these things down. He didn't know what he was up against.

"Go!" he screamed at her again.

One advanced on her and she instinctively punched him in the face. The pain of impact on her already injured hand shot up to her elbow, and she cried out again. The creature stumbled back as the other four bored down on Hank. He disappeared with a muffled battle cry under a heap of gray skin and the smell of decaying flesh.

Anka's heart pounded as her head swirled with a mix of emotions. She couldn't defeat these undead. Hank was buying her the seconds she needed to escape. As soon as they finished killing him, they would pounce on her. Her options were to make it to her car and flee while she had the chance, and Hank would certainly die, or fight back, and both of them would die.

CHAPTER

TWO

D enny slid off his stationary exercise bike, panting, and swiped a towel across his forehead as he glanced around his home gym. Tomorrow was weights day.

Forty-five minutes of cardiovascular perfection, he told himself as he gulped water.

Tossing the towel over his shoulder, he walked to his kitchen and opened the refrigerator. The leftover Chinese noodles from his poor decision-making yesterday stared at him. He needed to resist those carbohydrates and the urge to order a large, all meat pizza take-out. He hadn't lost thirty pounds in the last year just to fall off the wagon and gain it all back in moments of weakness.

After closing the fridge, he poured himself a glass of bourbon, contemplating a shower and a movie. Such had become most of his Friday nights.

A pounding sounded on his front door, frantic and forceful.

Possibilities of who would be so demanding formed a list in his mind as he made for the door. Storm Thoren didn't knock. Will Decker and Raine Thoren-Decker teleported directly inside their destination. Family called first. That left the dreaded other likelihood

—a patient. He kept his home address unlisted, but people had ways of finding out personal information.

Grabbing his phone off the counter in case he needed to call the police, he continued to the front of the house. When he glanced through the glass panes on one side, he spotted a slight woman in dirt-smeared clothing. Not one of his patients.

He opened the door. She was short, maybe five-five, with a punk styled dark-brown hair—shaved on one side and long on the other. Piercings decorated her nose and brow. She wore faux leather pants, worn, scuffed, black boots, and a white t-shirt that was torn in places. Her face was a medium brown with sculpted cheekbones. Pale gold eyes stared back at him. She was beautiful, despite the panicked look on her face.

"Are you lost?" he asked.

She walked past him, barging into his house with a pronounced limp. "Storm said you could help. We need to get an orb back from Helen."

Flabbergasted, Denny closed his door. Throwing the assassin's name around was probably the most effective way to keep him from calling the police, but if Storm had sent this woman to his door, why hadn't she called to prepare him?

He looked down at his phone, which was still on DO NOT DISTURB from during his work-out routine. Ah, she had called.

Shaking his head, he turned to the disheveled beauty. "There are so many things wrong with those statements. First, I'm a psychologist. I don't retrieve things, least of all from the evil woman who is so powerful that the two strongest women and their significant others I know are teaming up to take her down. And, mind you, they haven't succeeded for at least a year now—and not for lack of trying. Lastly, I don't even know you."

"I'm Anka Bashki, a descendant of Vali."

Like that explained anything. "Okay. Cool. Didn't take you for a valley girl."

Anka rolled her eyes. "Vali was the son of Odin and Rindr. He's best known for avenging the death of Odin and Frigg's son, Baldur."

"Not a fan of vengeance. Psychologists prefer talking through issues rather than resorting to violence."

He needed another sip of his bourbon, and Anka looked like she could use a glass of water. He walked toward the kitchen as she followed, limping behind him. A new injury or something chronic?

He was about to ask when she said, "Well, there's no talking to draugr."

"And those are—?"

"Undead. Helen's obedient servants."

Denny choked on his liqueur. "Are you serious? There are zombies among us?"

As he poured Anka a glass of water, he searched his memory, trying to recall if Storm had ever mentioned those. He thought not, but a lot of what she'd said to him was foreign because he'd known nothing of Norse mythology until the Valkyrie and her family had opened his eyes to the existence of supernatural magic lingering in this world from the fallen realms of lore.

Anka continued, "They aren't commonly walking the streets. They only emerge when they do Hel's bidding." When he handed her a glass, she drank eagerly.

"Handy, I suppose, to have little fetching demons. Don't guess they'd clean houses and pay bills on command."

She crossed her arms. "You're not taking this seriously."

Seeing the irritation and even hurt in her eyes, he sighed. "Humor is a defense mechanism. To be clear, I've been terrified of creatures lurking in dark alleys ever since I learned about the shadow world." He scrubbed a hand over his face. "Okay. Why don't you start at the beginning?"

"Do you have any food?"

Denny grinned. He liked a woman who thought of food amidst a crisis.

Five minutes later, he set a steaming bowl of noodles in front of

Anka and sat across from her at his kitchen table, holding his empty glass. He wanted another drink but was fairly certain this was a conversation for which he needed to remain sober.

Anka felt bone deep exhaustion as she sat in this stranger's kitchen. Her entire body ached and throbbed, though sitting still was a relief.

"I'm a tattoo artist. More specifically, I design tattoos for magical beings. Those of the light. Some inks are for protection and some are to enhance existing magical abilities. Anyway, I was at my shop when a man walked in and collapsed on my floor. He pushed this golden orb at me right before he died. He called it Odin's Orb. When I touched it, it was like it spoke to me, calling to my magic."

"Like the ability to make magical tattoos?"

She didn't hear skepticism or a patronizing tone but genuine curiosity.

She shifted uncomfortably in her chair, unaccustomed to sharing details about herself, much less with someone she'd only just met. But Denny had a compassionate demeanor, and she would trust that the Valkyrie Storm had led her toward someone who could help.

"I have telekinetic abilities."

Denny's eyebrows shot up. "Whoa. You can move things with your mind?"

With her mind, she raised the bottle of bourbon from the kitchen counter and drifted it through the air to the table.

His mouth fell open. "Cool. Hella cool."

She felt a blush at his amazement. "Small objects. Nothing earth shattering."

"It looks remarkable to me." His soft, caring tone conveyed he was not only genuinely impressed with her ability but troubled by her dismissal of the magic as minor or insignificant.

Perhaps she was dismissive of it, but then she wouldn't be the first.

"I was about to call for an ambulance when the man in my shop lost his pulse and three undead barged into my store. I reflexively reached for the power of the orb and killed them... or, you can't kill the undead, I crushed them."

"Crushed them?"

"With my ability to move objects plus the power of the orb, I folded their rib cages in on themselves, crushing their hearts and lungs, and they crumbled to the floor." She made a motion with her hand from open to a closed fist but stopped and grimaced from the pain.

Denny jumped up and leaned forward. "Oh, my gosh. Your hand! It's purple and swollen."

"They smashed it under a boot."

"You need ice on that thing. How are you not curled up in a ball of pain right now?" He grabbed a plastic bag and rushed to his refrigerator to fill it with ice.

"I shed plenty of tears on the drive here. Now it's mostly a dull throbbing as long as I don't move it."

"Here. Rest it on the table." He laid a towel down before gently, wedging her hand between two packs of ice.

When she sucked in a breath, he backed away and sat back down. "I should get you some ibuprofen. Do you want to lie down? No. You need a hospital and x-rays."

"Maybe," healthcare wasn't exactly in her budget, "but let me get through the rest of the story. I thought I could escape out the back, but I was ambushed. They knocked me down and took the orb." She thought about how she'd left Hank to die as a long silence hung in the kitchen.

Denny frowned. "I'm really sorry for everything you've been through. I don't know much about this Norse shadow world. While I can lend you a sympathetic ear, I'm not really sure why Storm sent you to me. I'm just a—what does she call it?—a hubble. Standard human bloodline. It sounds like those guys got what they were after with the orb. Are you worried they'll still come after you?"

"I was scared. I just moved to the area, and I don't know anyone other than Hank, and we only ever had one conversation. I think she sent me here just to have a safe place to go and regroup."

"Who is Hank?"

"The really sweet homeless man who used to hang outside the alley of the strip mall. The draugr killed him when he was fighting them off of me. He battled them in order to give me time to get away. I ran. I ran, and I left him there to die." She lowered her head to let the tears fall in her lap.

"Sounds to me like you would've died too if you'd stayed there." He tugged at his earlobe. "I don't know how you wanna play this. We don't really know each other that well. If Storm sent you here, then I trust she wouldn't send someone dangerous to me—especially to my residence. If you trust she wouldn't send you to someone dangerous, you're welcome to my guest bedroom. You need a good night's sleep, and you can regroup tomorrow."

"No, no, I'm a burden to no one." She stood.

"Nobody said anything about a burden."

When she went to take a step, pain shot up her hip, and she had to clutch the table to keep from falling.

In an instant, Denny was by her side with one hand on her elbow. His touch was soft, despite the calluses that brushed her skin.

"Yeah, let's start with the couch, some ice, some ibuprofen, and then you can argue with me about how you're ready to drive yourself to a motel when you can barely walk."

CHAPTER

THREE

Anka woke to the smell of bacon, eggs, and coffee. The strange bed she'd slept in was soft. Delightfully soft. She thought about the kind man who owned this bed. He'd been attentive, with ice and medicine, food and helping her hobble around his house.

He'd been compassionate and empathetic when hearing her story. She'd shed tears in front of that stranger, and she never cried in front of anyone. She didn't like the vulnerability of it, but she'd been exhausted.

She could fix it.

This morning, she would present herself entirely composed, thank him politely for his hospitality, and be on her way. They could both forget her emotional moment, and she could relinquish the sense of safety and security she felt in his proximity.

As soon as she moved, pain reminded her of her injuries. Her hip throbbed as her swollen hand sent tentacles of hot agony all the way to her elbow. He'd tried to insist she seek medical care, even offered to drive her, but she didn't want to use an emergency room and leave a trail of her whereabouts. She also didn't need a mound of medical bills.

Using her uninjured hand, she threw off the covers before sliding to the edge of the bed. Looking down, she was reminded Denny had given her one of his t-shirts so she wouldn't have to put her dirty clothes back on after her shower.

His shirt draped down to her knees as she stood. When she put weight on the leg with the hip injury, heat spirited through her buttocks like she'd been stabbed with the fiery crown of Sutr.

She bit back a cry.

She'd been in scrapes and had injuries before. The best course of action was to stay mobile. Attempting to go back to bed and sleep it off would be a mistake. Besides, she had places to go.

She hobbled out to the kitchen, well aware she looked like something the undead had dragged in—well, she kind of was.

Denny was in the kitchen flipping bacon. He wore sweatpants and a T-shirt as he whistled *What a Wonderful World*. When he glanced at her, he clearly noted her limp but didn't comment.

"Coffee?" he asked.

"Thanks." She sat heavily in the chair by the counter.

"Sugar? Cream?"

"Black."

He placed a steaming cup in front of her, asking, "Not a morning person?"

"No. But evidently you are."

"There's something about watching the sunrise every morning. Regardless of the roller coaster of life with the constant change and adaptation we all make, like it or not, that sunrise doesn't change. She greets you every morning. No matter what you did yesterday or what you'll do today."

"Okay." She regarded his cheery mood with wariness.

"There's no judgment from that glorious sun. Only light."

"He's a poet, a cook, a therapist, and a philanthropist."

Denny cocked his head to one side. "Philanthropist?"

"You took in a homeless person last night."

"Oh, so I did." He beamed at her before turning back around to stir the eggs. "And yet, still single. Who knows what it takes these days to attract the opposite sex?" The humor rang lightly in his voice.

Anka shrugged. "I can tell you it's not being a tattoo artist."

With a chuckle, he scraped eggs onto a plate beside hash browns and bacon and plopped the dish in front of her.

"Thank you. This looks delicious." She wiggled a finger at the strips of bacon. "I don't eat meat though. Eggs, yes. Pork, no."

As Denny scraped the crispy bacon onto his plate, he said, "Will it offend you if I do?"

"Not at all."

"Then I'll make you a trade. I'll take your bacon and you can have my hash browns."

He scraped the seasoned potatoes onto her plate.

"That's not necessary. But they do look good."

He shrugged. "I don't really need the carbs. I'm one of those lucky individuals who—in the world of carb-centric foods—reacts poorly to carbs. I was moving toward prediabetic until I cut the carbs and lost weight. Now my hemoglobin A1c is beautiful, so long as I win the battle against food addiction every single day."

He was tall with bulk that looked to be mostly muscle.

"You look like you're winning." As soon as the words were out of her mouth, she realized they sounded like a come on. Her cheeks grew hot.

Denny only smiled. "Don't be embarrassed on my behalf. A beautiful woman in my kitchen tells me I look good? She just made my day." He crunched into a piece of bacon before refilling both their coffees.

She relaxed. The sensation was unusual, since she seldom felt comfortable enough around people to relax. She avoided most social encounters because of her tendency to feel awkward around others. She suspected her awkwardness had to do with growing up on the streets where survival trumped socializing.

She took a bite of eggs, followed by potatoes. "These are delicious."

"Not too spicy?"

"I like spice."

"An artist, good taste in food, hard-core enough to fight through some tough injuries, and pretty. Seems like the full package."

"And yet still single," she mimicked him.

He chuckled again but was interrupted by the ringing of his phone. He set his fork down and fished his phone out of his pants pocket.

Holding it up, he waggled it at Anka with a shake of his head. "Seems Storm is checking up on you."

He laid the phone down flat and answered it, setting it to speaker. "Good morning, Storm," Denny greeted her.

"Is Anka with you? She's not answering her phone."

"She's here. It's probably dead. I didn't think to give her a charger last night."

"Hi, Storm," Anka said.

"I'll come over so we can talk about that relic." With that, Storm hung up the phone.

Denny rolled his eyes. "Well, at least she gave me a little warning this time." When rainbow colors shimmered in his living room, he added, "Only a little."

Storm teleported into his living room wearing black leggings and a black leather jacket. She had long dark hair and smooth light skin. Beside her was a man dressed in a navy suit with neatly combed brown hair.

"Something smells amazing," the man said. "Hi, I'm Will." He waved at Anka.

She nodded. "I remember. You transported Storm the last time."

"Yeah."

"Anka, you're okay?" Storm asked.

"Yeah. But we need to get that relic back from Helen's undead."

"Okay, okay," Denny interjected. "I get we're all about business and saving the world and what not. Can we just take a breather before we delve into magical relics and evil roaming the world? Will, there are some leftover eggs, hash browns, and bacon. You're welcome to help yourself."

Will brightened. "At least Storm dragged me along to somewhere with food this time."

"You can set boundaries," Denny retorted.

Will chewed on a bite of eggs. "Mmm. Good. Thing is, when she has me take her somewhere urgent, it's usually important. Or at the very least interesting." He scooped up a forkful of hashbrowns and filled his mouth.

Denny turned back to Storm. "Anka is not okay. She's been injured. Her hand is swollen like the Stay Puff Marshmallow Man and she's walking with a limp. And while I'm on a roll and nobody's interrupting me, let's get through some other normal human formalities. How are Bryce and Olivia?"

Anka knew Bryce, since she'd been the one to place the protection tattoo on his back. Olivia, she didn't know.

Storm relaxed slightly, as if conceding he was right to slow down the pace she had initially set. "They're good. Everybody's healthy and doing well. Bryce is learning to fight with his sword and his lasso, and Olivia is homeschooling between Bryce and Maddie."

"And what is Raine up to?"

"Surveillance. We found a nest of Midgard serpents on an island in the Mediterranean. It's a cell Helen planted for in-breeding. We're preparing an attack." She sat down beside Anka and inspected her hand.

He swallowed. "Surveillance. You could have stopped there."

Ignoring Denny's obvious discomfort with the idea of an island of snake-like creatures, she said to Anka, "I know a healer named Apollo. Will can take you to him."

Will tossed up his hands, a piece of bacon between his fingers. "There she goes again."

"The orb," Anka said, ignoring their banter. "It needs to be found. It needs to be confiscated before it reaches Helen."

"Start from the beginning," Storm suggested.

"This guy named Dune collapsed on the floor of my tattoo parlor, shoving the orb at me."

"Dune?" Will stood up straighter. "Young man with dreadlocks?"

"Yeah, you know him?"

"Raine and I met him. Well, we rescued him from a Dark Elf. Dune is a stag shapeshifter."

"Was."

"Oh, I'm sorry to hear that."

"He died in front of me. Internal bleeding, I think. Odin's Orb, he called the thing. Anyway, the draugr chasing him barged in and came after the orb." She shook her head. "The power of it. I crushed the rib cage of three undead as easily as squeezing a stress ball in my palm."

"Did what now?" Will asked.

"It enhances power. Tenfold. At least that's my guess. With my telekinesis I can move small objects. Add in the power of the orb, and I was able to collapse entire chest cavities. Can you imagine if the goddess of darkness wields it? The chosen won't stand a chance."

"I don't like the sound of this thing."

Anka resumed telling the story as she had to Denny last night, though with less blundering emotion compared to then.

"I agree. We need to get it back," Storm said when Anka finished.

Will turned to the cupboard and helped himself to a cup of coffee . "I can take Anka to Apollo for healing, then we can go to her shop. I'll scope out the place, talk to shop owners, see what surveillance footage I can get. Hopefully something on the ones who attacked you."

"Yes to all of that," Anka began, "but you won't get facial recognition off the dead."

"Somebody had to have driven them there," Denny interjected.

All eyes turned to him.

He shrugged. "At least, I've never seen a zombie movie where the undead can operate a car. Somebody drove them Anka's shop, right? And probably somebody who can pass for a normal human person has to get it back to Helen—who you think is somewhere in Europe, right? Maybe the camera caught that person."

Will nodded. "You're right. Also, delivery means a plane flight, which means passports and identification."

Anka looked around at the three people helping her. They were little more than acquaintances but trusted her about the importance of the orb and leaped at the chance to help. Their faith and willingness to assist were awe-inspiring.

"Let's do it," she said. "First, I need clothes."

Denny straightened. "Oh. I put yours in the wash last night. Should be all dry now."

He spoke the words matter-of-factly, but Anka was startled to think someone had washed her clothes for her. She'd never had a man wash her clothes. The act felt personal, intimate. She needed to reclaim her personal space despite the warmth she felt at his considerate behavior.

FOUR

After Will made a phone call to Apollo, Anka emerged dressed for the day in the clothes from yesterday. Now clean.

Will turned toward Anka. "Ready?"

Denny's brow furrowed. She was leaving already?

She nodded.

Storm straightened. "You need me to come with you? Ask witnesses what they saw?"

Will arched an eyebrow. "Are you kidding me? No, I do not need you intimidating and interrogating by-standers with no official capacity to do so."

Storm raised her hands in mock surrender.

With a salute, Will placed a hand on Anka's shoulder and shimmered into oblivion.

Denny waited until they were gone before leaning on the counter and addressing the Valkyrie. "You drop a beautiful woman in danger on my doorstep. I don't know whether to thank you or chastise you."

Storm shrugged as if to say her feelings would be unaffected regardless of which route he chose.

"How do you know her?" he asked.

"She did Bryce's tattoo. I went back to her on a case when I needed information on Norse markings. I figured who better to ask than a tattoo artist who understood the magic involved? Last night when she called for help, she was already in her car and away from danger. At that point, I thought she probably just needed a roof over her head and some friendly company."

He could see Storm's logic, respect it. If he was honest with himself, he was honored she regarded him as a reliable and trustable source for someone in need.

He also knew if he didn't set boundaries, she certainly wouldn't. "So long as this isn't a recurring event. I know you and your team are all doing important work, but when this crisis with Helen passes, I still need my day job—the one that keeps a roof over my head and food on my table."

"I won't jeopardize your job. This is a one-time ask. Anka is special. She's important to the cause."

"Special? In what way?"

Denny's limited understanding of the secret world of Norse bloodlines was that leaders of an organization called the Council of Mjölnir spanned across the world, and Shadow Guardians with different forms and levels of magic protected humans. Among the Norse bloodlines were prophets, who foretold of a forthcoming battle between Helen and the chosen ones.

"According to her grandmother, Anka helps the Shadow Guardians. I'm wondering if that moment is now, as it pertains to the orb."

"Her grandmother is also a Shadow Guardian?"

"Her grandmother is leader of the North American branch of the Council of Mjölnir. She's the woman who directly recruited and trained my sister, Raine."

"And how are things going with you?"

Storm gave him a sideways glance, and he knew she understood the question.

"I'm part of a team now. I see my family more regularly, and I have a new one with Bryce and Olivia. Life is good, or as good as can be expected while we work to try to track down Helen."

Denny had staged the intervention to help bring her out of isolation and rejoin her family, but he hadn't seen or heard much from her since that event almost a year ago. He hadn't been sure if the silence had been indicative of the success and she didn't need therapy any more or out of frustration toward him. Now he could see it was the latter.

He was admittedly happy for her. He sometimes missed her intrusions and impromptu counseling sessions; however, he would enjoy the satisfaction of knowing he played a role, though reluctantly at times, in helping a powerful Valkyrie coming into herself.

"Life is short and damn well ugly at times," he began. "Grab onto love and soak it all in while you have it. Take all that love into battle with you, because it's a kind of shield and a kind of power."

"I understand that now. I appreciate your help. Now and last year."

"That's what friends are for." He raised his coffee mug in salute before taking a gulp.

ANKA WATCHED in amazement as the rainbow colors faded around them. Less than a minute ago they were in Denny's home, now they were in someone else's home.

"That was the coolest thing I've ever seen."

"Thanks," Will said cheerfully.

The two of them stood in a house overlooking a sandy beach. Which shoreline, Anka didn't know. The view of lapping waves under the morning sun looked serene though.

Turning from the window, she noticed the owners of the home, seemingly unperturbed by their sudden appearance.

"This is Apollo and Rosalyn. Apollo is a healer and Roslyn is a shapeshifter with some pretty gnarly moves," Will announced with an easy grin.

Rosalyn had creamy skin with long white hair that contrasted her young appearance. Apollo was tan and a few inches shorter and broader than Will. His brown hair had sun-streaked highlights.

"Nice to meet you both. I've heard of you, Apollo. I think you're the only healer the shadow world knows. You're both Shadow Guardians?"

"That's right," Rosalyn said, her voice held a melodic English accent. "Chipping away at Helen's forces one demon at a time."

"They've been amazing," Will added. "This whole secret organization, the Council of Mjölnir."

"But you're one of them, aren't you?" Anka couldn't keep the slight chaffing out of her voice. She didn't like the thought of being surrounded by members of a group she'd been excluded from.

Will cast a sideways glance at her. "I'm not. I help them and they help me. They get rid of their demons, and I close FBI cases. It's a mutually beneficial relationship."

"So, you're like an honorary member?"

Will shrugged. "If people call me one it's because of my association with Raine, not from any official title. I'm happy in my role as an FBI agent. Anyone can contribute to helping to fight against Helen without directly being a guardian. Take Denny, for example. He was instrumental in bringing Storm into the fold—reconnecting her with her sister so she could join us. He's not a Shadow Guardian but helped us tremendously."

She thought of the tattoos she'd given Jake and Bryce—helping others without being a Shadow Guardian.

"How can I be of assistance?" Apollo asked, his voice light with a slight Southern accent.

Anka held up her hand. "I'm hoping for the use of my hand back. And I took a good blow to the hip."

"No problem. Let's see what we have here." Apollo approached, holding one hand out, palm up.

Anka set her injured hand on top of his. She felt warmth, followed by a burning sensation and then itching, and she sucked in a breath as her eyes watered.

"Almost done now," he said gently.

She thought of the orb and wondered what such a power might spew from the hands of a healer like him. Heal an entire cancer ward? A hospital? Perhaps. But as long as Helen walked Midgard, the orb needed to be hidden somewhere safe. A mass healing would certainly enable the goddess of death to track it down more easily.

Apollo moved a hand to hover over her injured hip. She started to ask him if he needed to see the injury in order to heal it, but before she could speak, she felt the warm itching and burning of his magic deep in the joint.

Relieved the pain had subsided and she would have no lasting injury, she flexed and extended her fingers.

"Thank you."

Apollo stepped back. "No problem. We're all part of the same team."

She thought he looked a little paler, like the use of his magic taxed his body a bit. Would use of the orb cause less consumption of personal energy or more?

"Is this the place?" Will asked.

Anka nodded and her heart sunk at the sight of the dead body on the floor of her tattoo shop. After they'd said goodbye to Rosalyn and Apollo, Will had brought her here.

"I think he's my age," she said sadly. She was twenty-eight. There was a time when she didn't think she'd live past twenty, but now she couldn't imagine dying so young.

Will looked down and shook his head. "I hate this damned war. Too many people are dying too young."

He pushed through the front door of her shop, gingerly stepping past Dune, neck craning in different directions as he looked around the exterior. She followed him outside the building.

"You can transport anywhere in under thirty seconds?"

"Most places," he said. "It has to be a place I've been, a person I've met more than briefly, or a place they know. For instance, just because I know of Helen it doesn't mean I can transport to her lair and launch a surprise attack. I don't know where she lives, and I haven't met her personally or spent time in her space enough to find her through the Bifröst."

"What about in a fight? Could you just move from one place to another, dodging the undead?"

"I'm not fast enough for that. I've tried. I've worked hard at making myself faster and managed it down from minutes to seconds. But dodging a bullet or a fist? No."

"I might be able to help with that. I'll think about it. There might be a tattoo we could do to augment the magic. Specific runes."

"Like Bryce's tattoo?"

"Not something quite so elaborate. His had to be large and more intricate because I was taking someone with no protective shield ability and giving him a powerful shield. For you, we're talking about a little extra something to enhance strong existing powers."

She followed him as he walked along the strip mall.

"I like the sound of that. Are there side effects or things that can go wrong with a magical tattoo?" he asked.

"Worst-case scenario is I don't get the magic right and it doesn't work. It's not as though I fumble the magic and you grow a third eye."

Will chuckled.

"What are you looking for?" she asked.

He pointed up at a lamppost in the parking lot and one corner of the strip mall where it made an L shape. "Security cameras. Like Denny said, if we can find whoever brought the draugr here, we can try to track that person. I'll hit up some shop owners and ask to look at their footage. See if I can get a photo. With that, I can have the FBI run facial recognition. I can't take you with me for this part."

She understood what Will was saying. If he was going to request information and look at video footage as an FBI agent, he might lose credibility if he brought along a civilian, especially someone as unconventional-looking as her. She took no offense because she liked her appearance and had no interest in tagging along with his investigation.

"Can you hang back in your shop? Maybe pack up some things you want to take with you since it's going to get shut down when I bring an investigative team here."

"Yeah. I want to check the cash register." She turned and walked away. She'd left the store unlocked all night since running for her life took precedence over her closing routine.

"Oh, and don't touch the body," Will called after her.

She glanced back at him to give him the most absurd facial gesture she could muster. Why on earth did he think she would? Gross.

She walked back into her shop and look down at Dune. Sadness swept over her. This poor man wouldn't have a regular burial for a while if the FBI was going to bag and tag him. Did he have a family? She wondered who would have to tell them. She'd seen dead bodies before, but none who had landed violently at her doorstep. She considered checking on Hank, but wasn't sure she could stomach what she might find.

She checked the register, thankful to see no one had taken the cash. She suspected if robbers had opened the door, they had probably left as soon as they noticed the body on the floor.

Tattoo artistry was, at best, a modest stream of income, so she couldn't afford a swanky place to rent and hang her shingle. In fact, she usually found slightly rundown strip malls like this one in sometimes sketchy parts of town. If she'd been robbed last night, it wouldn't have been the first time.

She gathered the cash, rolled it, and pocketed it before moving to the back room where she tugged a suitcase out from under a cot. After opening it up, she began dumping valuables and clothing inside. She could come back later for her other supplies when she found a new shop to rent, but for now, she couldn't sleep at this place. She definitely couldn't risk Helen knowing where she was.

As she was zipping up her suitcase, the front door chimed. Friend or foe? She thought she might now wonder that for the rest of her life when someone walked into her shop.

When she peeked around the corner, her heart gave a brief flutter to see a tall black man standing in the doorway.

Denny.

He looked down at the body on the floor and frowned.

She came out from the back office, lugging her suitcase. "Yeah. I try not to look at it."

"This is terrible." He swallowed. "I feel like we should cover him up, give him some dignity. But I suppose this is a crime scene, right?"

Anka nodded solemnly. "Will said not to disturb him."

"You had one hella terrible night."

"Yeah."

"All healed?"

"Yeah. What are you doing here?"

He shifted his weight on his feet. "You're going through a lot. I thought maybe you could use a friend. Or just somebody to lift heavy shit for you. Storm told me the name of your shop, so I found you on my GPS and drove over."

"That's very kind of you. And I'll hold you to that offer when I have to move all the rest of my things. For now, it's just a suitcase." She moved around the body and out the front door.

Denny followed. "Where will you stay?"

She shrugged. "Probably a motel. I can't rest until I know the orb is safe."

"You're welcome to stay with me until..." He let the word hang, making her wonder if he meant until she found the orb. Until she found a new place to live? Until either of them wanted to change the arrangement?

"You barely know me. Why would you help me?"

"Sometimes we get to know people by the quality of the time spent together, not the quantity. Have we spent less than twenty-four hours in each other's presence? Yes. But do I know you better than some casual acquaintances I've known for years? Also, yes."

She looked down at her packed bag as she considered his offer.

"You liked my eggs. Wait till you taste my homemade eggplant parmesan."

She laughed. "You clearly already know me well enough to know I can be bribed with food."

He chuckled—that warm, endearing sound she enjoyed. "I'll take that as a yes." As if it weighed nothing, he plucked her suitcase from her and they walked out the door to his car at the curb where he placed it in his trunk.

As he closed the lid, he peered around his car at her when she opened the passenger side door. "Anka, did you just pack an overnight bag from your tattoo shop? Are you living in there? In this place?" He gestured to the strip mall.

"I've stayed in worse." She rolled her shoulders and took a shaky breath. "Will you walk around back with me? I need to see Hank, and I don't want to do it alone. He saved my life. I would like to pay my respects."

"Absolutely."

CHAPTER
FIVE

enny drove back to his place, contemplating Anka's predicament. In one night, two men had died tragically in front of her. She was an entrepreneur on a tight budget whose livelihood was just shut down thanks to an evil she-demon with pet zombies. Right now, her only friend in proximity was a hubble with no magical abilities who probably couldn't do much to help her get back the orb she feared would land in Helen's hands.

Well, he didn't have magic, but he had compassion, good food, and a hella better place to sleep than a rented shop.

"Do you have family or anyone who needs an update on how you're doing?" he asked.

She shook her head. "I'm alone."

"By choice or circumstance?"

She glanced at him, and he took his eyes off the road long enough to give her an encouraging smile.

"Both."

"Sounds like a deeply honest answer."

She blew out a slow breath. "I was a difficult child—as you can imagine one would be when able to move objects with the mind. I was hell on my mom, who had no magical abilities. She couldn't exactly send me to daycare or school. We fought a lot. When I was seven, she threatened to put me in foster care, so I ran away. Living on the street was difficult but made easier by my abilities. I could steal whatever I wanted, and nothing could hold me—not handcuffs and not locked doors. My grandmother caught up with me when I was a teenager—one woman against the world with nothing to learn from anybody."

Anka sighed and shifted her weight in the passenger seat as she stared out the window. "She told me about my origins and the shadow world, adding to what I'd pieced together bit by bit living on the streets. I learned about how she trained Shadow Guardians, and I began having delusions that maybe I could be one." She fidgeted with the seatbelt. "You're way too easy to talk to, you know that?"

He took a gamble and reached over to hold her hand.

Voice unsteady, Anka continued. "My grandmother wouldn't take me in that way. Said being a Shadow Guardian wasn't in the cards for me. I assumed she'd meant I wasn't powerful enough. Being a pickpocket didn't create a robust résumé for a job of saving lives."

She turned to face Denny before looking down at their joined hands, her voice stronger as she said, "So I ran away again. I took odd jobs to make money, and I worked on becoming someone more respectable. She taught me that much. My love was of art, so I became a tattoo artist, and I learned how to infuse the ink with magic so the tattoo could be used by those with existing powers. Those with enough Nine Realms blood to activate the magic within the tattoo. Of course, those individuals are few and far between, so standard tattoos pay the bills."

She sucked in a deep breath, and on an exhale continued, "When word got out about my magical tattoos, I became a target, so I've had to move around a lot. My fear has always been I might be captured by Helen and put to work tattooing her creatures to strengthen them. I'd heard once about someone who lived in captivity for two years—a healer, forced to do her bidding. I think that was Apollo, whom Will brought me to today, but I didn't dare ask. I wouldn't wish something like that on my worst enemy."

"Maybe your grandmother kept you out of the Shadow Guardians directly so you could support them in a better way—with your magical art."

"Maybe."

"Sounds like your magic has been invaluable in making them stronger and more prepared to fight."

Anka nodded. "I found my niche."

"Self-made entrepreneur," he said with pride. "Still alone, though." Reluctantly withdrawing his hand, he pulled into his driveway and parked the car.

"Is this the part where you tell me I'll feel better if I reconcile with my past?"

He chuckled. "Some feel better visiting the people from their past. Sometimes it's closure. Sometimes it's a new beginning. If you decide visiting your mother and grandmother is part of your healing process, you don't have to do it alone."

She looked up at him with big golden brown eyes. He held her gaze, wanting her to feel the friendship he offered. This wasn't a counseling session; this was two friends in conversation. Except now that they were eye-to-eye in a confined space having just held hands, his thoughts turned less plutonic.

He glanced at her lips, wondering what they tasted like before he shook off the notion. He didn't prey on emotionally vulnerable women. Anka had been through an ordeal and didn't need him muddying the waters with his boyish infatuation.

ANKA'S EMOTIONS tumbled around inside her head as she tried to assess the situation. Denny seemed to have more than a casual interest in her. She found his easy compassion and broad features attractive, and the way his warm hand in hers offered comfort mixed with a simmering suggestion of something more. But she wouldn't let herself be swept away by some fanciful idea of a relationship with this man.

She followed him as he carried her suitcase toward his house. He started to set it down to reach for his keys when she unlocked the door and swung it open for him.

He chuckled. "If you're trying to impress me, it's working."

She opened her mouth in surprise. Was she? Damn, maybe she was.

He took her suitcase to the back room while she fixed herself a glass of water, drinking eagerly, unsure which emotions had her parched—her unprecedented recounting of growing up or the attraction she felt for a man she barely knew.

He set the suitcase down and busied himself in the kitchen. "Tea?" he asked.

"Uh, yes. Thanks"

How does he always seem to know just what to offer?

Maybe Denny had his own magic powers of a sort.

She slid into the barstool at the counter and watched him work. She couldn't help but admire his muscular form moving with easy grace. Mesmerizing.

He brought the steaming cup around the counter, and she raised her hands to take it, fingers touching his, but he didn't let go.

"You have no idea how incredible you are, do you?" he asked.

"Wh—what?"

"You have this amazing strength, enduring everything you've been through." He set the cup down and took a step back. "I'm sorry. I'm coming on strong because I like you. I don't want to make you uncomfortable."

She stood up, their bodies brushing, and positioned her lips just inches from his. "I like you too."

When he didn't move closer to her, she searched his face with her gaze. His eyes were wide, lips parted. He wouldn't move, she realized. He was too much of a gentleman, despite the heat his expression was emitting.

Less confident now, she stretched up and brushed her lips over his. Before she could enact a hasty retreat, he leaned closer, capturing her mouth and turning the chaste kiss into a scathing, scintillating experience. Her arms came around his neck as his hands gripped her waist. They deepened the kiss—all heady passion and a prelude to how this could escalate into something amazing.

When the phone rang, their lips broke apart. Denny's face looked as surprised as she felt.

He didn't move away as he withdrew his phone and set it down on the counter, placing it to speaker. "This is Denny and Anka."

"Will here. I've got everyone on speaker—Anka, Bryce, Denny, Raine, and Storm. You like how I did that in alphabetical order? Anyway, here's the situation: I was able to snag a photo off a security camera and had the FACE Services Unit run it through facial recognition. It came back with a name. Andrej Wølfe. According to Raine's contacts at the Council of Mjölnir, he's a known high-ranking lackey of Helen's. Here's the catch. FAA roster shows him flying out of three different airports tonight."

"Diversions," Raine said.

"Yes," Will agreed. "We have no way of knowing which airport the orb will be at."

"So, we pair up. Each couple stakes out an airport," Storm suggested

"Sounds like trying to find a needle in haystack," Bryce said.

"Fortunately, they're all private strips," Will said. "Less chance we risk public exposure or endangering civilians."

"Each couple?" Anka interjected. "You're talking about your friend, Denny, going into danger."

Silence hung in the air.

"I'm in," Denny said simply.

She looked up at him, speechless.

"Great. Thanks," Will said. "It'll be better to have pairs. I'll assign locations and a picture of the courier—this Andrej. The objective is to identify him and then alert the rest of us. We don't know what type of security force Helen will have in place to protect the orb, so reconnaissance only. Don't engage. Call the rest of us for back-up as soon as you spot the perp. We'll all converge and formulate a plan of attack."

"Yeah, that won't be a problem," Denny said.

"I mostly emphasized the call for help for Storm," Will countered.

She let out a huff.

"We'll call for help," Bryce assured him.

Will disconnected the call, and Anka blew out a puff of air, trying to deflate some of the tension she felt. She didn't want to go alone, but she didn't like the idea of putting Denny in danger either.

"So, tonight. He works fast." She strummed fingers on the counter.

"Tonight," he agreed, leaning forward and kissing the top of her forehead.

CHAPTER

SIX

Denny followed his car's GPS toward the hangar. He wore black sweatpants and a sweatshirt, unsure what tonight's events would entail.

Beside him sat a quiet Anka. She hadn't said much since their heated kiss. He wanted to talk about it but didn't want to push.

"Tell me about yourself," she said, interrupting his thoughts. "How'd you grow up and how did you choose psychology?"

"I had loving parents. Dad played football, so there was a lot of pressure for me to do the same. I enjoyed it, and my talents were good enough for a division three college on scholarship. But my real passion was talking to people, helping them reach their potential or deal with life's hardships."

"You're good at it. You definitely ooze trust-me vibes. In a day, you've learned more about me than anyone except my grandmother."

"I hope to learn more."

She ran a hand through the short side of her hair.

"Can we talk about that kiss?" he asked.

"No." She shook her head. "That wasn't a kiss. That was exploding fireworks and insta-flame."

"It wasn't a normal kiss for me either."

"We moved straight from sparks to roaring fire."

"My thoughts as well. Enough so that kiss will probably occupy my thoughts all night... maybe all the way up until the next one."

She smiled and laughed. The sight and sound so deeply moved him that he knew he would make it his objective to bring more joy into her life for as long as she'd let him.

THEY ARRIVED at the private hangar and drove past the guard gate beside a tall, closed, motorized, chain-link gate. A lone man sat on duty inside a square room lit by an interior bulb.

Denny kept driving, nerves growing edgier with the thought of breaking and entering private property.

"So, how do we do this?" he asked. "That guard probably has no part in any of this and is just working to earn a paycheck for his family."

"We passed a small gravel side road. We can park the car there in the darkness, cross the road, and sneak past the fence."

"Stealthy." He pulled a U-turn when there were no other cars around and drove back to the road Anka referred to with the headlights off.

After he parked, they hopped out and crossed the road, making their way down a ditch and up an incline to the edge of the fence. He followed Anka, who walked the length of the fence as if looking for an opening.

He said, "Can't go over it with the barbwire strips up top. Are you looking for a spot to go under?"

"I'm looking for a post where one section of fence ends and another begins. I can bend metal, but it's harder to snap it in half. When galvanized steel is in good condition and stretched taught like this fence, I don't have the power to bend a big enough section to make a path for us."

She found what she was looking for based on her abrupt halt and focused on a portion of fence near a pole as she mentally twisted the metal ties until they snapped. Once partially detached from the metal pole, she peeled back the bottom corner of the fence.

Denny stared in awe to see objects moving without hands touching them.

She went first, crawling on her belly under the fence. The lithe way her body wiggled had him envisioning her squirming over him in such a manner. Naked.

Get a grip, Denny, he told himself. One kiss did not give him the right to ogle her small, scrumptious body.

"I'll leave it bent up in case we need to make a quick escape through here," she said.

He cleared his throat and followed her, not nearly as graceful.

Denny stood, brushing grass off his pants, and with a sudden realization he officially trespassed and broke the law. He glanced around nervously.

When he noticed her waiting for him, he said, "This is a private hangar, right? They would still take security pretty seriously. I'd hate for my act of helping save the world to end with me behind bars."

"I'll take care of the cameras." She started walking, and he followed.

"Can you just snap a cable with your mind? Cut the power?"

"Any decent security system would have backup batteries for their cameras. Cutting the power would not suffice. I'll crush the lenses in each of the cameras as we go."

"You know a lot about security."

"Homeless and on the run, but I still had access to the public library."

Sticking to the shadows, they walked across the mown lawn, flanking the tarmac and making their way toward the one hangar with lights on like a beacon in the dark.

"With your skills, you could've been a master thief."

She shot him a look over her shoulder. "Who says I'm not?"

"If you are, you haven't mentioned it so far."

"I did my share to make ends meet, just to pay for basic food, shelter, and clothing. But I never had a taste for it. I prefer earning an honest living."

"Admirable."

"Is it? It's what most people do."

"Ah, but would most people, given your abilities, still be law-abiding citizens? You work hard at your artist craft and sleep in a cot at your workplace when you could steal Picassos and live in luxury. So, yeah, hella admirable."

She didn't reply, only kept walking.

Denny looked toward the hangar, a beacon of light spilling out into the surrounding darkness. There was a one in three chance this was the private airport Helen's goons intended to use. It had the right feel of creepiness, though that could be a projection of his own uneasiness.

The plan was simple enough—reconnaissance only, and if they had a whiff the big bad was here, call in reinforcements.

Following Anka's lead, Denny crept around to the side door rather than use the main large hangar entrance where they could have been more easily spotted. He watched her glance around with intermittent moments of concentration, which he suspected was her in the act of destroying camera lenses.

When they reach the side door, she tested the knob. "Locked," she whispered. Leaving her hand on the knob, a click resounded before she turned it easily.

"You are too cool. And one hella master thief," he whispered.

She turned around and grinned at him, sending his heart pumping harder than it already was.

They slipped inside, continuing to seek the shadows. A single plane occupied the hangar, facing the exit and with its steps down. The dual engine, sleek Learjet looked pristine and ready for boarding. Aside from a multi-million-dollar jet being ready to take off in the middle of the night, nothing specifically reeked of supernatural madness.

The sound of a vehicle had them both scurrying behind a stack of crates.

A limousine pulled up and parked, sleek and black. After a uniformed driver stepped out and opened the door, a handsome blonde man emerged, smoothing his navy suit.

Denny peered around the crates, but nothing unusual stood out about the wealthy-looking businessman. This certainly wasn't the goddess of death. Was he Andrej? Denny couldn't get a good enough look at him to compare the photo Will sent and be sure.

What now? he wondered.

Perhaps Storm and Bryce or Will and Raine were having better luck finding the orb.

Denny supposed he was partly relieved and partly disappointed. He didn't want to be in the midst of danger, but it would've been cool to be the one to make the phone call to assemble the Shadow Guardians and watch them take down Hel's minions.

The man in the suit reached back into the limo and withdrew a black box—a leather case with a handle. Denny glanced askance at Anka who peered with great interest at the object in the man's hand. Not a briefcase or satchel as a businessman might carry.

Was it the right size to hold the orb Anka sought? He wanted to ask her but feared noise might alert the driver or the man to their presence.

The man walked toward the stairs to board the plane when he abruptly paused, lifting his nose to the air and sniffing. A feral growl filled the room, and Denny quickly realized it was coming from the man in the suit.

He passed off the box to the driver before stepping around the plane and walking in the direction where Denny and Anka hid. Pausing, the man sniffed again. The two of them pulled back around the crate to remain out of view.

What is he smelling? Me and Anka? How is that possible?

The drawn-out silence had Denny's heart rate escalating as sweat trickled down the back of his neck.

Suddenly, something heavy landed on top of the crates he and Anka were hiding behind. A snarl, so close now, reverberated through Denny's body as he stared up and into the eyes of the biggest white wolf he'd ever seen. He'd never been so close to a predator.

Icy fear pricked along his skin before several events happened at once with dizzying speed.

Anka used her Jedi-like abilities to knock over the crates as she sprinted toward the driver. The thief's one-track mind had her bolting for the box. The orb.

The wolf was thrown off balance, but already twisting to pursue the moving target. Denny lunged at the animal, wrapping an arm around his furry neck.

He couldn't let the four-legged creature and his sharp teeth dripping with saliva give chase to Anka. If he could keep a grasp on the wolf, Denny could buy her time to get the box open and activate the orb to save them both.

With all his strength, Denny brought the creature to the floor and worked to restrain him. The wolf snarled, his eyes glaring murderous intent into Denny's.

The animal twisted in Denny's grasp even as he tried to adjust for a better chokehold on the beast. Hot, excruciating pain seared his bicep as the wolf sank deadly fangs into him. Someone unleashed a bloodcurdling scream, and Denny realized it was him.

Through the blinding pain and raking of the animals claws, he managed to keep hold of the wolf, though not tight enough to get him to loosen his jaws and remove the teeth clamping down on his arm. But if he let go, the creature would surely give chase to Anka. Denny couldn't let that happen.

He was no stranger to pain from his football years, but having a wolf chomp on his arm was a whole new level of agony no one could prepare for. He suspected he would have passed out from the pain if not counteracted by the adrenaline coursing through his body.

The wolf let go of his clasp on Denny's arm long enough to twist his neck and snap at his face. Denny jerked his head back but couldn't keep his distance and still keep his arms locked around the vicious creature. His grip loosened when he yanked back again, and the wolf squirmed free. Denny tried to reach for him, but the animal was already on the move.

When he tried to stand to give chase, he could barely move, only gasp for air. He reached for his phone, fumbled with it. When he looked down at the device, he only saw stars and the frayed edges of his blackening vision.

ANKA FELT POSITIVELY WRETCHED ABANDONING Denny to fight the shapeshifting wolf—a ruthless hellhound. She didn't have time for any other options. If she secured the orb in her grasp, she could crush the wolf. Without the enhanced magic, even she and Denny together couldn't take on the beast. She'd had to be decisive or they would both die.

As she dashed toward him, the driver took a swing at her with the box. He didn't transform, so she suspected he wasn't a shapeshifting wolf, but she was on alert for any other magic he might possess.

Dodging the object he swung, she countered with a kick to his balls. Yeah, street life had taught her how to fight dirty.

He dropped like a rock, the black box hitting the ground with a resounding thud. She reached for it, flicking the clasp and yanking it open. The orb gleamed, calling to her. When she grasped it, power immediately coursed through her.

From her peripheral vision, she saw the wolf launch through the air at her. She couldn't see Denny, didn't know if he was still alive, and the thought that this creature had harmed him brought hot rage to the surface of her mind.

Drawing on the power of the sphere, she lifted the body of the driver as if it weighed nothing and hurled it between her and the attacking wolf. The two bodies collided with a sickening crunch, and the animal slid across the smooth surface of the floor before colliding with the wall.

Anka glanced at the open driver's side door to the limo and glimpsed keys dangling. She needed only to get Denny in the limo and drive off to safety.

"Denny!" she cried.

Anka felt a brief moment of relief and joy when she saw Denny crawling out from behind the tumbled crates and pushing to his feet.

Her elation was replaced by horror and dread as she watched undead creatures pour in from the darkness and surround them. They came through the large hangar entrance and the side doors simultaneously, swarming forward like cockroaches.

Hand slick with sweat, she readjusted her grip on the orb and summoned magic to her, through her. Power like golden waves of warmth coated and dissolved the icy fear that had encased her. Magic poured out of her in waves, crushing two, four, six draugr at a time—those closest to her and Denny.

Denny picked up a large wrench and started swinging, even as he backed toward her.

She continued to crush and mangle the undead, bones snapping like brittle twigs, gray skin folding in on itself and shriveling, muscles contracting, curling like bacon frying on a stove.

But there were too many of them, and she felt the power of the orb taking as much as it was giving. She grew tired, weak.

So, we failed, she thought. *I failed.*

She had the orb in her palm ever so briefly. These creatures would kill them both, take the orb, leave, and find another means of transportation to deliver it to Helen.

If only I was stronger, Anka thought.

She suspected Helen was powerful enough to use something like this without it completely draining and exhausting her within a five-minute timespan.

"I'm sorry, Denny." Her voice was a strained, faint thing, like a whisper on the wind.

As she collapsed into his arms and the creatures descended on them—wreaking of decay—the world illuminated in a brilliant burst of color. Maybe death wouldn't be so bad if it was this beautiful. With that thought, she curled her body around the orb and sank into oblivion.

SEVEN

*Z*ombies, thought Denny. Never had he actually considered the possibility he might be killed by the walking dead. He hoped they choked on his flesh.

But what will happen to Anka?

She'd glowed golden and fierce as she defended the pair of them. But the magic seemed to have taken its toll. She still had a pulse and was breathing, but for how long? If she lived, would these things take her to Helen?

He sat on the floor, cradling the unconscious woman who clutched the orb as the creatures climbed over the fallen to get to them. They closed in, reeking of death and decay.

Suddenly, color danced around them, and Denny felt hope bloom in his chest. As the burst of light faded, his eyes focused on Will, Raine, Bryce, and Storm. His fumbling SOS call had reached them.

"I never thought I'd be so happy to see a rainbow," he told Will.

With spear, sword, and knives, the four cut through the hoard of undead.

Hella yeah.

If this was two-thirds of the six destined to battle the goddess of death, Denny was betting his money on the Shadow Guardians for sure. He wanted to help them, but his shredded, bleeding arm throbbed, and he wasn't leaving Anka and her orb unguarded.

After the dust settled, or rather the dusty bodies of the undead, he noted what was left. The limo and the shapeshifting wolf had vanished, but Anka still clutched the orb, eyes closed.

"She okay?" Storm asked.

"Recovering from a mega-watt use of magic, I think. Still, I'd like that healer you mentioned to check her out."

Storm nodded. "She took out a few dozen, it seems, before we got here."

"How bad is it?" Will asked, jutting his chin toward Denny's arm.

"Pretty useless at the moment."

"We'll get you patched up."

"I'd appreciate that."

"And the orb?" Storm asked.

"Anka still has it."

"I'll take you both to Apollo." Will placed a hand on Denny's shoulder.

The last thing he heard was Storm sizing up the plane and talking to Raine about stealing it from Helen.

DENNY SAT in the recliner he'd moved into his guest bedroom where Anka slept. He hadn't left her side since the hangar two days ago, even though she mostly rested.

He ran a hand along his healed bicep, still needing to process the last few days. He'd fallen in love with a woman with telekinetic powers, fought a wolf and zombies, thwarted a scheme of evil to retrieve a magical orb, transported via a magic rainbow, and watched a healer magically stitch his muscle back together.

The orb sat on the nightstand, closed within the black box. He wanted to make sure she was reassured of its presence when she awoke.

"Denny?"

He leaned forward. "Hey there, tiger. Can I get you anything?"

Her stomach growled. "I want some of that eggplant parmesan you promised me." Though her coloring was still pale, she looked infinitely better than when they'd left the hangar.

"Absolutely. I need a day though to pick up the veggies, marinate, and bake it. In the short term, I can make you a cheese quesadilla. Homemade salsa."

She reached out and took his hand as he started to stand. "Did Storm have any ideas about what to do with the orb?"

He glanced at the black box. "Will brought a dwarf to my house to inspect it. Name was Brok. He said the case is designed to shield the orb from those who can trace magical relics. As long as it's in the case, it's not a beacon to Helen." He wriggled his eyebrows. "Each day that passes without an army of evil arriving on my doorstep makes me more confident he's right."

He rubbed his jaw. "Storm asked that I hang on to it. I'm not so keen on the idea, but I get it. In the hands of a hubble—someone who can't be tempted to use it and won't take it out of the box."

"She's right to choose you. Thank you, Denny. Thank you for everything."

He swallowed. "Is this goodbye?"

"Do you want it to be?"

"No! Definitely no." He squeezed her hand and moved to sit on the edge of the bed. "I want this to be the start of something. You're such an incredible woman. I know you're accustomed to always being alone but take a chance on me. On us. We'll go as slow as you need to go."

After she showered, Anka arrived in the kitchen to find him cooking. He set the food down on the counter and she devoured the tasty quesadilla, washing it down with sparkling water.

As he cleaned the dishes, she came around behind him and wrapped her arms around his torso.

"Hmm. That's nice," his deep voice rumbled as he set aside the pan, dried his hands, and turned in her arms.

She stretched up and kissed him deeply, tasting and exploring his broad mouth. He kissed her back, arms winding around her and lifting her up onto the counter. She wrapped her legs around his waist, pressing their bodies together.

He groaned, lifted her up, and carried her toward the bedroom, where he resumed their kisses. He set her down on her toes but kept his arms firmly around her.

When she couldn't wait any longer and needed the feel of skin on skin, she took a step back. Using only her mind, her will, she lifted his shirt up and over his head. He obliged, raising his arms, and she took hers off the same way before letting both garments fall to the floor. He watched with fascination. Next, she slid off her pants and underwear while unzipping his.

"Is this okay?" she asked.

He licked his lips. "Woman, this is the most erotic thing I've ever seen."

She chuckled, stepping out and away from her pants as his fell to the floor, boxers and all. She gazed at his smooth, dark skin, exposed with his arousal, reinforcing the words he had just spoken.

Again, with only her mind, she unhooked her bra and slid the straps off her shoulders before letting it fall to the floor.

"You are so beautiful. Let me touch you, taste you."

"I hope you plan on doing a lot more than just that."

With a wicked grin, he wrapped his arms around her and lifted her off the floor, devouring her mouth in a heated kiss. She loved feeling his need and desire in the hungry way his lips moved and the roaming of his caressing touches. Never had a man shown her such affection.

When she lay down on the bed, he hovered over her, drinking in the naked sight of her once more.

"Sometimes when I look at you," he said. "I think I must be dreaming. I fear I'll wake up and you'll be gone."

The feel of his calloused hands gently stroking up her bare skin sent tantalizing waves of warm delight throughout her body.

"I'm not going anywhere, Denny."

He stroked his hand lower down, circling slowly and languidly. As he watched her expression, she closed her eyes and let out a little moan when his fingers found her moist warmth. She undulated her hips, wanting more, wanting him.

"I need you."

As a response, Denny took a breast into his mouth. Anka gasped with pleasure as she arched toward him. He worked his tongue and thick fingers mercilessly until she was crying out his name in shuddering ecstasy.

"Yes," he cooed. "Just like that. Now I need to be inside you. That's just the first one, gorgeous."

He stared down at her with heat in his eyes. She gazed back, running a hand along his firm jaw and feeling simultaneously satiated and ready for more.

She floated a condom packet at eye level. He chuckled, the sound reverberating through her.

"Perfect. You're perfect." He tore it open and slid it on.

Then she gasped in delight as he slid inside her.

"Let me know if it's too much. Tell me what you need."

In response, she angled her hips and pulled him down to her. "I need all of you."

He groaned in pleasure, tensing. His struggle for control gave her a thrilling satisfaction.

With bodies joined, they alternated speed and intensity—exploring the feel of each other until passion peaked in a firework explosion of tantalizing pleasure that had them both gasping and crying out.

He collapsed on her, panting as he buried his face in her neck and lavished her with kisses. "Good. Hella good."

ONE WEEK LATER

Denny and Anka sat on the couch, sipping coffee. She was stretched out with her bare, beautiful legs in his lap. The sun rose, shinning bright and brilliant through one window. He would make breakfast for them soon, but for now he enjoyed their proximity.

"Is it crazy I want you to stay with me? You don't have to. We've moved incredibly fast. You probably want your own space, are accustomed to having it. Tell me what you want. You know I'm all about open communication."

She had her shop moved and up and running again. She worked there, and he went to his clinic every day. They led very different lives, but that was something to be enjoyed and embraced, not feared.

"Is it crazy I want to stay? I've had my own space for twenty-years. I like occupying yours."

He grinned and placed a hand on her knee, enjoying the warmth of her skin.

"I'll need my own time, own space. Just sometimes. This is all a big change for me."

"Me too. I've never lived with a woman. Tell me when you need time and space, and I'll give it to you."

She sighed contentedly, a sound that sent his heart skipping. "You're too good to be true. And your eggplant parmesan was delicious."

"Ah, well. I'm sure you'll find the flaws if you stick around long enough. I hope they're not insurmountable next to good company and good cooking."

"I'm sticking around."

Expression turning serious, she set her coffee down and leaned forward. "Denny, I'm part of the shadow world. I'm helping the Shadow Guardians. My life will always come with danger."

His lips quirked. "So I've seen first-hand."

"My staying could put you in danger."

He nodded slowly. "I'm okay with that. Relationships come with risk—albeit not usually physical danger—but they also nurture strength."

She gave him a soft smile. "I love you. One day, when the six defeat Helen, we'll all breathe a little easier."

The six, Denny thought.

Storm had texted him that their campaign on the island had been successful—he guessed that meant many dead Midgard serpents. Yet, right now, they were four, not six. Sky Thoren still needed to be brought into the fold. And who was the mysterious third man?

"I love you too, Anka. I'm happy you'll stay."

THE SHADOW GUARDIANS TRILOGY

Raine Down, Book 1

Rosalyn's Run, novella

Storm Surge, Book 2

Anka's Orb, novella

Sky Fall, Book 3

CHARACTER LIST - BOOK TWO

Leads

- Storm Thoren - assassin and Valkyrie
- Bryce Chambers - physician and Vanir illusionist

Valkyrie Adversaries

- Bolverkr - Frost Giant and assassin
- Helen ógn (Hel) - descendent of the ruler of Helheim

Shadow Guardians Supportive Team

- Usha Bakshi - US representative on the Council of Mjölnir
- Brok Waldorf - dwarf and weapon's maker
- Denny Smith - psychologist
- Anka - tattoo Artist
- Avery - raven shapeshifter

- Jake - Vanir and UK based Shadow Guardian
- Apollo - Vanir healer
- Rosalyn - shapeshifter and Shadow Guardian

Main Characters' Family Members

- Will Decker - Storm's brother-in-law, descendent of Heimdall
- Raine Thoren-Decker - Storm's sister, Valkyrie, Shadow Guardian
- Sky Thoren - Storm's sister
- Maddie Chambers - Bryce's mother
- Olivia Chambers - Bryce's daughter

NORSE NAMES

Mjölnir - Thor's hammer

Yggdrasil - Norse tree of knowledge

Gungnir - the Spear of Odin

Mistilteinn - sword of Hrómundr Gripsson

Gleipnir - the silk ribbon that held Fenrir, Helen's fiendish wolf.

~~Nine Realms~~

Niflheim (Old Norse: "Niðavellir") - realm of frost and mist. This was the darkest and coldest realms and contained the spring Hvergelmir protected by the dragon Nidhug (Old Norse: Níðhöggr). The spring was the source of Élivágar, the seven rivers.

Muspelheim (Old Norse: "Múspellsheimr") - land of fire. Fraught with lava, flames, and smoke. Surtr reined over this land where Fire Giants and fire demons lived.

Asgard (Old Norse: "Ásgarðr") - home of the gods and goddesses (Aesir) and ruled by Odin. He was married to Frigg and possibly also Freya (some scholars postulate they may be the same woman).

Midgard (Old Norse: "Miðgarðr") - Earth. Midgard and Asgard were connected by the Bifröst, or Rainbow Bridge.

Jotunheim (Old Norse: "Jötunheimr") - realm of wilderness, forests, and snowy mountains. This is home of the Frost Giants (Jotun) who were the sworn enemies of the Asgardians. Utgard, the king, lived in a fortress of ice and snow.

Vanaheim (Old Norse: "Vanaheimr") - home of Vanir gods. Vanir were masters of sorcery, magic, and prophecy.

Alfheim (Old Norse: "Álfheimr or Ljósálfheimr") - home of the Light Elves. These minor gods of nature and fertility were known for having inspired poetry, art, and music.

Svartalfheim (Old Norse: "Niðavellir or Svartálfaheimr") - home of the Dwarves. Known for their master craftsmanship, these dwarves lived under rocks, in caves, and underground.

Helheim - home of the dishonorable dead. This realm was grim, cold, and devoid of happiness. Hel (daughter of Loki by some legends and daughter of Odin by others) ruled Helheim with her wolf, Fenrir, by her side.

DEAR READER

As I mentioned before, I would love to have you join my mailing list. Join at www.cbsamet.com. I promise I won't spam you. I only send an email when I have a new book released, giveaways, or special discounts. And I'll never sell your information. You can also unsubscribe at any time.

You can also follow me on any of these social media platforms. Check out my Etsy page for signed paperbacks.

Also, as an independent author, I rely heavily on readers to spread the word about books they've read. If you enjoyed this story, kindly let others know by posing a brief comment on social media or leave a review where you purchased it.

Thank you for reading,

www.cbsamet.com

OTHER BOOKS BY CB SAMET

The Rider Files

ROMANTIC SUSPENSE NOVELS

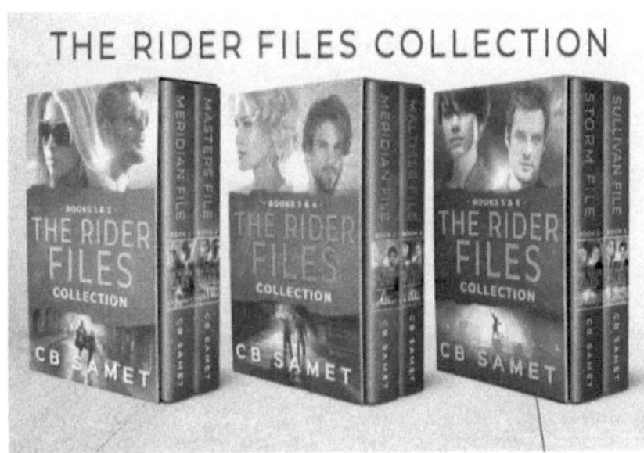

Join the Rider File protection team as they guard and defend their clients from deadly villains. Using their unique skillset and wits, they serve and protect

Meridian File / Masters File / Box Set 1

McMillan File / Maltisse File / Box Set 2

Storm File / Sullivan File / Box Set 3

~~~

The Dr. Whyte Adventure Novels

Perfect for thriller lovers!

Black Gold

Whyte Knight

Gray Horizon

~~~

Sweet Romantic Suspense

IN BOXED SETS

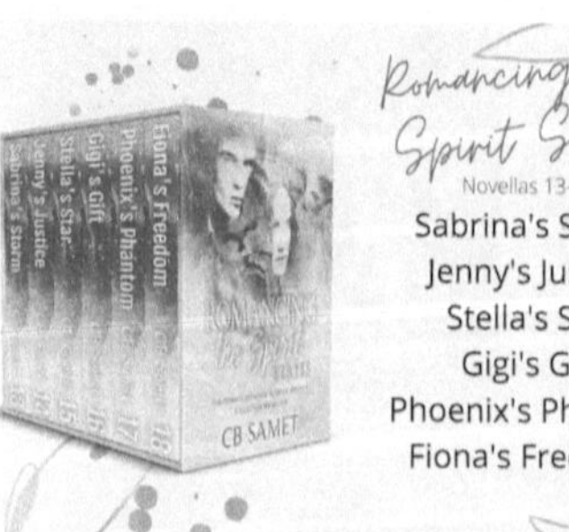

~~~

Love action/adventure and strong female leads in a fantasy world?

Check out my other genre:

THE AVANT CHAMPION FANTASY SERIES

The Avant Champion: Rising

Malakai: An Avant Champion Origin of Malos Story (prequel)

The Avant Champion: Honor

The Avant Champion: Ashes

Brothers' Bond: An Avant Champion Malakai Story

The Avant Champion: Conquest

Isabel: An Avant Champion novelette

The Avant Champion: Redeem